THE SEAGIRLS OF THE *IRENE*

KB TAYLOR

Full Steam Ahead!

www.kb-taylor.com

KB Taylor
11/19/22

BOOT TOP BOOKS

Lacey, WA

Library of Congress Cataloging-in-Publication Data
Bishop, Karen (KB Taylor), Illustrations: PB Taylor
LCCN: 2019948912
The Seagirls of the Irene/KB Taylor-1ˢᵗ ed.
p. cm: includes bibliographical references.
Summary: In 1898, after Daddy goes missing at sea, twelve-year-old Aggie and her two younger sisters are trapped aboard the *Irene* with thugs intending to steal their boat, but they outwit them at every turn.

ISBN: 9781733369701(print) 9781733369718 (ebook)

1. Self-reliance—fiction. 2. Steamboats and machinery—fiction. 3. Pacific Northwest (Washington State) 19ᵗʰ century—fiction. 4. Sisters—Fiction. 5. Boating, crabbing, fishing —fiction. 6. Spanish-American War—fiction.
Printed in the United States of America
October 2019
Boot Top Books, Lacey, WA

ACKNOWLEDGMENTS

Thank you to my dad and my grandmother for their love of steam, cherished stories, and enthusiasm to keep the Cline history alive.

My literary sister, Diane, for her proofreading, historical research, and keen insights used to captivate the reader's interest.

To my special friends who have been on this journey from the very beginning: Kathy McCracken, Cindy Norton, and Janet Pace. Other close friends who spearheaded me forward: Sandra Berry, Cecelia Black, and Heather Zarcilla. My critique group: Barb, Dave, and Jill for the final review.

Yvonne Nelson Perry, an accomplished author and mentor, whose guidance brought this book to life. Thank you, Yvonne. And thank you for pushing me to enter the San Diego Book Award contest.

Harv Lillegard and Stephanie Hylton of the Northwest Steam Society for their evaluation of all the steam references used in this book.

Lastly, my husband, for his love and support as my first reader, a re-reader, and knowing only-to-disturb with a fresh-brewed cup of his outstanding coffee.

THE IRENE'S LOWER DECK

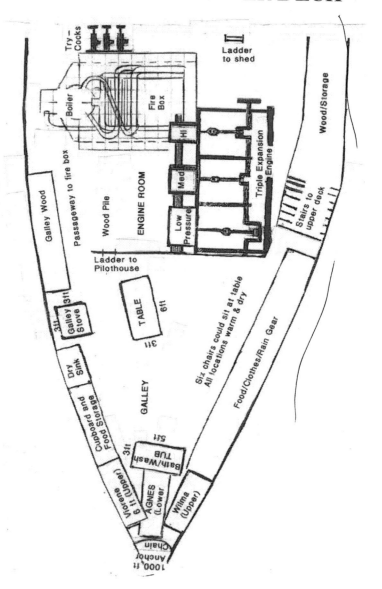

A TABLE OF CONTENTS

THE IRENE'S UPPER DECK

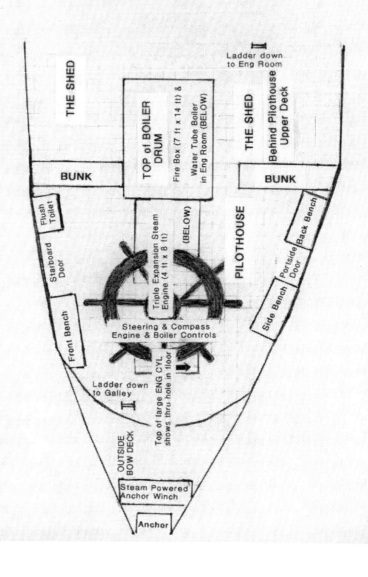

AUTHOR'S NOTE

Steam machinery has been a part of my life since I was a child. My father, Paul Taylor, a steam collector, inherited the love of steam from his grandfather, Fred Cline, and mother, Agnes Cline Taylor, the inspiration for this book.

My grandmother and her sisters were born in the early 1900's, but I pulled the timeline back to incorporate historical events that affected their parents: the Spanish-American War and the Alaskan Gold Rush. Even though the story is fiction, it's interwoven with facts of my family.

HISTORICAL BASIS FOR THE CHARACTERS:

The *Irene*, built in 1912 by my great-grandfather, Fred Cline, was named for his daughter, Irene, who died at age two.

At sixty-feet, the *Irene* was the largest of his nine boats and was manned by his three young daughters; one was my grandmother, Aggie.

My great-grandmother, Mary Belle, designed the interior, chose the boat's color: robin's-egg blue, and referred to the *Irene* as her luxury hotel. It had a bathtub and flush toilet, luxuries not found in their wilderness cabin, and a cast-iron stove. The engine room had a triple-expansion engine and an oversized upright water-tube boiler that could handle four-foot logs on long trips, unusual for this time.

The Clines lived winters in their Humptulips cabin and summers aboard the *Irene*. Artifacts of the actual *Irene* and the family history have been on exhibit in several Washington State museums.

The *Belle*, built in 1909 by my great-grandfather, was his first steamboat and named after my great-grandmother, Mary Belle.

Fern Hill School. In 1912, Agnes (eight) and Viorene (six) attended the newly-built Fern Hill School. The two girls rowed the school-rowboat up Gillis Slough, picked up other children along the way, and walked two miles on the railroad tracks. Wilma attended with her sisters two years later.

Humptulips (*Hum-tu-lups*) a Native American word meaning *hard to pole* or *chilly region*. Fred and Belle Cline homesteaded the region in 1897 and it remained the family homestead until Fred's death in 1959.

Old Betsy, the Polson Logging Train, was real. As the girls got older, they'd catch trains to and from town.

April 1896, the schooner, *W.J. Bryant*, transported prospectors to Hope City, Alaska (Turnagain Arm region). **Fred Cline** was a crewman on this voyage. His story was published in the *Alaska Sportsman* magazine in 1954.

Stories: As a boy, my father, Paul Taylor, sailed with Grandpa Cline, learned about steam engines, and gathered stories. He visited the Humptulips often and prowled the old decks of the *Irene*. While anchored at Pt. Grenville behind Bird Rock on the steamer, *Heather*, they set a crab pot and used water from the boiler for a feast. This actual event is depicted in the book.

CHARACTERS:

Agnes Beckman was based on my grandmother, *Agnes Cline*–also known in real life as *Aggie the Navigator and Captain Paddy*. By age twelve, she could man the boilers and the triple-expansion engine better than most seafaring men. In 1920, the *Tacoma Ledger* published the article *Captain Paddy–Pride of Harbor*.

Captain Paddy–Agnes Cline is the boast of Grays Harbor seafaring folk, and, what is more, a fact, can navigate the **Irene** *as well as Captain Cline himself.*

In the book, I first referred to Captain Murphy as Captain Paddy. Later, Aggie claimed the nickname as her own.

Viorene Beckman was based on my great-aunt, *Viorene Cline.* My grandmother described her sister as a sweet-natured, prim and proper girl who liked to read and cook.

Wilmina Beckman was based on my great-aunt, *Wilma Cline.* She was the only one of the three girls who inherited their mother's Portuguese looks. She loved all animals. A picture of her rowing a dug-out canoe with a cat inside followed by a pet goose swimming behind supported that fact. She also hated the smell of hot oil on the boats.

Captain Murphy was based on my father's friend, *Holger*—a hermit I knew when I was a child. He lived in a run-down shack along the Hoquiam River, rowed his rowboat to and from town, and always wore a crumpled captain's hat. Holger had a similar stature to Captain Murphy and spoke in a thick Danish accent. I made Captain Murphy Irish.

Mrs. Hill was based on a close friend, *Mrs. Cultee, a* Native American who lived nearby in the Humptulips region. Her description is fictional, but the friendship was real. Belle and the girls would visit often with fresh salmon and baked goods. Mrs. Cultee weaved cedar baskets and gifted several to Belle's basket collection.

Fred *Beckman* Cline, my great-grandfather, was born in 1874 Willamette, Oregon to German parents. After his father died in a steamboat explosion, Fred was raised by a Prussian family (Kleinsarge) and put to work in a chair factory. By age twelve, he ran away, dropped his birth surname *Beckman* and went by *Cline.* In the book, I used *Beckman.* During his life, he was a port-light tender, tugboat boiler-man, boat builder, sea captain, fisherman, inventor, and builder of pile-driven fish traps.

Mary Belle Cline (Belle), my great-grandmother, was born in 1880, Rainier, Oregon. Her Portuguese father died when she was two-years-old. It was Mary Belle who was ridiculed during the *Spanish-American War.* (In the book, I have this happen to Wilmina.) After Mary Belle and Fred wedded, they lived in a shack at the mouth of the Humptulips (*Hum-tu-lups*). For over thirty-five years, she cooked and washed without electricity or plumbing and knitted over 3,000 feet of netting for the fish traps. The girls also learned this skill.

The Clines had five daughters (no sons). Heather, 1898, lived two weeks, Irene (1902-1904), Agnes (1903), Viorene (1905), and Wilma (1907).

Grandma Margaret. Portions of her character were based on Mary Belle's mother, Sarah Elizabeth (my great-great grandmother). Sarah had been married three times. First, to my Portuguese grandfather who left her a widow at nineteen with two daughters, one was my great-grandmother, Mary Belle. A family historian stated that Sarah Elizabeth was a sweet woman, but a firm, devote Christian and a member of the W.C.T.U. (Woman's Christian Temperance Union).

When Fred and Mary Belle eloped, the *Grays Harbor Washingtonian* newspaper, 1897, published: *Wedded at Sea,* mentioning Sarah's disapproval of the marriage:

The bride being but 17 years of age, her mother strongly objected to the marriage and refused to allow a license to be issued...

Captain Hill was a real keeper at Destruction Island and a good friend of the Cline family. The Clines visited Destruction Island many times and Belle wrote to the lighthouse families for over forty years. On one of their visits, Agnes took pictures with her Brownie. One included two goats with the lighthouse in the background.

Lester Hanson was a half-brother to Mary Belle and fished with the Clines on the *Irene.*

THE SEAGIRLS OF THE *IRENE*

The *Irene* drawn by Aggie Cline (1920)

GRAYS HARBOR BAY

CHAPTER 1
HUMPTULIPS, WASHINGTON
APRIL 1, 1898

I HAD DEVISED A FLAWLESS ESCAPE, or so I thought. "Umtalah skalus," Mrs. Hill called out in her native tongue. It meant *Humptulips sun* for my yellow hair. "Boat, boat," she said, pointing to a canoe rowing up to her landing on Gillis Slough, a tributary off the Humptulips River.

Standing on her porch, I grabbed the binoculars, looked through them, and saw my skinny-as-a-stick fifteen-year-old uncle stepping out of a rowboat. "It's Lester," I gasped, my heart pounding clear up to my throat, "and his friend, Harold."

"Who?" She looked up at me with a quizzical stare, unique to her.

"Lester," I repeated. "He's a half-brother to my mama, but you wouldn't know it by his red hair and freckles. Please don't tell him I'm here. It's important that he *not* find me."

Mrs. Hill furrowed her brow, then gave me a quick nod.

With no time to spare, I raced down the steps and

1

crawled under the porch, looking up at her feet through the cracks.

Mrs. Hill, at eighty-four, was one of the wisest women I knew and had a distinguished look, not of any tribe seen in these parts, which made her even more special to me: stubby build, tan-leathered face, and a flattened forehead that extended down to a straight nose.

I had let her believe that I had rowed up the slough for a short visit, not that I had run away four days ago. Now I felt bad to have hidden the truth.

"Stay," she told me, then turned and trudged toward the boys as her thick white hair, tied at each side of her head like horses' tails, bounced with each step. "Welcome, hello," I heard her say.

"I know she's here," Lester said without a return *hello* or introducing himself. "That's Aggie's rowboat buried in the bushes."

I had done my best to camouflage my boat, and for all Lester knew, it could have been one of the communal rowboats or canoes borrowed and left for another to use, except my name, *Agnes Beckman*, was carved on the portside hull.

"Yes, yes," she said with a carefree tone. "Come, we'll have blackberry tea." She led Lester and his friend, Harold, to the porch steps, which provided me a close-up view.

"We don't have time for tea," Lester spouted. "We have to catch the logging train back to town."

2

Lester lived with Grandma in Hoquiam, the closest citified town, which was a six-hour steamboat ride depending on the tide, but sometimes shorter by Old Betsy, the logging train.

"I insist you get her now," he said, trying to sound grown-up, but truth be told, I, twelve-years-old, had a lot more savvy than fifteen-year-old him.

Mrs. Hill cupped one hand over her eyes and looked up at the sun. "Old Betsy doesn't blow her whistle for hours. Sit," she said, motioning the boys to two wooden chairs perched on her porch.

Lester wrinkled his forehead and scowled. "No. You produce Aggie right now."

Mrs. Hill smirked, making it clear that this red-headed string-bean had no scare in him. His friend, Harold, more lumpy than big, put his hands on his hips and gave Mrs. Hill a stern stare, which seemed to amuse her even more.

"Come along," she told them as she climbed the stairs to the porch. What the boys didn't understand was that if Mrs. Hill extended hospitality, she expected a visit.

Lester sighed, followed her up to the porch, and plunked down into a chair. Harold did the same.

"I'll get the tea," she said, disappearing into the house.

Breathing shallow as I could, I did my best not to move, but my heart was thumping so hard I feared they might hear.

"What's that woman's game?" Harold asked.

"Who knows," Lester said. "We'll play for a bit."

3

It seemed an eternity before Mrs. Hill returned with the tea. Soon as she handed them each a cup, she pulled a chair over to face them, but best of all, positioned herself so I could see her plain and clear.

"Why is it that Aggie can't visit? She comes all the time."

"She's a runaway," Lester said. "My mother was visiting the girls and planned to take them home with her, but before the ferry arrived, Aggie snuck out and hid."

"I see," Mrs. Hill said, darting her eyes downward at me, then back to Lester. "Aggie can stay here until her father returns."

"No. I was given strict instruction to bring her to town."

"But I have a letter that says she can stay with me."

From a beaded pouch hanging around her neck, she pulled out a coffee-stained note and handed it to Lester. I recognized it as the note that Daddy had written almost five-months back, right after Mama had died. He had requested that Mrs. Hill watch after my sisters and me, whenever needed.

Lester scanned the note. "This doesn't have merit. Her father's been gone almost six weeks and my mother believes that he's deserted the girls."

I gasped under my breath, *how dare she say such a thing*, and in my anger, didn't realize until too late that my leg had given way and pushed gravel beneath my feet.

"What was that noise?" said Lester.

4

I froze, my heart now pounding even harder.

I slowly looked up.

He glued his eyes onto mine. "There you are," he said.

I scurried from under the porch. Soon as I got to my feet, ready to run, he had stomped down the stairs and grabbed onto the back of my overalls.

"Where do you think you're going?" He chortled as I twisted back and forth, trying to get loose from his grip.

Mrs. Hill hurried down the steps. "Stop," she said, waving Daddy's letter in her hand. "She has permission to stay."

"Keep out of this old woman," he snapped, dragging me toward the trail. Harold followed behind.

"Lester," I pleaded, "please let me stay. At least another week to see if Daddy comes home."

"No. I've already wasted too much time looking for you."

I dug my leather boots into the ground, forcing him to stop, and looked for Mrs. Hill, but she was nowhere in sight.

Lester turned to Harold. "Get her feet, let's carry her down."

One good thing about being lanky, I had the flexibility of a monkey. Before Harold grabbed me, I kicked his shin. He jumped back.

"Ow," he mumbled, rubbing his leg.

I glared at Lester. "You owe me; remember when I caught you kissing Mary Jane Hawkins behind the bushes?

You swore me *not* to tell and I didn't. Not to one person did I spill. And when you took that dollar from Grandma's purse." I knew if I raked my brain, I could come up with a lot more negatives that he didn't want shared.

"No one's going to believe you."

"Maybe not, but Grandma will listen to Viorene."

Viorene, my middle sister and one-year younger than me, resembled a porcelain doll: blonde curly locks, dimples, and Daddy's perfect smile. I was blonde too, but my hair was straight as a yardstick and I had gopher-like front teeth.

"Viorene's Grandma's jewel," I added.

I could see by his face he was chewing on my words, but before he could respond, Mrs. Hill appeared and called out, "Better get your boat." Lester had left their canoe on the edge of Mrs. Hill's landing without tying it down. The out-going tide was carrying it away.

Lester gasped, studying the situation until a sneer crossed his face. He turned to Harold. "We'll use Aggie's boat." What he didn't know was that on my way to Mrs. Hill's I had hit a snag, putting a fist-size hole in my boat's hull. When I had reached Mrs. Hill's landing, my overalls were soaked up to my knees.

Mrs. Hill shook her head. "That rowboat is broken. Won't float with three people; you'll miss the train."

To catch the logging train did take some maneuvering. First, they'd have to row to the school landing, then walk two-miles along the rails to the watering tank, and hope with all their might, they got there in time before Old Betsy continued on to town. And she didn't go by a schedule. It all relied on the size of the logs and how long it took to get them loaded at the logging camp, which was a good hour or so farther back into the woods.

Lester looked at Harold. "We don't have far to row; the school landing is just around the bend. Let's get her into her rowboat and out of here."

When they grabbed me, I wiggled and kicked, but couldn't stop them from putting me inside the boat. And with one quick push, the boys got my rowboat into the slough. It was floating, all right, but water was gushing in and soaking my feet.

"Start bailing," Lester barked, motioning to an old bucket stuffed under the thwart.

"Don't squirm," Mrs. Hill called out from the shore, as if she was providing friendly advice. I knew better, recalling the time she had sabotaged her grandson's boat ride.

After she figured out that her grandson, John, was taking her to his home to live, she fidgeted side to side until the canoe tipped over, landing them into the river. Luckily, they were near our dock and my daddy fished them out.

"What are you doing?" Lester growled as I shifted back and forth, forcing more water inside. "Stop it." He looked at Harold. "I'll row; you bail."

Just as Harold reached for the bucket, I tossed it overboard.

7

Lester narrowed his eyes. "Why can't you behave?"

Harold poked at the bucket with his oar, but the tide had taken hold and the bucket was floating away. We were still in sight of Mrs. Hill's landing, but water was now up to my calves.

"Too much weight, we're sinking fast," I said.

Lester clenched his teeth. "You're impossible. I should let you drown like a rat." He looked up at Harold again. "Row back to shore."

Once we reached Mrs. Hill's landing again, I stepped out of the boat into water and waded back to dry land. I turned to Lester. "One thing you should consider is how angry Daddy will be with you for aiding Grandma's plans. His letter does have merit."

"Don't care," he said. "Mother's expecting you."

"Please, Lester," I begged. "Grandma plans to send me to Cousin Ella and Wilmina to that evil Aunt Harriet."

Wilmina, my eight-year-old sister and the only one of us three girls who took after Mama's dark Portuguese looks, was a ragamuffin, just like me, which was considered bad in Grandma's eyes.

"Wilmina's having a hard time with Mama's death," I continued, "and sending her to Aunt Harriet so far away is the worst that could happen. Aunt Harriet will crush her spirit. You know I'm right." I had pleaded the case before to Grandma, but had to try again with him. "Daddy has to know this news soon as he arrives and he'd be furious with you, if leaving me here could have stopped it."

He paused and pulled on his lip. "Aunt Harriet can be strict; I'll give you that."

Strict was an understatement. My Aunt Harriet, Grandma's oldest sister, was meaner than a riled bull.

"Grandma wants only Viorene living with her, but with me gone, there's a good chance that she'll keep Wilmina too. That's why I ran away."

Mrs. Hill interjected. "Her father's note says that Aggie can stay; tell your mother that I'll take all the girls."

Harold spoke up. "She's going to run again, might as well leave her here. Besides, that boat won't hold the three of us and we need to get to the train."

Lester sighed, "Fine," then he looked at Mrs. Hill. "Do you have another pail?"

"Yes, yes," she said, pulling out a rusty bucket buried in the nearby bushes. "Bail it now and go."

After they emptied the water from the rowboat, they pushed it back into the slough. Harold did the bailing as Lester pulled on the oars. "You may have outwitted us this time," he hollered, "but we'll be back. And next time with the authorities."

THE NEXT TWO mornings, I mentioned to Mrs. Hill about going home to see if Daddy had returned but she told me no need for now. Today, we spent most of our time in her garden. As she planted more rutabagas, carrots, and potatoes, I spruced up her faded scarecrow and even fixed the split-rail fence built by her late sons.

The fence showed its sixty years of wear but I straightened it upright with rocks and re-nailed the chicken wire attached to it, to keep out the rabbits. When a kingfisher flew overhead shrilling its dry scolding rattle, she looked up.

"Listen," she said. She believed our spirits intertwined with animals and birds.

"It does have an unusual chatter. Reminds me of a rattlesnake, shaking its tail before a strike."

She gave me a puzzled stare.

"It's a poisonous snake. Saw one when we visited my Cousin Earl's farm in Yakima."

"Yes," she replied, still looking confused.

"Is there something special about the kingfisher?"

"Smart bird."

"It is one of my favorites. Funny looking too, the way its feathers stick straight up on its head. Reminds me of someone waking up and not combing their hair."

"Big head," she added.

She was right on that. The kingfisher, about a foot tall, had a head twice as big as its medium-sized body, but it had pretty coloring: slate-blue with a white collar and underbelly and a blue needle-sharp beak.

Holding my hands, she gazed into my eyes. "Learn from the kingfisher."

"I know they have patience. I've seen them grip onto a tree-branch for close to an hour before taking after a fish."

"Good. Keep watching."

THAT NIGHT while sitting on the porch, my sisters popped into my head. I ached to see them.

Mrs. Hill smiled and patted my hand. "Everything will be fine. Tell me some stories about your sisters."

She especially liked the ones about our one-room school—what we had learned, skits performed, and poems recited. I always shied away from anything that required me to stand up in front of a group, but not my sisters. Especially Wilmina, if it had to do with her being center-front, she'd take the lead. Mrs. Hill laughed when I told her that.

I pointed to her cut wood. "John was here. He must've come when we were in the garden." He was the only one of her nine grandchildren who visited on a regular basis. Both her sons died, long before I knew her.

She grunted and waved one hand across her face. It appeared she still held a grudge about John tricking her into his boat. I wondered if his kind acts of checking on her and cutting her wood would eventually wear her down, but I wasn't going to tell her to forgive him. She had to come to that conclusion on her own.

"I have a sudden urge to row home and see if Daddy might be back. Maybe tomorrow, okay?"

She shrugged and stood. "No more talk. Time for us to sleep."

CHAPTER 2
THE HUMPTULIPS

ACCORDING TO MRS. HILL, a person awakened by cawing crows set a negative omen to their day. She believed in all types of omens and told me to trust them whenever they come, good or bad.

At the break of dawn, she kicked my straw mat. "Up, up."

I wanted to tell her that I preferred their caws to her kicking foot. I sat up and stretched. "Good morning."

"Spirits all around. Crows wake you?"

Must be having dreams again, I figured. Whenever she did, she'd talk in whispers. Like she was doing now. "No," but the truth was, I *was* awakened by the crows but I didn't dare tell her that. Last time I admitted to it, she chanted at me for what seemed hours. After breakfast, I gathered up the dishes, but she stopped me from washing them.

"Come. Let's go."

"Where are we going?"

"No more questions. You'll see," is all she added.

I followed her down the trail to her old rowboat covered in grass. It took some doing to get it free from the mud. When I got it into the slough, it floated but had four leaks. Luckily, there was a rusty pail inside. I looked across at Lester's boat. It had settled in the bulrush grass on the other side of the slough.

"How long since you've used this boat?" I said, thinking I should retrieve Lester's rowboat instead, which was actually one of Daddy's sturdy-built ones that Lester had taken from our dock.

She shrugged.

"Maybe I should get Lester's boat now."

"No. Let's get going."

"Hope you're good at bailing," I told her.

I helped her inside the boat, pushed it out farther and climbed into it. Water sloshed on the bottom boards. Quick as it came in, Mrs. Hill scooped it out. I decided right then we would be using one of Daddy's rowboats to take us home. We always had at least seven or so tied to our dock.

At the last bend of the Humptulips River, I saw our cabin. My heart fluttered with excitement, hoping that since Mrs. Hill had agreed to come, it meant that Daddy might be home.

"Wonder if he's back?" I mumbled, scanning the dock to see if the *Belle*, Daddy's oldest steamer, was tied on.

Mrs. Hill didn't answer and continued bailing. She had done a good job keeping the water below our ankles, but soon as I helped her out and onto the dock, the rowboat filled up like a bathtub.

"Sorry, but your boat's a goner."

She stared at it like a person in a trance, nodded, and walked away. Her odd behavior made me wonder if she considered the sinking rowboat an omen? I shook it off.

On the way up the dock, Mrs. Hill stopped beside the *Irene.* I stood beside her and touched the *Irene's* hull. "Daddy used to say that people would never recognize the *Irene* as a powerful sixty-foot steamer. Instead, they saw her as an albatross—an awkward bird with black-webbed feet—all because of her littered deck."

"Ah, yes," she responded.

"He told me to watch the albatross the next time we're in the open sea. Said, that it may be a clumsy bird on land. At sea, it's breathtaking. Same as the *Irene.* I believe that too."

"Pretty boat, color of a robin's egg," she added.

"Yes, robin's-egg blue was Mama's favorite color."

When I saw the empty slot where the *Belle* usually moored, my stomach tightened. Holding Mrs. Hill's arm, I tried not to show my disappointment as I guided her up the trail.

"Voices sleep," she said, batting her head from side to side. Soon as we reached the cabin, she walked around to the front porch, looked down at the river, and surveyed the dock. She scowled and pulled on her chin.

"Something wrong?" I asked.

"Last night, the bear entered my dreams. Coming here, confirms it."

"What does that mean?"

"Searches for the truth, but the crow plays tricks."

Normally, her theories entranced me and were fun to hear. Now scared, I feared what they might reveal.

15

She latched onto my arm. "We must go."

I pointed to our porch bench. "Please sit. I have to leave Daddy a note."

By the time we got back to the dock, her rowboat had sunk and only the line remained. Thankfully, we had plenty of spare rowboats and skiffs.

I got Mrs. Hill into a rowboat, picked up the oars, and headed downriver. We didn't talk. Instead, she chanted, over and over, the same monotone verse. She'd stop a bit, start in again, and did it all the way to her home. By the time we reached her landing, I shivered with exhaustion.

Sliding out of the rowboat and into knee-deep cold water, I guided the boat to shore. Once it grounded, I held Mrs. Hill's hand as she stepped out and we hiked in silence up to her porch. Must be something to those morning crows, I decided. It had promised to be a bad omen day and it sure turned out that way.

I sat in the wooden chair next to her. "Mrs. Hill, what did your omen mean?"

She sighed. "In my dream, the bear is truth, but the crow is a trickster. You are the bear."

"Me?"

"Yes. Don't let the crow mislead."

"If I'm the bear, who's the crow?"

She shook her head.

"But you must have an idea."

She shrugged.

"Only person who comes to mind is Grandma."

16

She shrugged again.

"I'm not sure what to think, but now I'm truly worried. I need to head to town now and face Grandma."

"Yes," she said, "you must go."

STANDING AT HER LANDING, Mrs. Hill handed me a basket she had filled with berries, bread, and smoked fish. I reached in and took a bite. Within minutes, energy surged through me. I wasn't sure if it was anxiousness or the food itself, but nonetheless, it supplied me fuel.

"Thank you for the food." I set it in the boat. "I'm sure I'll get hungry along the way."

She removed her beaded necklace and placed it over my head. "To keep you safe." She held my face and kissed my forehead.

I touched the necklace. "I'll carry it with me always."

She smiled.

I turned and pushed my rowboat into the water, climbed in, and sat. Just as I picked up the oars, I hollered to her. "I love you, Mrs. Hill. Thank you for the hospitality and for being my friend."

"Yes, yes," pumping her hand over her heart. "Trust the signs. Think like a kingfisher. Don't let the crow trick you, your father *is* alive."

I shipped the oars and called out. "What do you mean? Did something happen?"

"Only you can find the answer."

She waved and walked away.

CHAPTER 3
HOQUIAM

AT THE SCHOOL LANDING, I stepped out of the rowboat, pulled it to shore, and rested it in the bushes, next to my damaged rowboat that Lester and Harold had used. There were two more rowboats in the grass. I could see by the hull branding—*Beckman,* our last name—that they belonged to us and were part of our communal practice: borrowed by a neighbor, left for another to use, and eventually ending up back at our dock.

On the climb up to the railroad tracks, I spotted a blue ribbon stuck to a leaf and picked it loose. "That's Wilmina's," I said aloud, remembering her fit when she lost it. I tucked the ribbon into my pocket and restarted up the graveled grade.

Fern Hill, our one-room schoolhouse, was two miles up the tracks, and just beyond that, the logging train's water tower. The instant I stepped onto the tracks, I smelled the thick-tar-scented creosote. It saturated the air. As I walked along, I imagined my sisters with me. Wilmina hopping to each slat like leapfrog, Viorene reading a book, and me balancing on the rail inching one foot before the other as I teetered with extended arms.

I loved my sisters and missed them something fierce, but sure didn't relish a visit with Grandma. Maybe Viorene smoothed things out, I hoped. A whistle blast interrupted

19

my thoughts and I stopped cold. It's too early for the afternoon train, looking up at the sun and guessing it was now close to two o'clock. Depending on the load, the train ride to town could take two hours or so. When the whistle blasted again, I took off into a full run. As I neared the water tower, I felt the vibration of Old Betsy under my feet, quickly stepped off the tracks and stood back.

Old Betsy, not sleek like the passenger locomotives, had a bulky rectangular body, funnel-shaped stack, and a front light that resembled an enormous eye. She was no beauty, but according to all the engineers, could out-pull any other engine.

With a final whistle-blow, Old Betsy rounded the corner, and in a slowed-down chug, sand spilled from her belly for traction as her brakes screeched and loaded cars twitched back and forth, sparks flying out from behind her skidding wheels.

*Huff...huff...huff...,*clouds of steam hemming her sides.

I waited until the crew started filling her boilers and then walked over to the cab. "Hello, Engineer Tyler." He was my favorite of the three engineers who had this route. Short and tubby with strands of gray covering his balding head, his rides to town included story after story. So many, that sometimes my head would spin trying to keep up.

"Aggie, my girl. No sisters?"

"Just me today."

I climbed in, sat underneath the side window, and looked back at the cars piled with logs. "Why so early?"

20

"Got a steam donkey at the camp and it speeds up the work."

Just as we got underway, I heard the full history of a steam donkey.

"Iron oxen," said Engineer Tyler. "It's got enough power to rig up trees, pull loads, and haul giant logs from the woods. Even has one that stacks the logs onto the train. Steam's a magical thing, that's for certain."

I smiled and nodded, but the truth be told, I already knew all about steam from our over-sized boiler on the *Irene*. Daddy had taught me how to stoke the boiler's firebox and to bleed the try-cocks, but I decided out of politeness to let Engineer Tyler explain it all.

The next two hours had rushed by so fast I never realized we had reached the outskirts of Hoquiam until Old Betsy slowed her pace. As she headed into the sawmill yard, her chug-a-chugs panted, then she skidded, and finally halted between rows of stacked logs. Before I could thank Engineer Tyler, he had hopped off the engine and was already talking with a group of men.

I stepped off the train and headed down Eighth Street, but instead of turning to Grandma's, I walked two more blocks. Much as I wanted to see my sisters, I had not figured out how to approach Grandma, and plus I needed to check the dock to see if Daddy's boat, the *Belle,* was there.

Crossing the bridge, I saw a few boats tied up, but only recognized the *Molly Mae*, Captain Murphy's scow.

Barely longer than a skiff, she had a tiny pilothouse atop the deck and two miniature portholes at the bow. Her deteriorated whitewash, now gunpowder gray, covered her from stem to stern.

I hadn't considered visiting the captain, but seeing his boat drew me to it. I hurried to the end of the dock. "Captain Murphy, you here?" No reply. I tried again.

"Who's there?" He climbed up to the deck.

For being a pint-sized man, he sure had a loud bark. Not used to seeing him without a rumpled sea-captain hat, I giggled when I saw one side of his thick white hair sticking up like a porcupine. Must've been napping.

He waved me aboard. "You alone?"

"Yes." I followed him down to his galley.

"Where's ya dad and the rest of ya family?" he said in his thick Irish brogue.

I hadn't anticipated being asked questions and paused before answering. "Daddy's still fishing and my sisters are at Grandma's."

"Why aren't ya there?"

"Umm..., mmm..."

He pushed his face into mine and it smelled of tobacco.

"Actin' odd. In trouble are ya?"

"Yes...with my grandmother." I held up my basket. "Have food. Want some?"

Dirty plates and clothes covered his table. He swiped his hand across it, pushing most of the clutter to the floor.

22

"Put it here."

"Bread, smoked salmon, and berries," I said.

"No pie? Thought for sure there'd be pie." He scratched his chin and gave me one of his what-are-you-up-to stares. "Ya a runaway and lookin' for a place to hide?"

"I hadn't thought of it, but would sure appreciate if I could stay."

"Nope. Not right to worry the family."

"It's only Grandma and she's so mad at me, she won't care a lick."

"She's family, all the same. Can't allow it."

Not meaning to, my lip quivered and tears welled in my eyes.

"Now don't do that."

"I can't go to Grandma's house. She doesn't even know I'm in town."

"What's this? Where've ya been?"

"I've been staying with Mrs. Hill at the Humptulips. I came to town to visit my sisters, but now I don't know if I should go near Grandma's."

"No need to tell me more. Sleep where ya can find a spot. I'll bed down in the pilothouse tonight."

The next morning, the smallness of the *Molly Mae* exaggerated every sound—Captain Murphy's footsteps on the deck above my head, his stepping off the boat onto the dock, even the tapping of his cane. I sat up, looked out a porthole, and as daylight approached, I watched Captain Murphy limp down the dock.

Stiff from sleeping on the wooden bench, I leaned over arms outstretched and touched my toes. Sitting upright, I scanned his galley. *Wonder when he last cleaned?*

I went to his galley table, gathered food-covered dishes, found more under clothes behind the ladder, and on the floor. Locating a pail, I filled it with the dirty dishes and lifted it up the ladder, one rung at a time. He had rainwater collection jars scattered around his deck. After I used the water to wash and rinse, he had nothing left but twenty empty jars. I lined them up against the pilothouse to catch the next rain.

When the captain returned, he found me in the galley hanging up the last of his shirts.

"Well, I'll be. Sparkles better than a new coin."

"Least I could do, for you letting me stay, but I used all your water."

"No matter. Got two filled flagons in the pilothouse. Here." He handed me a lumpy napkin. "Brought ya a biscuit."

"Thank you," I said, unfolding it. "Blueberry, my favorite." I took a bite. "This tastes good."

He pulled out his pocket watch, squinted, and looked at it with one eye. "Ten after seven. Time for a nap."

"I best be on my way."

"Have ya a plan?"

I nodded. "Grandma's got a shed out back. Figured I can hide in there. She always has a gathering to attend."

24

I MADE IT HALFWAY UP First Street before I saw Grandma and uppity Grandpa James standing in her rose garden.

Grandma, a petite woman with thick gray hair and often complimented on her looks, had a long angled face. Just seeing Grandma so close, filled me with panic. I spun around and started back up the block, but coming up the street, right at me, was Mrs. Tucker, laughing and talking with two others. Mrs. Tucker was more of a social acquaintance of Grandma's than a friend, but true competitors. Even when marching in their long black skirts, white tops, and stern faces for the W.C.T.U.—Woman's Christian Temperance Union—they'd try to outdo one another's sour looks. And believe me, Grandma didn't need more practice, she already had a permanent scowl.

Stuck on which direction to go, I turned back around. That's when the holly hedge caught my view. The eight-foot hedge separated one side of Grandma's front yard from her neighbors. I darted into the neighbor's yard, and without a moment to spare, I pulled back a spiky branch and crawled inside the hedge to an open space where my sisters and I used to hide. We called it our secret fortress and even had a jar for keeping notes. Soon as I sat on the ground, I looked through the branches and saw the women standing at Grandma's picket fence.

"Hello Margaret and James," Mrs. Tucker said. "Ready for today?"

"Yes Clara," Grandma answered. "Just making final selections. Time to get last year's blue ribbon replaced," Grandma said smugly as she pointed to the old one hanging on the porch beam.

What a blessing, I thought. The flower show must be today.

"You might have to settle for second place this year," Mrs. Tucker said in a smug tone similar to Grandma's.

"Is that right?" Grandma huffed. She turned her back and carefully cut another rose. The women walked away. I would've been scolded for such rudeness, but Grandma played by different rules. "Over here," she told Grandpa James as she strolled through the pinks in shades from pale to hot vibrant, handing him her cuts.

I turned when the screen door slammed and watched Viorene and Wilmina cross the porch. Even though Mrs. Hill reassured me that Wilmina was with Viorene, it relieved me to see her. They sat in the swing, pushed with their feet, then extended their legs as it swung back and forth. My stomach twitched with excitement. I sure missed my sisters, and being so close it was hard for me not to race over to them now.

"You girls behave," Grandma said, pulling on her white gloves.

"Good luck," Viorene called out.

"Luck has nothing to do with it," Grandma said. "I have superior roses and those judges better see it that way."

26

I hoped for everyone's sake the judges agreed, remembering the year she took second. It made her angry as a caged bear. Mama tried to calm her with tea but I learned, real quick, the only medicine that cured her mood was saying the judges didn't know spit.

After Grandpa patted his top hat onto his overly round head, he carefully squatted down, stiffly lifted two baskets overflowing with flowers, and almost toppled over.

"James, watch how you lift those," Grandma said, rearranging the bouquets.

I waited until my grandparents left and crawled out into Grandma's yard, removing stickers from my hair. Wilmina saw me first. She skidded her feet, stopping the swing and leaped up. "Aggie!" she said, racing down the stairs.

Viorene ran to the picket fence and craned her neck. "No one in sight. Hurry inside."

In Grandma's house, I plopped down onto the sofa. "Sure feels good to sit on something soft. Why didn't you go to the flower show?"

"Grandma said I had the sniffles," Wilmina said, "and didn't want me near her."

"This might cheer you up." I pulled the blue ribbon from my pocket and handed it to her. "Found it at the school landing." She started to tie it in her hair, but Viorene snatched it.

"That's dirty," Viorene scolded.

I smiled at my sisters. Such opposites.

27

Viorene, our blonde porcelain doll, so prim and proper, perfect grades, and nose always in a book. And Wilmina, a dark-haired Portuguese chatterbox who liked to climb trees, but at other times, played dress-up and paper dolls.

"I sure missed you both."

"We missed you," Wilmina said. "I cried for days."

"It is good to see you," Viorene said, "but I'm surprised you'd come here. Any news on Daddy?"

I shook my head. "What'd Grandma say about me?"

"Very little after Lester said he couldn't find you," Viorene replied, soft as a kitten's purr. Sometimes, I had to strain to hear her.

"Good," I said. "Back to Daddy. Mrs. Hill had a vision, said the truth was in town. To watch and listen like a kingfisher, for anything unusual at all."

Viorene grimaced. "The bird? What does a bird have to do with this?"

"I studied their habits. The way they grab a fish from the water takes patience and skill."

Wilmina interrupted. "Grandma got a special delivery letter last week. After she read it, she locked it in the bookcase. When I asked her what it was, she told me to never mind."

"That's the kind of observation we need." I headed to the bookcase. "Maybe she has the key hidden."

The tall oak case had two top shelves, a fold-down desk in the middle, and two locked drawers at the bottom.

I jiggled the drawers, ran my hand alongside the case, and underneath it.

"She wears a key around her neck," Wilmina said.

"Stop it...both of you," Viorene insisted.

Ignoring Viorene, I studied the lock. "We have to open this cabinet. I could try to pry it."

"No. If she saw it broken, she'd go into a fit."

Wilmina stepped forward. "I'll break it. She's always nipping at me."

Viorene thumbed me toward the kitchen. I knew it meant she wanted a private talk.

I put my hands on Wilmina's shoulders. "Wait here and keep watch while we fix a snack."

At the kitchen table, Viorene stood next to me and buttered jelly on a piece of bread. "I'm worried about Daddy too," she whispered. "After I persuaded Grandma to let Wilmina stay here with me, everything seemed fine, but...something has happened. Yesterday, Grandma told me that Wilmina's going to Aunt Harriet's after all. She wouldn't tell me what changed, but I think it has to do with Wilmina's Spanish looks."

"That doesn't make sense."

"It's the Spanish-American War. The newspapers have turned negative opinion into a rage against the Spanish. Grandma's keeping Wilmina locked away. She won't even let her go to the library with me."

"What excuse has she given to Wilmina to keep her home?"

"Said there's an outbreak of measles and doesn't want her exposed."

"Wouldn't that apply to you too?"

"Yes...but Grandma convinced her because I'm older I'm not at risk."

"Grandma's right to keep Wilmina hidden. It'd be awful hurtful if someone said something rude. We have to get into that cabinet."

"What does that have to do with any of this?"

"I trust Mrs. Hill. She said I was to find the truth. And I believe it's hidden in Grandma's bookcase."

Wilmina rushed into the kitchen. "Grandpa James is coming up the walkway."

"Quick... out the back door," Viorene said, opening it. She handed me the sandwich and I shoved it into my pocket.

"I'll be on Captain Murphy's boat." I looked at Viorene sternly. "Keep Wilmina with you, at all costs. I'll come up with a plan."

I RAN TWO FULL BLOCKS before I slowed down. My heart pounded, partly from being winded, and the other, from scared of being seen. I took side streets to downtown until reaching the Hoquiam River Bridge, then sped across it and hurried down the gangplank to the dock. On the step off, my foot buckled and I landed on the ground.

"Ow," I moaned, trying to stand.

Down I went again.

I unlaced my boot and pulled it off. My ankle throbbed like a toothache. I rubbed it, stood, and hobbled one-booted toward the captain's boat. "Ow, ow, ow."

The *Molly Mae's* starboard hull butted next to the dock and made it easy to get aboard. I stepped down onto her deck and called out for the captain. When he didn't answer, I looked through the pilothouse door, but he wasn't there. I hobbled to the hatch and called down. No answer again. Must've gone to town, I figured.

I went to the pilothouse and sat down on a bench. I had never been inside his pilothouse and it reminded me of a cluttered closet—greasy tools scattered about and machine parts, some in buckets, slapdashed all around the room. Cobwebs hung everywhere, and except for a section Captain Murphy had scraped off for viewing, dirt caked all the windows. When I spotted two blankets under the wheel, I pulled one out to the cleared space on the floor and made it into a bed. With my hurt ankle, all I could do was nap. Not sure how long I slept, but it was getting dark when I awoke to loud voices. I sat up, peeked out the pilothouse door, and saw the captain on the dock with two other men.

The captain blurted out in a slurred Irish accent. "You manky thieves, get away from my boat." He started hopping and boxing, same as a kangaroo I had seen in a picture book. Knowing he had a bad leg, I was surprised to see him jumping about, but decided I had better stay hidden.

31

Every time the captain threw a punch, the men swayed to one side then to the other before he could get one hit back. The larger man pushed him, and the captain staggered and fell to his knees. Then he grabbed the captain's arm, pulled him up to the gunwale, and pushed him over onto the *Molly Mae.* He landed on the deck with a loud *thud.* The captain groaned, but the two men laughed as if they'd heard a joke.

I'd never witnessed a scuffle before. I shook and worried for the captain. But when I heard one of those men yell, *Murphy. Have my money in a week or I'll set this old boat afire with you aboard,* I nearly leaped out of my skin.

CHAPTER 4
THE *MOLLY MAE*

AFTER THE MEN DISAPPEARED, I crawled to the captain.

"Captain Murphy," I said, shaking him.

"You'll get your money," he mumbled.

"No, it's me. Aggie."

"Go away," he moaned.

"Are you in pain?"

"No...," he said before passing out.

Hoping to get him into the pilothouse, I shook him again but he didn't move. I got a blanket and covered him with it, then went back into the pilothouse and bedded down for the night. Awakened by a thunderous crash, I jolted up like a spit of steam. My brain hadn't connected to my whereabouts until I heard his voice.

"Ya bleedin' kettles."

"Captain Murphy, are you all right?"

"Who wants to know?"

"Aggie," I called out.

"Thought ya left."

"I came back. Are you hurt? I heard a terrible noise."

"Fine. Tangled on my trap."

Across his aft deck, pots and pans dangled from a clothesline. One end attached to the pilothouse rail and the other end angled down to a mooring bit at the stern. I figured that's how he kept his pots from being lost, but now saw that it served as an alarm for intruders on the boat.

"Do you need help?"

"No, go back to sleep."

When the sun peeked through the window, I reached for the wheel and pulled myself to my feet. Luckily, only a twinge of pain remained in my ankle. I hobbled out to the captain.

Snuggled under the covers, he had his eyes closed tight. What a sorry sight. His rounded snout, weathered from the sun, was peeling, drool leaked from his mouth, and his chin bristled like a hairbrush. Apart from hair strands sticking to a dried gash on his forehead, his coarse white hair cut-short was his only presentable part.

"You'll need coffee," I muttered, shaking my head.

"Eh?" Squinting his eyes open, he looked at me. "Diddya say brew?"

"Yes. I'll go make it." I headed to the galley hatch.

I grasped the top of the ladder and stepped down, putting most of my weight on my good foot. When I reached the bottom rung, and turned and faced the galley, I gawked in disbelief. The galley I'd cleaned yesterday, had clothes piled everywhere, but that wasn't the worst of it. It was the two mangy river rats, the size of moles, gnawing on a half-eaten sandwich.

I clapped my hands. "Git." They looked at me with beady eyes as if I was the intruder, then continued eating.

I was used to rats. We had plenty of them along our river. It didn't mean I liked them. Especially in a galley. I hurled a fry pan at them. When it landed on the tin plate, they scurried across the floor. Their long skinny tails, stiff as hard-leather razor strops, followed behind them as they disappeared through a hole. I found a rubber boot, shoved its toe into the opening, then grabbed the broom and swept up every crumb in sight.

After the coffee boiled, I poured it into a tin cup, steadied it in one hand, and climbed up the ladder with the other. I popped my head through the hatch and saw that Captain Murphy had moved. Slouched against the pilothouse with his legs stretched in opposite directions and hands resting on his belly, the captain looked like a portly sea lion basking in the sun.

"Barks like one too," I whispered, going over to him.

" 'Bout time." He squirmed, sitting up.

I handed him the cup. "You have rats down there."

"Eh, you should be used to that. Part of livin' on a boat."

I saw no point in continuing the rat discussion so I changed the subject. "I sure detect your Irish accent."

"Must be the wee leprechauns whisperin' in your ears."

He reached into his coat pocket and pulled out a bottle.

"Is that liquor?" I asked, watching him pour it into the coffee.

"Skin of the hog that nips you."

35

"What does that mean?"

"Pulls the tooth of a hangover. Hasn't ya dad ever had one?"

"No," I said very matter-of-fact. "My father's never touched a drop. He said nothing good ever came from drinking."

"'Tis grand advice, but too late for me."

"Is that why you're in all this trouble?"

"Trouble?"

"I saw two men drag you here and throw you aboard. That's why your head's bloody."

"Oh," said Captain Murphy, feeling his forehead. "Diddya talk to 'em?"

"No... I had the good sense not to let them see me. They sounded awful mad and they threatened to burn your boat. You don't recall any of that?"

"Hmm...'tis a bit of a fog, but I do believe I was gamblin'."

He handed me his cup. "Fetch me some more. Grander yet, bring up the pot."

"I will, if you let me wash your forehead. Where's your fresh water?"

He pointed to a jug in the pilothouse. "In the flagon."

I found a new handkerchief in the pilothouse, cleaned his wound with it, and rinsed it out. Then, I retrieved the coffeepot.

He drank two more cups and seemed more alert when he slanted his eyes toward me. "What's the story?"

36

I paused. "Story?"

"Why're ya here again?"

I wasn't sure where to start or how much to say, but figured him knowing the truth couldn't hurt. After I finished, he scratched his chin and studied my face.

"'Tis odd for ya dad sailin' off on the *Belle*. But this misgivin' with ya grandmother, I'll need to bite on that a bit. Not right sneakin' behind her back."

"Are you going to turn me over to her?"

"Probably not. If ya dad put you under Mrs. Hill's charge, as ya say, then that's the way I see it. But I don't need more problems. Got my own." He pointed at my foot. "What's wrong with your bootie?"

"I fell, but it's better."

"Soak it in some salts. Don't need both of us gimpin'."

"Do you mind if I stay a few days? To rest my ankle."

"Should be safe for a day or two, but I'd hide that yellow hair. There's a cap in the galley. And bring back some fixins'. The old belly's growlin'."

"All right, but first, I'm going to board up that rat hole." I grabbed a small board from the woodpile. "Where's your hammer and nails?"

"Down below, under the bench. I wouldn't be countin' on it doin' much good. They'll gnaw right through it. Besides, I named 'em after me scoundrel brothers, Timothy and Donegan O'Murphy."

"Well, your brothers are uninvited. Got any poison?"

"Peek under the stove."

37

THE NEXT MORNING after breakfast, I spotted two dead rats lying in a corner. They were sprawled on the galley floor next to the poisoned food. I grabbed a bucket, scooped them inside, and climbed to the deck.

"Whaddaya got there?" Captain Murphy asked, leaning out the door as I passed the pilothouse.

"Your brothers. They're going for a swim." I tossed them overboard.

"Fare-thee-well," he said.

"I'll get you more coffee."

I barely got to the stove when he yelled down through the hatch. "Better hurry back up. Your sister's comin'."

"Really? My sisters?"

"Just the one. With the yellow hair."

I climbed up to the deck. Viorene had already stepped aboard and was talking to the captain while he rubbed his neck, looking up at her.

"Don't recall you bein' so tall," the captain remarked. Viorene's growth spurt made her my height and half-a-foot taller than the captain. "Here's your sis," he said, turning her toward me. "You two go below to do your visitin'."

I handed him his coffee, then hugged Viorene. "It's wonderful to see you."

"Why the cap?" she said to me. "You look like a boy with all your hair tucked under it like that."

"That's the idea." I pointed her to the hatch. "Watch your head," I said as she started down the ladder. "It's a tight squeeze."

38

"Tiny space down here. I don't believe I've ever been aboard."

"Probably not. It's the perfect size for the captain. How's Wilmina?"

"Fine," Viorene responded. "And if you're interested, Grandma won first place at the flower show."

"That's good, should keep her in a good mood for a bit."

Viorene nodded. "I can't stay long. I have a ten o'clock appointment with the dressmaker."

"Dressmaker?"

"Umm ..., yes," she said, straying her eyes to her feet. "Grandma wants me fitted for a new party dress. Mine's too short and she doesn't want me wearing yours."

"Why not? It's nice and I've only worn it once. And what party are you attending that would require a special dress?"

"Grandma pulled me aside this morning, told me that we're sailing to San Francisco in two weeks and there are parties to attend. I tried to get Wilmina included, but Grandma said no." Viorene paused. "On our way to the ship, we're dropping Wilmina off at Aunt Harriet's."

My anger flared. "While she sends Wilmina away to that evil woman, you get a trip and a new dress?"

"It's not my fault," she stammered. "This should please you." She pulled letters from her pocket and handed them to me. "Last night while Grandma bathed, Wilmina snuck into Grandma's bedroom and removed the key from her bedpost. I was in the parlor with Grandpa James when she stole it. After everyone fell asleep, she crept downstairs and opened the case."

"Really?" I stared at the letters. "That was brave of her. You didn't know?"

"No, I would've stopped her."

"Where's the key now?"

"She slid it under Grandma's bed this morning, hoping Grandma would think she dropped it herself. My stomach's been in a knot ever since she told me."

"Tell her I'm proud of her. Mrs. Hill said I was to find the truth and I'm hoping it's in these papers."

"What I hope is that you have a plan on how to get them back into Grandma's bookcase."

CHAPTER 5
THE *MOLLY MAE*

I KNEW PRYING into Grandma's private letters was wrong, but was thankful for Wilmina's courage to steal them. And for prim-and-proper Viorene to bring them.

My hands trembled as I unfolded the telegram from the U.S Lifesaving Service. "This is to save my family," I told myself. I froze when I saw Daddy's name: *Captain Fred Cline* with Grandma's listed below his: *Lindsay.*

OFFICIAL NOTICE – MAY 8, 1898
Vessel: B*elle, Tag #555577B*
Registered: C*aptain Fred Cline,*
Humptulips, W*ashington*
Secondary: M*argaret Lindsay,*
598 First St, H*oquiam, Washington*
Condition*:* DESTROYED

I paused and re-read the line. *Destroyed?*

Location: *The Strait of Juan de Fuca-West*
Cause: *Storm; Starboard hull washed ashore.*
No life aboard—lost at sea

I paused again. Lost at sea. My brain wasn't connecting to the words on the page.

"No, this can't be true," I said, shaking my head. "Mrs. Hill said Daddy was alive." Is this the truth I'm supposed to find? There must be more.

Rifling through the stack, I snatched a loose letter with Mama and Daddy's names attached and scoured every word. I relooked at the date. This must be the letter Wilmina saw delivered by messenger:

June 1, 1898 - Hoquiam, Washington
RE: Fred Beckman and Mary Belle Beckman

Dear Margaret,
I forwarded the guardianship paperwork to our San Francisco office with a note explaining your circumstances. Once the legal department reviews your request with a determination of your son-in-law's disappearance, it will be treated with haste to have you added to his account.

I can state as your friend, I will do all I can to aid you. Please find comfort in knowing substantial funds exist in this account. After these papers are approved, contact John Mason, a good attorney, to assist with the transfer of assets and broker an agent to sell all boats.

Sincerely,
Ned Randall, Vice-president
First National Citizen Bank

That's why Grandma's going to San Francisco—to rush this through. "How dare she do this," I muttered. I scurried up the ladder, and soon as I reached the opened hatch, I stopped on the middle rung and inhaled the cold air. Rain sprinkled my face. After a few more deep breaths, I climbed out onto the deck, walked over to the pilothouse, and peered inside. I moaned at the sight of the captain fast asleep on the floor. I sure needed to talk to someone. Oh, well. *Maybe it's best I rake this through my brain first.*

I leaned down, reached for the tarp next to the pilothouse door, and slowly pulled it to me. In a dry spot under the pilothouse eave, I tented the tarp over me and sat as raindrops plopped. It seemed forever before I spotted Viorene coming from the dressmaker. I stood and gave a hurry-up wave, but she was too preoccupied balancing her umbrella and avoiding mud puddles to notice me. By the time she reached the boat, my stomach had tied into knots, raising my anxiousness even higher.

"What a terrible change in weather," she said, clasping my hand and stepping aboard.

As she closed her umbrella, I held the tarp over her head and followed her with it until she reached the hatch, then I wadded it up, placed it back into the pilothouse, under the wheel, and looked over at the captain, still fast asleep.

43

As I stepped off the ladder into the galley, Viorene was already below next to the warm boiler, shaking water from her raincoat. "Any news in the letters?" she asked, hanging her dripping outerwear on a coat hook.

"Plenty." I latched onto her arm and pulled her with me, and sat next to her on the bench.

She furrowed her brow. "What's wrong?"

I bit my lip and grabbed her hand. "Grandma got a telegram from the Lifesaving Service." I paused, trying to calm my racing heart and jitters in my voice. "The *Belle...*," I hesitated again, "was destroyed in a storm."

She gasped and her eyes widened into a piercing stare. "Destroyed? Are you sure?" she said, speaking barely above a whisper.

I nodded and pointed to the letters on the table.

"What about...Daddy?" Panic rose in her voice as tears cascaded down her cheeks.

I squeezed her hand. "No mention of him, but...I know in my heart that he's safe. Mrs. Hill said so, and she's *never* wrong. He's too good a sailor."

I saw no need to mention what the telegram said: *no life aboard—lost at sea.* They were words from someone who didn't know Daddy or realize the power of Mrs. Hill's visions, for that matter.

Viorene studied my face, then nodded. "That's true. Daddy is resourceful."

44

She pulled a hanky from her pocket, wiped her face, and then blew her nose. I waited another moment and cleared my throat. "There's more."

"More?" she said in a shaking voice.

"It's Grandma. She's even more of a threat than I figured." My words spilled faster than I knew I could talk. "She's acting like Daddy's never coming back. She even petitioned the bank to have her name added to his account. She's trying to steal his money, take our home, and sell our boats." I pulled the letter from my pocket. "Look."

Viorene narrowed her stare, but didn't speak, and I could see by her expression she was theorizing in her head.

Oh, oh, I thought, did I wake up Viorene's black and white views? Mama used to tease that whenever Viorene got serious, it was her old soul paying a visit, making her seem three times her eleven years.

"We have to stop her." I insisted. "Don't be getting your brain wrapped into your right or wrong thinking now."

"I'm sensible," she snapped, "unlike you, who always jumps to conclusions without all the facts."

"Facts are in those letters. Grandma's a no-good thief."

When I saw the whites of her eyes turning blood-red, I knew I had sparked her temper. Grandma had that same trait whenever she got fuming mad.

"That's a disrespectful thing to say," she spurted. "And why is that letter in your pocket? Give it back."

"No, I might need proof."

"That doesn't prove a thing. I'm guessing Grandma needs the money to care for us. Daddy would understand."

"How dare you defend her, she's only caring for you. She's sending Wilmina away to earn her keep and planned to do the same to me. Grandma has a taste for new dresses, trips, and whatever grabs her fancy."

Viorene huffed. "I wish I never got involved with this. Grandma's going to know we broke into the cabinet. And for what? Some foolish notion Mrs. Hill gave you?"

"There's nothing foolish about Mrs. Hill. And knowing where to find Daddy, gives us hope."

"How? We wouldn't know where to search. Nothing's changed from seeing these letters, except now, Grandma will mistrust me."

"It's Wilmina you should be concerned with."

"Of course I'm worried for Wilmina, but crossing Grandma doesn't help any of us."

"I don't trust Grandma and neither should you."

"I don't know what to think. My only concern now is getting the letters back."

I handed the bundled envelopes to her. "Put them in the kitchen drawer, next to the pantry."

46

"How's that going to help? If Grandma finds them there, she'll suspect us."

"I've seen her put papers in there before. Hopefully, she'll think she was absentminded."

"Hopefully?" she said, pulling on her coat. "Just like Wilmina *hoping* Grandma believes she dropped her own key."

"Deny knowing anything. If she continues to press, tell her that I must've taken them."

"The sooner these are out of my hands, the better. I might just drop them into the trash. Will you give me that bank letter?"

I sighed, placed it in her hand, and followed her up to the top deck. "I'm going to Mrs. Hill's to figure out a plan. I'll return next week; look in the hedge jar for instructions."

Inside the giant hedge, separating Grandma's yard from her neighbor, was our hiding spot with a buried jar for secret notes.

"Don't include me in your plan." She handed me her umbrella. "Hold this over my head," she snapped, and grabbed it back when she stepped off the boat onto the dock. "You need to accept situations. And let them be." She turned and walked away without a hug or goodbye.

As I watched her hurrying up the dock, rain splattered my head, but I didn't care. Seeing her fade away left me empty as if I had been starved for days.

When she reached The Eighth-Street Bridge, I didn't pay much notice when two shadows passed her, because my focus was on my sister until she disappeared. Just as I turned to go back to the galley, two figures caught my gaze. I realized from the larger man's build that they might be the same two who had brawled with the captain. I hurried to the pilothouse.

"Captain Murphy," I said, shaking him hard. "Get up. Now!"

"What's the ruckus?" He squinted as he sat up.

"Two men are coming toward the dock. I think they're the same gangsters who threatened you."

Attempting to stand he grabbed my arm, but it took a few tries to sober his feet. "Get off the boat."

"Wouldn't it be best if I greeted them? And told them you were gone? They aren't going to hurt a kid."

"Don't argue with me. Get off now!"

CHAPTER 6
HOQUIAM DOCK

THE CAPTAIN TUGGED on my arm, pulling me over to the gunwale.

"Might as well let me stay aboard. They're halfway here and there's no place to run."

"No," he said. "Keep your head low and no lollygaggin' when you pass 'em."

I stepped onto the dock. Increasing my gait, I kept my eyes glued to those two men. One of them, a giant, had brown hair and fuzzy whiskers that looked like a lion's mane. All I could tell about the other man was he was skinny, had dark, slicked-back hair, and looked awful odd next to the big one. Luckily, they were talking and not looking my way, so I raced to two wooden crates on the dock and squatted down between them, then held my breath and prayed they'd pass me by.

Their footsteps neared. The dock swayed and so did my stomach. Sour bile rushed up into my mouth and I gagged. Coughing, I swallowed it back. No matter, because right then was when I saw the toes of their boots.

"What do we have here?" a voice said.

I looked up and saw both men staring down at me. The skinny man leaned forward. With his pointed features—nose, chin, pencil-thin lips—he reminded me of a weasel.

"You jumped from Murphy's boat." He grabbed my sleeve. "Did the old Irishman send you for help?"

"No. I was feeling sick. You must've heard me gagging."

The weasel yanked me up like a puppet. "All I hear is a smart-mouthed kid."

My insides quivered, but I didn't take my eyes off his bony face. "I don't know what your problem is. I'd appreciate you releasing me."

"Looks like a sick waif to me," the fuzzy-bearded man blurted.

A disgusted look crossed the weasel man's face. "That's why you don't make the decisions." He dug his fingers into my arm and pulled me with him.

I stumbled alongside.

When we reached the *Molly Mae*, weasel man yelled, "Murphy. Got a present for you." Then he threw me toward the boat.

I tripped, fell down, and skinned my arm.

"Leave her alone," the captain barked. "Here's your money." He tossed a coin-filled black sock at their feet and extended his hand to me. Pulling me up to the gunwale, he grabbed the seat of my pants and slid me onto the deck.

"Where's the rest?" the weasel man said. "You're eating and drinking on something."

"My check only comes once a month."

Daddy had told me that the captain had injured his leg during the Civil War and was living on a small pension.

The weasely man straightened up and glared at the captain. "You have two days left. And don't think about playing any games, or else ...." He drew his fingers across his neck, like a knife cutting a throat, then turned and walked away with the brown-haired man.

"No good drifter hooligans," the captain whispered under his breath. He turned and looked at me. "Ya hurt?"

"No. They sure are mean."

"That's for certain. Desperate too. That's what makes 'em so dangerous."

"I have a five-dollar coin piece." I reached into my pocket. "You're welcome to it."

"Appreciate the gesture. I need a wee grand more than that. At least ten times as much."

"Will you have it by this Friday?"

"No."

"They threatened to burn the *Molly Mae*," I said as I stood.

"Aye. A serious threat."

"This is your home. Where would you live?"

He shrugged. "It's my worry not yours. You'll be leavin' tomorrow."

"You can come with me on the mail boat. To the Humptulips. They won't find you there."

"My leg can't make the hike from Damon's Dock."

"If we paid extra, they'd take us right to our dock."

"The mail boat left two days ago. Won't be back till first of the week."

I paused a moment. Maybe the logging train? Then I remembered the two-mile hike on the tracks, his leg couldn't do that either. We needed a boat. Suddenly, an idea popped into my head. "What about the *Molly Mae*?"

He scowled at me disbelievingly. "Are you daft?"

"You have a boiler, don't you?" Every steamboat had to have a boiler to convert the water to steam to power the engine. "An engine too?"

"Aye, but her sailin' days are long gone. If ya haven't noticed, she's stuck in mud."

"So? When Daddy dry docks a boat, he works the propeller to get it out."

"It's not that simple. Her hull's in sorry shape. Full of holes."

"We'd only be going into the harbor, then up the river. A little leaking isn't going to hurt us."

"Too tall of a task to have her ready in two days."

"It's worth a try."

"Can't pilot on my own anymore. Watchin' the firebox is a full-man job."

"You have me."

"I thank ya for the offer, but you're just a tyke and a colleen, for that matter."

"I've helped my daddy plenty on the *Irene.* I can stoke a fire and man the gauges better than most."

"Even if ya could, we don't have fresh water for the boiler or dry hardwood either."

"What about the tugs? How do they get their water?"

"Hook to the spring with a hose."

"We can do the same thing, and I'm betting they have plenty of dry wood in their hold."

"We can't take their wood. That would be stealin'."

"Not if we leave my money. This is an emergency."

"You're wearin' me out. This ain't fairyland. It won't work." He headed to the pilothouse, opened the door and slammed it closed.

AT FIRST LIGHT, Captain Murphy hollered through the hatch. "You up?"

"I am now," I said, sitting up and sliding off the bench. "Already dressed. Wore my overalls to bed."

"'Tis a grand mornin'," he called out.

I climbed up the ladder. "Why're you in such high spirits?" I stepped onto the deck.

He pointed at the river. "Tug will be here shortly."

"Tug?" I spun around and saw a black and white tug vibrating in the water. As dark smoke spewed from its tall stack, it rumbled backwards straight toward us.

"Keep out of the way," the captain told me. "A lot of movin' parts."

I hurried to the pilothouse and leaned against the outside rail.

With a slight bump, the tug butted our bow and pulsated like a beating heart. I instantly smelled the fresh-tarred decks permeating the air, covered my ears, and watched the two crewmen leap aboard, dragging chains.

53

One of the men shook the captain's hand. The captain smiled and patted his back.

After the men secured the iron hooks to the *Molly Mae's* bow bits, they jumped back to the tug. The tug chugged forward, then stopped a good distance from our boat and turned on its towing winch. As the chain's iron links wrapped around the spool, the *Molly Mae* rocked back and forth.

Captain Murphy grabbed my arm and pulled me into the pilothouse. "Get braced," he said, sitting down on the bench clutching to it. I stood at the wheel gripping tight as I could.

Suddenly, a loud suctioned *pop* released the *Molly Mae* from the mud and she catapulted into the middle of the river like a shooting stone. The force knocked me against the wheel and landed the captain on the floor.

"You, all right?" I said, going over to him.

"Fine," he replied. I helped him up and followed him outside.

The tug now at our stern lurched back and forth as the two crewmen jumped aboard, unhooked the chains, and dragged them back to their boat. And with our sterns aligned, the tug pushed us back to the dock.

Quick as I'd ever seen Captain Murphy move, he tied the *Molly Mae's* lines to a piling and waved the tug off.

The tug blasted its whistle and pulled away.

I pointed to the piled wood on the deck. "I see they left us dry alder."

"Also hooked up the hose," he added.

"I can't believe they did all this."

"Seadogs help one another."

"I know, but this is beyond normal. How'd you coax them?"

He sighed. "If you must know, I used to be their captain."

"You?"

"Don't act so surprised," he said, brushing past me.

"I'm sorry, I'm sorry," I repeated, chasing after him. "I knew you were a captain, but I thought it was of the *Molly Mae*. It takes a lot of skill working the tugs. Before my parents married, my daddy was the fireman on the tugs, working the boilers."

"Who do you think taught him?"

I froze and gaped in disbelief. "What?!...YOU?"

"Better close that mouth before a mosquito flies in and chews up ya tongue."

I was having a hard time imagining my daddy captained by him. I wanted to ask more, but I knew I needed to be awful careful with my questions.

"No disrespect intended. *Sir*," I said, remembering the crewmen calling him *sir*. "Should I fill the boiler? Sir?"

"No," he snapped. "Need to verify no corrosion. Just because it's been sealed with lime, doesn't mean it's good."

"What would you like me to do? Sir?"

"Stop callin' me sir. Go clean the pilothouse."

"Sorry, just trying to be respectful. Did you say clean?"

"Is that a problem?" he said, raising his eyebrows.

"No," I stammered. "But ... isn't there something more important to do?"

"I'll not be explainin' my reasonin'. If you're not interested, we'll drop this whole sailin' idea."

"No, no. I'll get right to it."

After he disappeared down the hatch, I stood in the pilothouse doorway. Even though I'd spent time in the room, looking at it now, it seemed in more disrepair. I figured that was probably due to me having to clean it. I went on deck, dipped a bucket into the rain barrel, and filled it with water. With a scraping knife, I chiseled the windows. Dirt sprinkled the floor, and after I washed the glass, overcast daylight gleamed through. He was right. Sailing with those windows would've been impossible.

I hadn't seen him in a long spell, but he was awful noisy. Pounding away, like my daddy used to do when he prepared for a trip. Halfway down the ladder, I stopped and looked through the rungs. He was on his knees working on the firebox.

"Hungry?" I asked. "I'll warm up the stew."

"Suppose so." Holding on to the boiler, he pulled himself to his feet. "I've made good progress."

"Me too. Even found your engine under the wheel."

"Only a one cylinder, but a powerful little machine."

"It could sure use a polish. I'll spit clean it after lunch."

"Before doin' that, I'll need your help installin' the gauge glass."

"Is it cracked?"

"No, but, ya can't trust its looks. Seen too many burst and scar men for life. Taught ya dad to change the glass on every trip."

"Come to think of it, Daddy does keep a supply on the *Irene*. Said he learned from ...the leprechaun. That's you?"

He nodded.

"So that's why Mama and Daddy are so fond of you. You helped my daddy become a sea captain."

"Ever think they might've liked me for my charm?"

I shrugged, fearing if I answered, it might come out impolite. Even if I didn't mean it to.

"Ya dad was one of the best I've ever trained. A good worker and only talked when needed. Too bad *you* didn't inherit that trait," he said, wiping his hands on a rag. "Wasn't there a mention of stew? Any chance it might be today?"

CHAPTER 7
GRAYS HARBOR BAY

CAPTAIN MURPHY BENT DOWN, grabbed my boot, and pulled me out from under the wheel.

"Whew, what'd you do? Bathe in kerosene?"

I sat up. "Just polishing the engine."

"Looks grand from here; shiny as a gold piece," he remarked and scanned the room with a nod. "Ya got the whole pilothouse sparklin'. I'd say we're ready to sail."

I stood and dusted off my overalls. "No. The boiler still needs fresh water and wood."

"Already done; bled the valves too. Come along, help me get her untied."

I followed him outside. "But it's three o'clock. Isn't that too late for us to leave?"

"Don't get dark 'til nine," he said, untying another line from a piling. "With high tide, it'll be an easy cross into the Humptulips."

The Humptulips, the most northern river that flowed into Grays Harbor, was cursed with sand pits at the mouth. Daddy only crossed it at high tide.

"Tide's been high for a long while. Maybe we should wait until morning."

He furrowed his brow. "You questionin' my skills?"

I gulped. "No." I followed him into the pilothouse, sat down on the bench, and watched as he turned the throttle.

With a low hum, the engine cylinder pumped up and down, and as it stirred the propeller, the captain gripped the wheel and guided the *Molly Mae* away from the dock, slower than a snail.

"By golly," he said, slapping the wheel. "Never thought she'd test the waters again."

I smiled, but my stomach twitched something fierce. Much as I wanted the *Molly Mae* to sail, she sounded awful creaky.

As we crossed from the Hoquiam River into the harbor, I watched storefronts, Victorian houses, and tidewater mills, fade into the distance. Now stretched before us was the wide-open bay, and along its border, wind-blown trees, crabapple brush, and in the distance, hilltop after hilltop of giant spruce and Douglas fir.

"The bay's choppy today," I remarked, looking out the pilothouse window.

"A little bounce won't hurt us. Sailed in worse."

I focused the binoculars on a boat. "Schooner way off, being towed by a tug. Can't tell if it's the same tug that helped us this morning."

"Doubt it. That line up began at dawn."

"You mean the tugboat war?"

"Aye."

With lumber in such high demand, San Francisco schooners arrived almost daily to pick up from the mills, but the Grays Harbor Bar, the entrance from the ocean into the bay, was plagued with mountains of sand heaved by the sea and reshaped with every rise and fall of the tide. And much too dangerous for clipper-type ships to cross on their own. They needed tugboats to guide them.

"Even seen the tugs ram one another, to get the fare," the captain remarked.

"Heard the stories, Daddy witnessed plenty. Any last instructions, before I go below?"

"Watch the water in the boiler. And the fire in the box, keep it to a low roar."

He seemed pleased giving me instructions, but the upright truth was, I probably knew more about boilers than most sailing men did.

At the hatch, I swung one leg over onto the ladder, started down, and stopped when I heard the captain bellowing an Irish jig. He was grinning so wide, years disappeared from his face, but I didn't want him to catch me watching, so I ducked my head and quickly climbed down to the galley.

Behind the ladder in an alcove on two bolted-down iron sleds, sat the boiler. It was smaller than the boilers on Daddy's boats, but nonetheless they all functioned the same: converting water to steam to power the engine. When I looked through the firebox peep-hole and saw a low flame, I picked up the work gloves, pulled them on, then opened the furnace door and threw in more wood. A moment later, a yellow-red blaze toasted my cheeks. The warmness put me into a trance until the *Molly Mae* started rocking. I quickly closed the furnace door, hurried to the

61

galley bench, and sat. As waves splashed against the portholes, I held my breath and slowly let it out.

I never liked staying below too long—the engine room with all its oily smells and a swaying boat could turn me queasy, lightning-fast. Even when I sailed with Daddy, I'd rush with my galley chores and skedaddle up to the top deck. I didn't dare share this news with the captain. No siree...I'd have to fight it, and thankfully, my stomach agreed.

After a bit, our whistle shrieked high-pitch and shrilled two more times. I stood, looked out the porthole, and saw a tug towing a four-mast schooner, approaching from the left, portside, for a red-to-red pass.

Portside, the exterior lantern lens was red. And when both vessels passed on their left, it was called a red-to-red pass.

The tug rumbled loud as thunder and parted water with such cascading force that backwash streamed over its bow like flowing rivers. The turbulent wakes splashed our portholes and swayed the *Molly Mae* back and forth with a vibrant force. Suddenly, another incoming wave smashed our hull and the *Molly Mae* bucked like a wild horse.

I sat down, gripped the bench, and prayed I wouldn't puke.

The captain's trunk slid across the floor and banged into my leg. I bent to catch it. It slipped away too fast. Coming back at me, I stopped it with my foot and held it in place. Back and forth, we rocked. I reached for a bucket under the bench, just in case. Finally, the boat steadied but I didn't move until the sloshing in my stomach stopped. I wobbled to my feet, dragged the trunk over to the stove, and shoved it into a gap until it wedged.

When the boat bobbed up and down again, I hurried back to the bench and plopped down. Water splashed and soaked my britches. I jumped up. "What's all this about?" I muttered, staring at the puddle. With one finger, I followed the stream to a cracked board in the bulkhead. All the tossing must've caused the wood to give way.

I knelt down on the floor and pulled out the toolbox from under the bench. I remembered the toolbox from my rat-hole repair. It had everything I needed—a hammer and nails in a jar, and next to it on the floor, a stack of thin boards. The leak took little effort to repair, but in less than a frog's jump, three more dribbles emerged. I patched them too.

Finally able to sit again, I plunked down on the bench. I wasn't there more than a minute when I heard gushing behind me. I jumped up, turned, and saw a jagged rupture in the middle of the hull. Grabbing three boards, I hammered one over the hole and crisscrossed the other two, but now the water just squirted cockeyed. I pounded in more boards and angled them every-which-way, but what I'd truly accomplished was turning the bulkhead into an odd-patterned quilt. I sighed and scurried up the ladder.

"Leaks," I hollered, climbing onto the deck.

The captain leaned out the pilothouse door. "How bad?"

I hurried toward him. "I boarded up some. This last one, I couldn't fix."

"Take the wheel," he said, hobbling past me. "I'll go below."

Overheated, I dripped with sweat until I stepped into the pilothouse. It was as cold as a block of ice and chilled me fast. I closed the door. Sure isn't like traveling on Daddy's boats, I thought, shivering. He always had heat piped up from the boiler and coffee warming on the engine top.

I kept rechecking the captain's pocket watch that he had hung near the wheel. He'd been gone a long while, but I decided to give him ten more minutes. That is, until one of Daddy's *never, never* reminders popped into my head. *Never* leave the helm unattended.

"But what if it's an emergency?" I remembered asking Daddy.

"If such an occurrence arises, and only in dire need," he had said, "steer to mid channel and reduce knots."

I concluded the captain being gone concerned me, but didn't constitute an emergency. I gripped the wheel and kept us at a steady pace. When we turned into North Bay, I throttled down, spun the wheel north, and decreased to three knots. All seemed fine until the engine knocked.

"Oh, oh. Hope it's not dirty water," I muttered.

I knew if water deposits carried into the engine, it'd

choke in an instant. I quickly closed the throttle and steered to center. I raced to the hatch, knelt down, and called out.

"Captain, the boat's losing power. Can you help?"

When he didn't answer, I climbed onto the ladder. Halfway down, I saw the captain sitting on the floor submerged in water up to his chest. His head was propped up against the bench.

In knee-deep water, I trudged over to him. "What happened?"

"Hammerin' on a leak, I stepped up onto the stove," he said, shaking his head. "Should've had it bolted to the bulkhead. It tipped over, dumped me off, and it landed on my claw. Didn't you hear it fall?"

Truth was I was too overwhelmed piloting the boat to pay much attention to noises below. "Yes, but I thought it was you making repairs." I glanced down at the stove again. "Can't you pull your foot out?"

"Think I'd be lyin' here, if I could? Get the screw jack. Should be under the wheel."

The jack was where he said and the same design as my daddy's: short four-legged stool with a large center screw that rose up and down with a crank.

I set the jack into the water, felt for an opening, and then shoved the jack under the stove. I cranked and cranked until it released the captain's foot, then quickly pulled his leg out. Soon as I got him to the bench, I lowered the jack and put it atop the stove.

"Best I wait here," said Captain Murphy.

"Yes," I replied as I surveyed the room and saw all the leaks, too many to count, spurting through the bulkhead. It reminded me of a rain barrel shot full of holes. I sloshed over to the boiler. With bilge water just below the air opening under the grates, I knew it'd be a short time before it reached the flame. This is a serious situation, I told myself, glancing over at the captain.

His teary-eyes and clenched lips told me I had to handle this on my own. I figured him safe for now, but with a struggling engine and rising water, I knew we'd be losing power real soon and I sure didn't want to be adrift with all the leaks.

"I'm going up top," I told him. "Be back shortly."

As the engine clinked and clanked, I opened the throttle, then closed it to rest the engine and let the boat glide. Close to thirty minutes, I repeated these steps. By the time we reached the Humptulips, I had a knotted-up stomach and tight-grip hold on the wheel, and was certain if I let go, I'd fall straight to the floor. I babied the *Molly Mae* into the river's mouth, and just as I spotted a sand pit beyond our bow, I realized I was in an outgoing current and crossing at low tide. I spun the wheel, but instead of closing the throttle and shifting the lever to reverse, I panicked and throttled to full steam.

With low tide, portions of the river had become a grassy marsh. The *Molly Mae* veered portside, then she leaped into the air, and belly-flopped into the middle of a pasture of bulrush grass, skidding across. Startled geese fluttered out—*honk, honk, honk*—wildly flapping their wings as they flew in all directions. Their confusion dazed me, and when the boat finally stopped, I froze and stared out in disbelief.

Suddenly, I remembered the captain. "Oh, *no,*" I repeated as I raced over to the hatch, down the ladder, and landed in water.

"You, all right?" I asked, coming toward him.

"What happened?"

"I...I...I..."

"Spit it out."

"I shipwrecked the *Molly Mae.*"

"What?!" he remarked, shaking his head as if he had misheard. "Did ya say shipwrecked?"

"Uh-huh."

"Can't be. Better see for myself."

Using me as a crutch, he got to the ladder and inched up backwards on his butt. Once on the deck, he slid out onto it, but kept hold of my hands. "Bit of a slant to her," he said before letting go. Skidding down, he banged into the gunwale. I climbed out onto the deck and slid down too, but he caught me before I hit.

"She's a sinker for sure," he said in a solemn tone.

Tears welled in my eyes. "Captain, I'm so sorry." I stared down at my hands, afraid to look at him. "If I hadn't talked you in to sailing...none of this would've happened." I hesitated, taking a full breath. "It's all my fault."

He sighed. "Well...," taking a long pause, "at least she died at the hands of the sea. Not some spiteful hooligans."

I glanced up and caught his gaze. My lip quivered. "How can you forgive me? The *Molly Mae* was your home."

He shook his head. "Nothin' to forgive."

"But..."

"Nope..., but what I won't excuse is that gloomy face. Get it gone."

CHAPTER 8
THE HUMPTULIPS

BY EARLY MORNING, low tide exposed gooey mud and it stunk bad as rotten eggs. The *Molly Mae,* now partially perched on bulrush grass, tilted to one side.

"Be back in a few hours with the rowboat," I told the captain.

"See you then," he said as he sat up in the make-shift bed I had made for him in the pilothouse.

I climbed over the gunwale, slid down into waist-high grass, and footslogged toward dry land. Mud sucked my boots, and with every step, suctioned them down like quicksand and splattered my overalls.

Straggly spruce trees lined the entry into the deeper forest. I headed in and tromped through underbrush so thick, it seemed I got stuck more than I moved. When I encountered a patch of devils club—the curse of the forest—that was plain unfortunate luck. Every inch of its maple-like leaf and crooked stem was covered with needle-sharp spines. Some plants, reaching high as my waist, brought back memories of the dreadful day when I tripped and landed on one. Mama had to use Mrs. Hill's skunk-cabbage remedy to get all the slivers out. First, she had to dig up the stinky skunk-cabbage, boil its root, and wrap its warm stock around my wound, drawing out the splinters and thorns. I wasn't about to go through that again.

As I slowly passed through the spiny devils-club plants, I held my arms above my head. No matter, one still caught on my overalls and forced me to stop and pinch the corner of its leaf, carefully peeling it off. Getting snagged three more times, cautioned me even more not to let it touch any of my flesh.

When I finally reached our cabin, I hurried to the front porch, but stopped and listened as a chickadee warbled in the distance. It was one of Mama's favorite songbirds and hearing its sweet-pitched call made me think of her. How could so much have changed in such a short time: Mama's death, separation from my sisters, Daddy missing, and now Captain Murphy's shipwrecked boat. If only I could rewind it all. I hesitated a moment longer, then headed down to the dock. Soon as I passed the *Irene*, Daddy popped into my head. A sea captain with a crew of girls, he sure didn't fit into traditional ways. Right then, I vowed I'd find him no matter how long it took.

I continued up the dock to one of our rowboats, stepped inside, and sat. As I pulled the oars, the incoming current had taken hold, and going against it, forced stronger strokes. Once I reached the river's mouth, I saw that the rising tide had turned the bulrush grasses into mushy pastures. Smack in the middle was the *Molly Mae* sagging more than before. Rowing, pushing, and poling, I zigzagged around grass clumps and carefully butted up to her hull.

"Captain Murphy?"

He popped his head through the hatch, placed his trunk in front of him, and let it go. It slid down and banged into the gunwale. He climbed out and skidded down behind it. Watching, I wondered why he'd endanger himself going below and how he managed with a bad foot in waist-deep water.

I stood, reached for his hands, and steadied him into the rowboat. It rocked something fierce, but we quickly sat before it tipped. I leaned for the trunk, but it was too heavy for me to lift.

"Leave it," he said. "Foolish of me to think I could bring it. Can't keep mementos forever."

"Maybe at another angle, we can hoist it into the boat."

"Nope. Get away from the *Molly Mae* before she takes us with her."

When we got a good distance, I shipped the oars.

"What're you doing?"

"Thought you'd like one last look."

He turned his head and took a long deep breath. " 'Tis a grand restin' place for her." Sadness lagged in his voice."Goodbye, old girl." As he faced me, wetness glazed his eyes.

I quickly looked over my shoulder, slid the oars into the water, and pulled. At the final bend of the river, the *Irene* came in view.

With her robin's-egg-blue hull, stark-white pilothouse, over-size boiler stack, and two tall masts, forward and aft, the *Irene* looked as elegant as a sailing ship.

71

I turned and faced the captain. "I didn't think to ask. How's your foot today?"

"Painin' some, but at least it's my gimp leg."

I nodded, remembering he had injured it in the Civil War. "Maybe I should go to Mrs. Hill? She has all types of natural medicines."

He frowned. "Don't need her foolishness. A good soak in a washtub will do it."

"All right," I said.

Once I got him into the *Irene's* pilothouse and onto the back bench, I pulled out the duck-feathered mattress stored underneath and sat it atop the bunk. He lowered onto it.

"Always admired this pilothouse," he said.

The U-shaped pilothouse had whitewashed planked walls, long-arched windows, and inside the glass-horseshoe curve, a well-equipped pilot station, but the prize of the room was the polished eight-spoke mahogany wheel, standing front and center.

"Daddy added extra touches," I said, covering the captain with a blanket.

"Even two pilothouse doors, I see. Thought of everything, didn't he?"

"Yes," I agreed. "I'll go below and fix you something to eat now."

"Aye. My belly's been callin' but I could use a bit of a rest too."

"Okay," I said. "I'll be up shortly."

AFTER I STOKED the galley cookstove, I pulled the coffeepot from the cupboard, filled it with grounds and water, and placed it atop the burner. I started a pot of oatmeal too. While waiting for it all to boil, I leaned against the table, looked around the room, and thought about Mama. She called the *Irene* her luxury hotel. It had features we didn't have in our cabin, like the bathtub at the foot of my bed and the flush toilet attached to the pilothouse.

Daddy built the galley, but it was Mama's design: the over-sized cupboards and closets edging both sides of the room, and bolted to the floor, a table that comfortably sat six. The only part that resembled a standard boat was our bunks. Mine, doublewide and floor level, sat toward the point of the bow. Viorene and Wilmina's upper bunks hung on each side of the bulkhead, and they used my bed as a step to get up on theirs. Mama and Daddy slept in floor-level bunks located in the pilothouse.

I turned off the oatmeal, but the coffee wasn't done, so I went next door to the engine room. The air smelled oily. I breathed it in and felt inspired because it reminded me of Daddy. He loved his iron workhorses: the steam steering mechanism with chains, cranks, and worm gears, the boiler, and the triple-expansion engine. And when it all came to life—snorting, hissing and blowing off steam—it was as if an angry dragon had arisen and was crazed for a fight.

Thinking about my parents now, gnawed an emptiness inside me. So bad, that it hurt.

73

THE NEXT DAY, I rowed to Mrs. Hill's, but she wasn't there. Her great-grandson had left a note.

Mrs. Hill gone to help with the new baby.
Back in one week - John

As I rowed along Gillis Slough back to the Humptulips River, I thought of my sisters, how we'd laugh and jabber on our way to and from school. Now so quiet, not even a chirping bird.

At the river, I shipped the oars, drifted into it, and cross-stroked—pushing with one oar and pulling with the other to angle the boat—but instead of heading upriver toward home, I pointed the bow toward the *Molly Mae*.

"Goodbye *Molly Mae*," I whispered, looking out at her.

Flopped on one side, pots, pans, and a barrel had floated off her deck and bobbed in the water. When I spotted the captain's trunk in a clump of grass, I rowed over to it. Coming up to its side, I tried to lift it, but couldn't. I leaned over my gunwale, opened the trunk's lid, and pulled out items one by one, examining each as I set them on my bottom boards: four crocheted doilies, a hand-painted vase, linen table cloth, and a picture album etched with O'Murphy on the front. My curiosity overtook, so I opened it and looked at the pictures inside.

The first page displayed a portrait of a young man and woman, maybe in their twenties. The round-faced woman, dressed in a lacy gown, had wavy hair tied up in a bun and a flower garland around her head. The man wore a sea captain's coat and hat. I looked at it closer. Staring back at me was a young Captain Murphy. I flipped to the next page and saw the couple again. In this picture, they appeared older, at least by ten years. The woman held a baby girl, and standing in the front was a young boy outfitted in knickers.

He never mentioned that he had a family. I closed the album, put it down by my feet, and shut the trunk's lid.

I looked up at dark clouds shadowing the river. A moment later, plop, plop, plop, raindrops hit the water. Then in the usual Humptulips fashion, the clouds opened up into a downpour. I pulled out a tarp from under the thwart, covered the captain's things, and picked up my oars. Rowing home, cold rain pelted my head.

I carried the captain's tarp-covered belongings onto the *Irene* and debated if I'd give them to him now or wait for a special occasion. I opted for the second, especially since I figured I might be scolded for going back to a sinking boat. After hiding his mementos in the galley closet, I headed up to the pilothouse.

"You look like a drowned muskrat," the captain said as I walked through the pilothouse door.

"Took a hike." I didn't want to admit that I had rowed to Mrs. Hill's or visited the *Molly Mae*. "How are you feeling?"

"Bit feverish. Must've caught a bug."

"This weather doesn't help. I'll throw more wood in the firebox, get changed, and then bring up coffee and some of Mama's jarred potato soup."

"Grand. My stomach's been a rumblin'."

After he ate, I walked him to the privy that was built into the pilothouse wall. It resembled an outhouse but had a flush toilet. And with a pull of the rope, the collected rainwater from the roof traveled down to the bowl, filling it up and flushing it out into the river.

"Quite a contraption," the captain said, coming out the privy door.

I nodded, grabbed his arm, and steadied him back to the mattress. I looked out the window. "Rain's let up. I'm going to check the boiler's water level."

Daddy had taught me to *never, never* let the boiler run low on water. He had piped water from a natural spring to a shut-off valve spigot at the dock. There, he connected a fifty-foot fabric hose. I dragged the hose onto the *Irene*, snaked it down the boiler tank-hole, and turned on the spigot. After the glass gauge measured full, I turned off the water, pulled the hose back to the dock, and wound it around a spindle. Just as I stood, a familiar voice called out.

"Aggie."

"Who's there?" I said, looking side to side and up at the trail.

"Me," the voice said. "On the river."

I raced to the end of the dock. "Wilmina?"

Rowing up to the dock, she threw me her line. I reeled the boat in and tied it to a piling. The instant she stepped onto the dock, I hugged her tight. She wrapped her arms around me too.

"I'm so happy to see you," I said, rocking her back and forth. I pulled her back at arm's length. "But what're you doing here? And where's Viorene?"

"I waited for Viorene to fall asleep, then I snuck out. When I saw the *Molly Mae* missing, I knew you'd be here, so I went to the sawmill yard and slept on the logging train. Engineer Tyler was sure surprised to see me."

I put my arm around her. "I'm glad you're here, but Viorene must be worried sick."

"Don't care. She can't be trusted. She squealed on you."

I sighed. "Start from the beginning."

"While Viorene was at the dressmaker, Grandma opened her bookcase, then yelled for me to come downstairs and asked if I'd been in it. I said *no*, but she made me wait in the parlor anyway. Soon as Viorene came through the door and saw the case open, her face burned fire-red and she started shaking. She didn't even wait for Grandma to say a peep, just handed over the letters, then burst into tears and told Grandma the whole idea belonged to you."

I nodded. "We had an agreement. If caught, she was to blame me. And you know Viorene gets jumpy as a jackrabbit and spills every last drop without meaning to."

77

"She's a turncoat. I think she told Grandma about me too. I caught them whispering in the kitchen, but their lips sealed shut soon as they saw me. I'm certain Grandma's convinced Viorene to spy on us."

"Why would you think that?"

"She's been acting odd, asking me if I knew any secrets that she should know. I said no, then I asked her what she and Grandma where whispering about. She told me nothing important for little ears. So, I decided to find out for myself."

"Oh, no, what did you do?"

"I waited until Viorene took a bath, then I snuck down the stairs, sat on the steps, and listened in on Grandma and Grandpa James. Lester and Harold are coming to fetch you. Grandma even mentioned sending you and me away to a special school for unruly girls. What're we going to do?"

"Don't know, but we'll think up something. For now, let's keep this to ourselves. Get changed while I fix you a bowl of soup."

Wilmina rifled through our wardrobe closet, stuffed full of dresses, pants, shirts, shoes and boots, to name a few, and found a pair of overalls and a similar green-plaid shirt like mine and slipped them on. She strung her wet clothes over the bathtub, which sat at the foot of my bed, and then she plopped down in a chair at the galley table.

"Except for our hair, we look like twins," she said, tugging the sleeve of her shirt.

I smiled and nodded. "No harm in that," I replied, dishing up her soup.

While she ate, I told her about Captain Murphy's hurt foot and the sinking of the *Molly Mae*.

"That's awful," she said, taking her last bite, and then washing her bowl and setting it out to dry.

I placed the teakettle and a tin cup on a tray and picked it up. "If you're ready, come say hello to the captain."

The captain, sitting up and examining his toes, looked up as we walked through the pilothouse door. He scowled when he saw Wilmina. "What's she's doing here?"

"She's in the same pickle as me," I said, setting the tray down on the front bench. "Ready for a cup of tea?"

"No," he barked. "Two runaways? Can't be associated with that."

"We'd never make you a part of our problems," I said.

"Fact you're both here, ya already have. Can't bother with it now. Need to soak my claw. Get the washtub."

After we got him over to the bench, I retrieved a tub, set it on the floor in front of him, and poured hot water from the teakettle. Wilmina bent down and looked at his toes. "They look like slimy green slugs."

"Get back. Don't need an opinion."

I looked at them. "Captain, they're infected."

"Aye," he said, and then he lowered his foot into the steaming water.

"I'll go to Mrs. Hill. She has natural remedies."

79

–

"Told ya, I don't believe in that magic."

After a bit, I handed him a towel. He blotted his toes. Wilmina leaned in for another look.

"They're worse," she said.

The captain narrowed his eyes at my sister, but I interrupted before he snapped out words.

"Wilmina, give the captain air." I pulled her to the wheel. "No more comments, you're getting him riled." I turned to the captain. "We'll let you rest."

"Aye. Need my strength to sail tomorrow. To see a doctor and to get ya back to your family."

Wilmina and I looked at each other.

"Only solution possible," he said.

"No," Wilmina spurted. "We're not going back to Grandma's. And you can't make us."

The captain looked at me with pleading eyes. I nodded, but only to give him a response.

Wilmina piped up. "Doctor Simpson's gone for two weeks. He told Grandma that when he dropped off her medicine."

When the captain's expression showed concern, I spoke up. "Aberdeen has a doctor."

Aberdeen, twice the size as Hoquiam, was four miles beyond the Hoquiam River entrance.

"Is the boiler ready?" he asked.

"Yes, watered and wooded up."

"Grand. We'll leave at dawn."

We helped him back to the bunk, and then we carried

the washtub outside to the gunwale. "He can't force us to go back to Grandma's, can he?" Wilmina asked in a panicked tone as we tossed the water overboard.

"No, but for now let him think that we are. Aberdeen's a safe port. No one there knows us or the *Irene*."

"Can he sail this boat? He looks awful pale."

"Should be able to." Truth to be known, I wasn't sure either. And after sinking the *Molly Mae*, I was gun-shy from trying on my own, but with Lester and Harold coming and the captain needing a doctor, we had no choice but to sail. He'll be fine, repeated in my head.

That night, Wilmina snored in the bunk above me, but no matter, I worried so much about tomorrow's voyage and tossed from one side to the other. Even tried sleeping with my head down where I usually had my feet. Finally, I sat up.

Through the portholes, the moon beamed a golden hue into the galley, enough light for me to see by. After I dressed and put on my socks and rubber boots, I shuffled quiet as I could to the table, lit the lantern, and headed to the engine room. As I heightened the lantern's flame, it turned the room to a glowing pumpkin orange and magnified the giant workhorses three times their actual size. Crossing the steel floor to the boiler, I opened the firebox door and tossed in more wood. Moments later, the fire rumbled inside. Leaving the door open, I stood in front of it as it warmed me and the surrounding coldness.

Wilmina called from her bunk. "Is it time to get up?"

"No." I closed the furnace door and hurried to the galley. "Sorry I woke you."

"You didn't," she said, sitting up. "Smells like hot oil. Comes through the vent below my bunk."

We always kept the boiler damper, blower, and hinges well oiled, and with a full roar inside the firebox, they burnt off a scent.

"I never knew it got this strong," I said.

"That's because you were always in the pilothouse with Daddy. It's especially bad after a fresh oiling." Sliding off her bunk and pulling her boots on, she wrapped herself in a wool blanket. "I'm going up to the pilothouse. It should be warmer there. And it doesn't hold on to this terrible smell."

"I'm coming with you," I said.

Once inside the pilothouse, I glanced at the captain, still fast asleep, then I motioned Wilmina to the front bench.

"It's so warm in here," she whispered, sitting and covering up with her blanket.

"Nothing like boiler heat," I said, snuggling next to her on the bench.

Soon as the sun gleamed through the windows, I crept to the wheel pedestal and squatted down behind it.

"What're you doing?" Wilmina asked.

"Making sure the worms aren't loose."

"Worms?" She hurried over and crouched down next to me.

82

"The steering gears. Daddy calls them worms. See the chain on the wheel's axle?"

"Yes," she said, leaning over to watch me.

"It's hooked to the steering cylinder that controls the rudder. Everything looks in good order." I stood.

"I never knew you knew so much," she said.

"I've always been fascinated by the inner workings of this boat. Daddy was pleased to teach me."

She pointed to the brass boat controls on the wall. "I know that's the compass and the other one, the engine gauge."

"That's a good start. But as my first mate, you'll need to learn more."

Her eyes widened. "I'm first mate?"

"Yes, and you'll be a good one. How about I teach you to bleed the boiler? Always has to be checked before we sail."

"What's all the racket?" The captain barked.

"Uh, oh," Wilmina said. "He sounds grumpy."

I smiled and pointed her back to the bench, then headed to the captain. "Good morning. Tide's up. How're you feeling?"

"Fine," he said. "Have the little one start the brew. You, help me to the privy and get workin' on this boat. Want to be out of here within the hour."

Wilmina and I fixed the captain two cups of coffee and fried up some bacon. After we wolfed down our breakfast, we headed to the engine room.

83

I grabbed two pair of work gloves from a bucket and handed her a pair. "Whenever dealing with the boiler, *always* wear work gloves," I told her. After we pulled on the gloves, the tips hung over our fingers.

"These gloves look funny," she said, holding up her hands.

"Never bothered me, but do the best you can. Next time we're in town, we'll get smaller sizes."

On the side of the boiler were three try-cocks—water spigots positioned one above the other and four inches apart. I pushed a bucket under the spigots. "Always, *always* open the bottom try-cock first."

"Why?"

"You can't open the middle try-cock, draining out scalding water, then go for the handle below," I said. "You'd burn your hands good. I'm not even sure the gloves would protect you. There's a proper order to opening the try-cocks. Bottom, middle, and the top valve, last."

With my hand atop of hers, we twisted the bottom valve. Steam hissed, then water flowed. "Good," I said, closing the valve. "If it'd been *only* steam that would've meant the boiler was low on water." We followed the same process with the middle try-cock.

"So both valves get *A's*, just like school," Wilmina said.

"That's right," I assured, moving her hand with mine to the top try-cock. "Now, we're looking for just steam."

She slowly turned the valve, but she stopped.

"It's *thquealing.*" Whenever she panicked, she lisped. "And it's coming out water and *theam.*"

"Needs to be blown off."

She followed me to the drain valve, a separate spigot off to the side of the boiler. I set a bucket beneath, turned the spigot, let a tiny bit of water out, went back to the top try-cock, and opened it again. Water flashed into steam.

"Still under pressure," I said. "One more draining should give us pure steam."

"There's so much to learn. What if I muddle it up?"

"You did great. Better than my first time."

"Really?" she said, with a hopeful look.

"I'm telling you the truth. Every boiler's unique. In no time, you'll know this one's call."

She grinned. "You sound just like Daddy."

CHAPTER 9
CHEHALIS RIVER

WHILE THE CAPTAIN stood behind the eight-spoke wheel fiddling with the gauges, Wilmina and I headed outside to untie the *Irene*.

"The Irene's ready to sail," I told the captain as I followed Wilmina into the pilothouse and sat down next to her on the front bench.

"Aye, so she is." He gripped the wheel with quivering hands.

Wilmina nudged me and whispered, "He looks nervous."

"He's fine." But truthfully, I had noticed his shakiness too. "Captain, with all the snags and turns, the Humptulips can be a tricky switchback."

A switchback river would start in one direction, and then switch to the other, back and forth, like a slithering snake, and never truly straighten until it emptied into a bay.

"Ya forgettin' I captained the tugs."

"No, just wanted to remind you that once we start down, there's no turning back. It isn't wide enough to make a spin."

"Git up here then and give me your eyes."

As I stood next to him, he slowly turned the throttle, looked out at the river again, and then opened the throttle wider, increasing our knots. The engine's steady putt-putt-putt, sounding like Mama's foot-pedal sewing machine, guided us out. When the captain pulled a rag from his pocket and dabbed his forehead, I didn't think much of it until I saw sweat beading on his brow and his cheeks now crimson-red.

"Are you feeling all right?" I asked, looking at him then glancing back to the river.

"Jitters."

"We still have time to turn around and dock."

"Don't be tellin' me how to sail."

"Okay. Sorry."

Nervousness filled my belly as I watched him head the *Irene* into the first bend. He throttled down, and much to my relief and maybe a bit of surprise, was handling the boat good as Daddy. I sighed under my breath, but all that changed in less than an eye's blink.

He latched onto my arm. "Feelin' a bit weak-kneed. Take a hand to the helm."

"What?!"

He let loose of the wheel and stumbled toward Wilmina on the bench. She jumped up and helped him sit.

"Leg gave out. Just need a bit of a rest."

I grabbed the wheel, but my hands were trembling so bad that it took every bit of strength to hold on to the spokes.

Coming into the next curve, I opened the throttle, but

too much and the *Irene* lunged, just like the *Molly Mae* before she shipwrecked. With no time to spare, I cranked the wheel and forced the bow into the razor-sharp turn. The next couple of switchbacks came so fast, they challenged my skills, but the *Irene* handled them with ease. By the time the river widened into the mouth, I don't know what was worse, my rolling stomach or shaking hands. I looked over at my sister and saw that the captain was missing.

"Where's the captain?"

"I got him aft, just in time before he collapsed onto the mattress. His forehead's on fire."

I sighed and shook my head. "I should've trusted my gut. He didn't look good and now we're stuck at the mouth."

"At least it's high tide," Wilmina said.

"Yes, but that means I have to take her into the bay. Last time I was here, I sank the *Molly Mae*."

The captain hollered from the back. "Sorry, Aggie-girl. Appears I'm sicker than I thought."

I turned around and gave him a frail smile. "Just rest. We'll get you to a doctor."

"Thank ye," he said, and then closed his eyes.

I turned back to the wheel and glanced over at my sister, who was now staring out the window at the *Molly Mae* sagging in the grass.

"Is that the captain's boat?"

"Yes, not much left of her," I replied in a somber tone.

"Glad he didn't have to see her like that." Guilt rushed through me. I clasped the wheel and took a deep breath. "Keep your eyes sharp for sandpits."

With tidal rivers, sandpits were a constant menace. One day they'd appear, disappear the next, and ground a boat faster than a flick of the eye. The *Molly Mae* was proof of that.

Wilmina opened the side window and stuck her head through it. "What is it I'm looking for?"

"A faint shadow or rippling water hints to one too. Anything that looks odd."

Inching the *Irene* through the brackish water toward the crossing, I leaned out the pilothouse door watching for humps of sand. As the wind blew off the bay and swayed the yellowed sedge grass along the shore, I cupped my hands over my eyes, blocking the sun now hazing behind clouds.

"The water's so cloudy. I can't see a thing. Not even the Lone Tree," Wilmina said, closing the window.

The Lone Tree, a magnificent Spruce on the point near the Grays Harbor Bar, had been used as a navigation beacon for over one-hundred years. Daddy called the Lone Tree our spiritual guide.

Wilmina slid off the bench and stepped over to me.

"The bay's grizzly too," I added, "but this tide can't get much higher. I'd say it's safe to cross. Here we go."

Gripping the wheel and the forward-reverse lever, I advanced the *Irene*. Water splashed against her hull.

90

Soon as we entered the bay, I went limp, slowed our knots, and shook out my arms.

"I knew you could do it," Wilmina said.

PASSING EACH BAY MARKER: James Rock, Brackenridge Bluff, and Grays Harbor City Pier, I looked at Daddy's pocket watch hanging from a nail near the compass, and silently thanked God for getting us this far. In an hour, we'd be passing the Hoquiam entry to town, but instead of turning the wheel portside into the Hoquiam River, we'd be keeping a straight course on the bay, inland four more miles to Aberdeen along the Chehalis River.

When we reached the Chehalis' mouth, the waterway had shriveled in size, but not all the watercraft—tall ships, lumber schooners, ferries, barges, tugs, and fishing boats elbowed side by side along the wharves. A towing tug pulling a barge signaled for a green-to-green pass—both of us passing starboard on the right—I pulled our whistle, spun the wheel, and waved. I didn't show my nervousness, but passing in such a tight space shivered my insides as if dunked in ice.

"Over there," Wilmina said, pointing to an empty dock.

"Good eye," I told her as we headed toward it.

The river bordered Aberdeen, a bustling lumber town known for being good and bad. The town center, frequented by normal folk, had clothing establishments, eateries, hotels, general stores, and a post office, to name a few. But along the wharf, there was nothing but saloon after saloon, run-down flophouses, and dance-halls that catered to loggers, transients, and sailors from the tall sailing ships.

After we tied up, I saw the dock's neglected state. It was leaning sideways and had rotten pilings and missing boards.

"I see why it's vacant." I told my sister. "Looks dangerous to walk on. Stay with the captain while I go for the doctor."

"Okay," Wilmina said. "Be careful on the dock."

"I will. Keep your fingers crossed that the doctor will give me medicine."

"Too bad we're not in Hoquiam," Wilmina remarked. "Grandma's got a cupboard full."

Grandma did have cures for every ailment known to man: bursitis, abscessed tooth, dropsy, even typhus, or so she claimed. Only the best medicines would do. All special ordered from San Francisco and stored in her bedroom closet.

Two hours later, after I returned from town, the captain awoke. Groaning, he pushed himself up and leaned against the wall. "Where are we?"

"Aberdeen," I said.

"I was out that long?"

"Yes. I've already been to the doctor, but his sign said that he won't be back for two days."

The captain frowned, lifted his foot, and examined his toes. I tried to look, but he shooed me away. Then he sighed. "Get me somethin' to write a note."

"Here you go," Wilmina said, handing him paper and a pencil.

After he scribbled out a message, he folded it up. "Aggie-girl, take this to my brother. Go with him to get supplies. He's a scoundrel, so don't tell him a thing or let him talk you out of money. And *don't* bring him back to this boat."

"Why don't I get the supplies, then we don't have to bother with him."

"No, he'll know what to get. Don't read my note, understand?"

"All right."

"His name is Donegan. He lives in a run-down hotel at the edge of town. Believe it's called the Laurel."

I stuffed his note into my coat pocket, then headed to the door.

"Wish I could go with you," Wilmina said, walking with me out to the gunwale.

"Me too, but you gotta stay with the captain. Don't worry I'll be fine."

In town, I stopped into a feed store to get directions to the Laurel. "Careful," the clerk had told me. "Bit shady over there."

When I got to the hotel, I stared in disbelief. Captain described it as run-down. More falling down would've been my words. Broken windows, tattered curtains, and a tilted porch—and that was seeing it from one angle. I pushed on the lobby door, went inside, and stepped onto a worn tapestry rug that partially covered a scuffed-up wood floor. As I glanced around the large room, I noted three dirty overstuffed chairs and faded pink-striped wallpaper peeling off the walls, but what was still intact was a magnificent curved staircase leading up to a second floor.

"Hello," I called out, climbing up the stairs. "Is there a Donegan here?"

A door opened. "Who wants to know?"

"Have a note to deliver."

"Three doors down," the man said, closing his door before I could respond.

At Donegan's door, I knocked, then knocked and knocked again. Finally, a voice hollered. "Stop pounding." The accent matched the captain's, and when the door opened, so did the weathered face. Only difference, this face didn't possess the captain's kindness. Hard and cold, this one was.

"Here," I said, extending my arm.

He scowled at me. "What's this?"

"A note."

"I can see that. Who's it from?"

The captain said not to offer any extra words, so I didn't speak.

He grabbed the note from my hand and slammed the door. A moment later, the door cracked open, but instead

94

of the old man, there stood a boy not much older than me, but scrawny as an unfed cat.

"Hello," I said.

"Get away from that door," Donegan said to the boy, pushing him aside. He looked at me. "Where's the man who sent this?"

"I'm only the messenger," I stammered.

"It says for me to get you supplies. You must know where he is."

"Uh ... uh, all he said was to get your help and he'd find me."

"Find you where? He's asking for odd things. Says he needs a handsaw, sharpened hunting knife, fishing line and needle. Plus clean wrap and whiskey."

"A handsaw?"

"Sounds to me, he's planning on sawing off a leg. Had to do it once. To a man on a sailing ship. Not a pleasant thing to do."

I froze. Is the captain's foot that bad? His toes were awful green.

"I have to go." I turned around, but before I took my first step, he grabbed the back of my overalls.

"Not so fast. You'll be takin' me to him."

"Don't know where he is."

"You have two choices. Either I tie you up until you talk or you take me to him now. Billy-boy," he called out to the boy inside. "Get the rope."

I paused and found myself in a stare-down with this

man. And I knew in my gut that he wasn't bluffing. "Fine," I said. "I'll take you."

"Never mind the rope," he said to the boy. "Get out here. We're goin' for a walk."

Sandwiched between the old man and the boy, I didn't offer any words. Neither did they, so I studied the boy. Dirty clothes, wiry brown hair, oblong face, and droopy eyes. Can't be more than eleven or twelve. Looks outcast to me.

The whole time, I tried to figure out an escape but nothing came to mind. I decided the captain seeing his brother couldn't do any more harm than the captain cutting off his own toes. If that was his plan.

"Where you leadin' us?" the old man said.

"To the dock. There," I said, pointing to the *Irene.*

"Nice vessel. Who owns it?"

I ignored his question. "This way. Careful where you step."

I zigzagged from board to board. The boy copied me like *Follow the Leader.* Not the old man. Built same as the captain, but with no limp, he marched across the dilapidated dock without a thought or a care until his foot broke through a board. Down his leg went. Words, some I recognized, others I knew I shouldn't, flew out of his mouth.

The boy snickered, turned back, and helped him up.

I stepped aboard the *Irene* and raced into the pilothouse. "Captain, your brother insisted on coming."

"What?" he said, sitting up.

Before he added another word, in walked Donegan and the boy.

"Captain Paddy," the old man said, walking toward the captain. "What type of fix you in?"

"None to concern you," the captain replied.

Seeing them together—same stubby build, white hair, and round nose—they looked like twins.

"You young'ns git, while me brother and me talk," Donegan said.

"Not until the captain tells me," I replied.

"Gotta a tongue sharp as a spike, don't you?" Donegan spouted. "Listen here, Little Spike, I don't take sass from anyone, especially kids."

I looked at the captain.

"Go below," Captain Murphy said. "Take the boy with you. Looks as if he could use some eats."

The boy followed me down to the galley.

Wilmina stood at the cookstove stirring a pot.

"I'm back. With a guest." I pulled out a chair at the galley table. "You can sit here," I told the boy, then I stepped to Wilmina at the stove. "His name is Billy. He's with Donegan, the captain's brother."

"Hello," Wilmina said, craning her neck to look at him. "I fixed salmon chowder, if you're hungry." Mama had jarred all types of soups and chowders: clam, potato, and salmon, to name a few.

"Yep," Billy said.

Soon as she set the bowl on the table, he lifted it to his mouth, slurped, and swallowed the chowder down in chunks. "Got more?" he said, belching.

Wilmina spun back around to the stove and leaned to my ear. "Should've told him to wash up. He has more dirt on his face than his hands." After she filled his bowl again, he didn't hesitate to lift it to his mouth.

"We have spoons," Wilmina said.

He ignored her and kept eating.

I sat down at the table across from him and asked, "What's your association with Donegan?"

He didn't answer.

"Grandson?"

He shook his head.

"Nephew?"

Shook his head again.

"Don't you have a tongue?" Wilmina said. "You don't have manners. That's for sure."

He put down the bowl, wiped his mouth with the back of his hand, and burped again. "Donegan ain't no relation and I earn my keep."

"Are you an orphan?" I asked.

"Ain't answerin' no more."

"You're not suppose to use *ain't*," Wilmina said. "Our teacher says it's not proper."

He stuck a finger in his ear and pulled out a ball of wax. "This probably *ain't* proper either." He grinned, showing her the wad.

I giggled to myself. If Wilmina had been in the mood, she would've showed him up. Instead, she gathered our bowls and carried them to the washbasin. But my sister Viorene would've been outraged. Me, I couldn't have cared less.

"Little Spike," Donegan yelled from the hatch. "Captain wants to see you."

"Stop calling me that," I said as I passed him. When he smirked at me, I knew I'd made a mistake showing my dislike for the nickname. He followed me into the pilothouse.

"Did you plan on cutting off your toes?" I asked the captain.

"Never mind that. I've made an agreement with me brother. Go to town with him for supplies. Still have money on you?"

In addition to my five-dollar gold piece, I had pulled another five dollars from a gunnysack that Daddy had hidden in the boiler shed. I was planning to use it for the doctor. "Yes," I told the captain. "I have money."

"Pay it only to the clerk."

"Don't trust me, little brother?" Donegan said.

"You'll get your pay when the deed's done."

WHEN WE GOT DOWNTOWN, I followed Donegan into a general store. He picked out a saw and knife, set them on the counter, and asked the clerk for a bandage to wrap a leg, plus fishing line and needle. He turned to me.

"Pay the clerk." He headed out the door.

Carrying a bag with the jagged teeth of the saw sticking out, bothered me. Not because it looked odd, but because I knew what it was meant to do. I caught up to Donegan and walked beside him. As we turned the corner, two men brawled in front of a saloon, and from an upstairs window, a dance-hall lady shouted to passers-by. She wore so much red, I couldn't see past it—red hair, red cheeks, red lips, and a feathered red boa around her neck.

Donegan walked us to mid-street, stopped in front of a saloon, and held out his hand. "I'll need money for a bottle. Give me a dollar and I'll get two."

With reluctance, I reached into my pocket and removed half a dollar more than I intended. He snatched every cent out of my hand and disappeared into the bar. I strolled to the end of the block and sat down on the planked sidewalk. After a bit, I pulled out Daddy's pocket watch. From the last time I'd checked, another half hour had passed. I stood, brushed off my overalls, and headed to the saloon. Once inside, I found Donegan leaning on the bar, drink in hand.

"Thought you were coming right out."

"Don't like being rushed," he barked. He swallowed down his drink, slammed the glass on the counter, grabbed the bottle sitting in front of him, and headed out the door.

"Thought you needed two bottles."

"Nope."

"Then give me my change."

"None comin'."

I could see the captain was right not to trust him. So dishonest, he'd steal from a kid. I wondered if he made Billy steal. Maybe that's what he meant by earning his keep?

Back on the *Irene*, I hurried into the pilothouse with Donegan at my heels.

"I'm starved," Donegan said. "Like to eat first."

"There's salmon stew below," I said. "Captain, can I get you some?"

"No, your sister fed me earlier. Donegan, go eat."

After Donegan left, I sat down next to the captain. "Are you cutting off your toes?"

"Just two. Turnin' black, might be a sign of gangrene."

"Let me check on the doctor," I begged. "Maybe he's come back."

"Don't want to wait, it spreads fast. Besides, I've seen this done plenty. On clipper ships. Even performed it on several men, more than once. So has me brother. It's over fast."

"You trust him to do it? He's been drinking."

"Even better. It'll give him courage."

My eyes filled with mist. "I should have never made you sail. Please forgive me. This is all my fault."

"Stop it. The *Molly Mae* was a goner whether we sailed or not. Those hooligans were determined and would've burned her down. Accidents are just that.

Besides, it's on my gimp leg. I already walk with a cane. Two missin' toes ain't goin' to make a difference. What I need from you now is five dollars, but not your special gold piece. Do you have any extra on the boat?"

"Yes. Daddy stashed money all over this boat. There's a gunnysack in the shed behind you."

"Make it quick. Don't want Donegan knownin' you got more."

Behind the captain was an opening into the boiler shed. I crawled through it and pulled a five-dollar coin out of a hidden sack, and then I quickly backed out and sat beside the captain again.

"Once he's done, pay him," the captain instructed. "And get him *off* this boat. Give me the whiskey, then get goin'."

I pulled out the cork and handed him the bottle. As he gulped and gulped, I swallowed the nervous lump in my throat. Suddenly, I gagged. "Sorry, captain. Have to go." I rushed out the door to the gunwale, leaned over and threw up.

"Looks like you're the one who's been drinkin'," Donegan said on his way into the pilothouse.

I staggered as I stood, wiped my mouth with the back of my hand, and inhaled a deep breath in and out until my stomach calmed. Rushing down the steps into the galley, I grabbed Wilmina's hand and pulled her to my bed.

"Sit down and cover your ears," I said, handing her a pillow. "You too, Billy."

"Why?" Wilmina asked.

"Do it."

When she sat down and pulled the pillow around her head, I was relieved she listened to me. I turned to Billy, but he didn't seem fazed by what I said. His only interest, eating more chowder.

I sat next to Wilmina and covered my ears with a pillow too. After a bit, Donegan entered the galley. Shaking, I set the pillow in my lap and watched as he approached, hand extended.

"He chickened out," Donegan said, "but I'll still take that five dollars for my willingness to try."

I hesitated, ready to tell him no, but the truth be told, I was relieved that the captain had changed his mind. And I sure didn't want to cross Donegan, otherwise, he might just go through with it for spite. I pulled the money from my pocket and handed it to him.

"Got any more in there?" he said.

"No."

"Say, whose boat is this?"

I squeezed Wilmina's hand and said nothing. Only problem, Donegan wasn't leaving without an answer. I saw that as clear as I saw dried chowder bits in his stubby beard.

"I could get use to livin' on a boat like this," he remarked, scanning the room. "Maybe we'll stay awhile. Might be good if we do, then I could keep an eye on me brother."

103

"Our father's coming in on the train. Tomorrow," I blurted. "It's his boat, and we'll do fine watching after the captain. Time for you to go."

"Told you, I don't take sass. But I'm feeling generous from all this extra pay. Don't try it again, Little Spike. Come on, Billy. I'm ready for more grog."

I followed them up to the deck, watched until they disappeared off the dock, then I checked on the captain.

Passed out and lily-white, the captain looked dead. His foot reeked of whiskey that had been poured on his toes.

Looking at him, I felt helpless. Tears stung my eyes, and as they cascaded down, I wiped them away with my sleeve. I pulled Daddy's watch from my pocket. I was surprised to see it was only six o'clock, but exhaustion hit me. All I wanted was to sleep.

"Are they gone?" Wilmina asked as I entered the galley.

"Yes, thank goodness."

"Why'd you make me cover my ears?"

I sat next to her on the bed and told her about the captain's toes, but that he had changed his mind.

"That's good," she said.

"I'll sleep in Mama's bunk tonight," I said. "To keep a close watch on him." Mama's bunk was at the back of the pilothouse on the starboard side, next to the privy.

"Can I sleep up there too? Mama's bed is wide enough and I can spell you."

"Sure," I said. "A second set of ears would be helpful."

The next morning, before dawn, the captain's moans woke me. I hurried to him.

"Is he all right?" Wilmina asked, coming up behind me.

"He's burning up," I said, feeling his forehead. "I'm going for the doctor."

"Now? Nothing's open. Besides, I thought the doctor wasn't back until tomorrow."

"Might've gotten back early. And doctor's are used to people waking them up. I better take more money." I crawled into the boiler shed, reached for the burlap sack, and pulled out five dollars in coin, then I headed out the pilothouse door.

With a lantern, I maneuvered along the dock to the road. Except for howling cats, the empty streets—solemn as a tomb—magnified shadows at every turn. Luckily, streetlights guided me along. When I got to the doctor's house, I put down my lantern and knocked on the door again and again.

"Hold on," a voice called out. A tiny bell jingled as the door opened. There stood a round-bellied, middle-aged man with a brown beard, glasses, and a head bald as a shiny rock.

"I have an emergency, sir. My grandfather is burning up with a fever. He has infected toes."

"Let me get dressed and grab my bag." The doctor kept up with me, huffing most the way. At the gangplank leading down to the dock, he stopped.

"He's on the boat," I said.

"I know this dock," he said, shaking his head. "Years back, my brother used it for his boat. Last I knew, it was condemned. Surprised it's still here."

"It's fine. Just have to be careful with your steps. Follow me, I'll go first."

"Not safe for someone of my size. Sorry, I'm the only doctor in town. Can't take the chance of getting hurt. Can you bring him to me?"

"No, he's too sick. Please come."

"Best I can do is provide you medicine." He set down his bag, pulled out a bottle of tonic and wrapping. "This is for his toes. Pour it on twice a day and apply clean dressing. I'll only charge a half dollar for this bottle; it's hardly used."

"What about his fever?"

"I've run out of that medicine. Expecting the order by train, sometime next week. All I can advise is fluid and rest. Don't let him up. Otherwise, the infection could spread. And don't move the boat. He doesn't need any rolling waves. Keep him down until the fever breaks."

CHAPTER 10
ABERDEEN

AFTER TWO LONG DAYS, the captain showed no improvement. Sweat poured off him. He blurted out words, saw things that weren't there, and flailed his arms in the air. Several times, he thought we were his children. Another time, girls from his school days.

"We can't wait six more days for the doctor's medicine to come in," I told my sister. "I'm going for Grandma's, but I'll need Viorene's help."

Wilmina frowned. "After what happened with the letters, I don't think she'll do it."

"Then, I'll sneak into the house myself."

"But Lester's there."

I shrugged. "He's usually gone with Harold."

"You might find Viorene at the library. She goes early to meet friends."

"It's worth a try. If I hurry, I can catch the first trolley."

AT THE ABERDEEN TROLLEY STATION, I sat on a bench and waited. When I heard the trolley coming, I stood behind two others who had already formed a line.

"Whoa," the driver said, pulling the horses' reins.

Soon as it stopped, we boarded.

The red trolley had open-air sides, green poles for those standing, and wooden benches on each side of the aisle. After I paid a penny, I hurried to the back bench and scooted over to the outside. Once more people boarded, the driver snapped the reins and off the horses went. With no one getting off or on along the way, the bumpy ride took less than forty minutes. I rode to the last stop—downtown Hoquiam—and walked two blocks to the library.

The yellow three-story library, once the home of a well-to-do family, was as large as a house could get before being a mansion. Its covered porch, enclosed by a white, spindled railing, extended the full length of the front. A black and white sign, *Public Library*, hung from the porch beam. A smaller sign dangled from the front door: *Open at ten a.m. Close at four p.m.*

To keep out of sight, I sat on the back steps, checking the time on Daddy's pocket watch. At five minutes to ten, I inched along the side of the house to the front and peeked around the corner. Sure enough, six girls huddled together on the sidewalk. One of them was Viorene. My stomach fluttered from excitement as I watched her. She appeared to be having a joyful time, laughing and talking. Seeing her, I realized how much I missed her.

I pulled my captain's hat down to my brow, checked for loose hair strands sticking out, and then sauntered over. "Excuse me, Viorene?"

She turned and looked at me. So did the other girls. Her eyes widened.

"Cousin Elmer," I said, lowering my voice to imitate a boy. "Can we talk?"

Before she could answer, the library door opened. She turned to her friends. "Go ahead, I'll meet you inside." Once the girls disappeared, I hugged her. When she didn't hug me back, it hurt my feelings, bad.

"Is Wilmina with you?"

I nodded.

"Thank goodness, I've been worried sick. Where is she?"

"She's safe."

She sighed. "I'm guessing she told you I got caught with the letters."

"Yes. I'm sorry."

"Lester and Harold left this morning for the Humptulips. If they don't find you, Grandma plans to alert the police. I heard her say she's going to post a reward and have the newspaper print the Christmas picture taken of us last year. You better come to Grandma's with me now."

"No."

"Haven't you heard a word I said?"

"I heard you, but there's something more important. I need some of Grandma's medicine, really bad. It's probably best I don't tell you much. That way, if caught, you really won't know what's going on."

"Caught? If you think I'm trying anything again, you're wrong."

"Please, Viorene. It's for someone real sick and we can't get to the doctor."

"It's not Wilmina, is it?"

"No, but it is best I not say anymore. Please, please. I'm begging you as your sister. Please, help me."

She started shaking. "You've got me so worried now. I don't know what to think."

"I only need one bottle. I'll hide in the hedge while you get it. You know I wouldn't ask unless it was important."

"Why do you do this? Always make situations worse than they need to be? Grandma could help."

I slowly nodded, wondering if she might be right. What if the captain died? All because of my stubbornness not to face Grandma. I decided, right then, if the captain didn't improve after taking the medicine, I would go to Grandma.

"If it's Wilmina and you're not telling me, I'll never forgive you."

"It's not her. Trust me on that."

She huffed. "Wait here." She stomped off. A moment later, returned. "Let's go."

"Thank you for helping."

"Don't be thanking me yet. I'm not promising anything."

SITTING INSIDE THE HEDGE, I focused on Grandma's porch. What's taking her so long? My stomach twisted and turned, same as a dog chained to a tree. I didn't hear her when she approached from the back, in the neighbor's yard.

110

"You still in there?" she said, bending down and looking through the thicket.

"Yes." I backed out and stood.

"Here." She handed me a bottle of elixir as I stood. "This one says typhus. Grandma has three bottles, so might not notice one missing."

I hugged her. "I love you. Thank you." This time she hugged me back.

I started to leave, but she put a hand on my arm. "I need to know your plans."

"It's best you don't."

"At least, tell me who's sick. You owe me that. If it isn't Wilmina, then it must be Captain Murphy."

"I do owe you, but prefer not to say. Can't you just trust that I need this medicine and leave it at that?"

"No, I can't."

"What's going on out here?" a woman's voice said behind her.

Viorene spun around. "Mrs. Mathews," she stammered.

Mrs. Mathews, Grandma's neighbor, owned the other side of the hedge dividing the two yards.

"Who are you talking to?" the woman said, peeking around Viorene.

Before Viorene could answer her, I bolted toward the street. Viorene called out, "Wait, wait." I looked over my shoulder, saw it was only her running behind me, so I slowed down and stopped.

111

Panting, she halted beside me. "Mrs. Mathews asked if it was you, but I didn't answer," Viorene said, gulping in air until she caught her breath. "Mrs. Mathews rushed over to Grandma's, telling her to come outside. I knew this would turn out bad. What're we going to do now?"

"Go home," I said. "Tell her you saw a boy hiding and confronted him."

"Grandma's not going to believe that."

"I need to get out of here."

"I'm coming with you."

"No."

"Either you let me come along or I follow you. Makes no difference to me."

"Fine."

Once we reached the trolley station, I checked the schedule on the window, then sat down on the bench next to Viorene and removed Daddy's pocket watch, looking at the time. "Doesn't leave for another fifteen minutes."

"You're taking the trolley?"

"I've already said too much."

"What do you mean by that?"

"You know I love you, but...you've never been able to hide a secret. No matter how you try. I suggest you leave now."

"I want to see Wilmina. To make sure she's safe."

"I'm telling you, she's fine."

"She needs to come home. Now."

"If I could trust Grandma wouldn't send her away, I'd

112

see to that myself." I got up and paced back and forth while looking up and down the street.

"Stop worrying, no one will think to look here."

"Oh, good," I said. "I see the trolley now."

When the driver pulled on the reins, slowing the horses, the trolley teetered then it stopped.

I leaned down and hugged Viorene. "I love you."

"Love you too," she said, patting my back.

Soon as I stepped aboard, I felt a poke in my shoulder. "Pay for me," Viorene said. After I dropped two pennies into the jar, she followed me to the back bench and scooted next to me in the seat.

"Much as I know you shouldn't, I'm glad you're coming." I waited until the trolley crossed the bridge before telling her all that had happened. It wasn't until we got off in Aberdeen that she finally spoke.

"Look at the trouble you've caused. Seems to me, the worst for all this is Captain Murphy. You lost his home and made him sick."

"I may have saved his life. Those robbers threatened to burn his boat. With him in it." But the truth was, I couldn't defend my actions, and now she had me feeling so low, I wanted to run and hide, but that was Viorene's way. As sweet as she could be, she had that black-and-white view, no gray in between. Once she made up her mind, it took some doing to get her thinking any other way.

In less than two blocks, we had reached the wharf.

113

"I never knew the Chehalis to be such a busy river," she remarked, following me toward the dock.

Sunlight reflecting off rocks spotlighted the dock's rickety state. "This way," I said, leading her down the gangplank.

"Is it safe to walk on?"

Even when rowing a boat, Viorene feared we'd fall out and drown. I could only imagine her panic now. "I'll go first. Grip the back of my overalls."

Walking across, every word out of her mouth was either *oh, no* or *watch out.* At the *Irene,* I held her hand and helped her aboard.

Wilmina raced out of the pilothouse. "Aggie, you're back." She saw Viorene and stopped mid-step as if she'd been roped.

"Shame on you for running away," Viorene said, going up to her.

"Glad to see you too," Wilmina said in a sarcastic tone. She turned to me. "Did you bring the medicine?"

"Right here," I said, pulling it out of my pocket. "How's the captain?"

"No change. His head's still on fire."

"Maybe after he drinks this, he'll feel better."

"He sounds contagious," Viorene said. "I'm not going anywhere near him." She grabbed Wilmina's arm. "Neither are you. Let's go to the galley."

"I've already been exposed," Wilmina said.

"Not anymore," Viorene quipped.

114

When I came downstairs, I found my sisters sitting at the galley table. I sat next to Viorene and looked across at Wilmina. I could tell from her scowl that Viorene had been giving her an earful.

"Good," Wilmina said. "You can listen to her for awhile."

"The captain needs a doctor," Viorene said to me. "Sail to Hoquiam now and take him."

"Won't do any good. Wilmina heard Doctor Simpson tell Grandma that he won't be back for two weeks."

"Maybe Grandma can help."

"Trust me, the captain is my number one concern, but a doctor already told me *not* to move this boat."

"How do you intend to get *me* home? I will *not* walk across that dock again."

"Why don't you stay with us?" I said.

"No. I came to get Wilmina. I'd like to convince you to come too."

"I'm not going with you," Wilmina said. "Grandma plans to send me away."

"You need to accept your punishment and get it behind you."

"Sorry, Viorene, but I agree with Wilmina. You've never had to face Grandma's wrath."

"She may now," Wilmina said as she turned to Viorene. "What if she wants to send *you* away?"

"She wouldn't do that. She'll be pleased with me for bringing you home."

"So that's what this is all about?" I said. "To get more praise from Grandma? Aren't you concerned about us?"

"You two are impossible. I've been fretting about you both. I'd rather know you're somewhere safe than off to who-knows-where."

"We don't mean to worry you. But with Daddy missing and Grandma wanting only you, Wilmina and I are like orphans."

"You don't have to be. I believe Grandma's come to her senses."

"Uh, huh," Wilmina said, shaking her head. "I heard *all* about her plans."

"Eavesdropping again? You sure you got it right?"

"No wax in my ears." She stuck an index finger in each ear, twisted them around, pulled them out, and held them in front of Viorene's face. "See? Nothing there."

I giggled under my breath, remembering Billy doing the same thing to Wilmina, except he had wax.

"Don't be so disgusting," Viorene said.

Suddenly, heavy footsteps pounded on the deck above our heads.

"Who's that?" Wilmina said.

I got out of my chair. "I'll let you know in a minute."

"Little Spike, you down there?"

I looked at my sisters. "It's Donegan and he sounds drunk. Wait here." Before I could get to the stairs, he and Billy were standing in the galley. "Can I help you?"

"Came to check on me brother."

116

"He's resting, but he's on medicine now so should show improvement soon."

"Good," he said, stumbling toward the stairs. "Need to talk to him. Keep 'em down here," he told Billy.

I started up after him, but Billy held me by my arm. "Let go of me." I jerked loose, pushed him against the bulkhead, and raced up the stairs. Billy followed me, trying to grab me from behind.

I rushed into the pilothouse.

"I tried to catch her," he told Donegan.

I looked at the captain bedded down on the back bunk. He was lying on his stomach, motionless.

Donegan, with his back to me, stood above the captain and tapped his dirty boot on his brother's ample butt. "Roll over. Need to talk."

The captain groaned, but didn't move.

I yanked on Donegan's arm. "Leave him be."

He spun around. "Don't be messing with me."

My insides fluttered like a jellyfish, but I held strong and glared at him. "Get off our boat."

"Awful bold talk for someone in a fix."

"You don't know what you're talking about."

"Funny thing about me brother. When liquored up, he talks. Made mention about your father missin' and you girls on the run."

"You're mistaken. Our father arrived yesterday by train. He should be back here shortly."

"Then you don't mind if I sit a spell and wait for him."

117

He plopped down onto the bench, leaned back, and folded his arms.

"What is it you want?"

"Bargaining, are we?" he said. "Maybe you have more money. Better yet, I'll ask your father for some. Except we *both* know he's not coming. Isn't that right, Little Spike?"

I tightened my fist. "Stop calling me that name."

He looked at me and smirked. "I knew the other night when I asked who owned this boat. I was testing to see your answer. You're a sharp one, I'll give you that."

Dirty old fox, I thought.

"Seems I'm in a bit of a fix of my own," he said. "Could use a quick ride to Westport. Take us there. Add another five dollars and we'll be gone."

"What makes you think I have money?"

"Nice boat like this? I'm sure you got more squirreled away."

"How do I know I can trust you?"

Donegan got off the bench and stood in front of me. "You don't. But I'd take this offer, if I were you. The next one won't be so generous."

CHAPTER 11
WESTPORT

BLACKMAIL—only word to describe it.

"Take this to mind," Donegan said. "We're not leaving this boat. If you want to get rid of us, Westport's your only choice." Westport was a seaside hamlet on the Pacific coast.

I looked down at the captain, hoping he'd wake up to give me a sign, but his sweat-soaked shirt and motionless body showed he couldn't help. "The doctor said the captain can't take a rolling boat."

"Think I care?"

I bit my lip. *What a terrible person to act like that to his own brother. Must be awful bad blood between them.* "We have to fill the boiler, stoke the fire, and bleed the valves." Truth was, I had already filled the boiler tank, had a good fire burning, and checked all the gauges, but I needed time to think this out.

"Best you get to it, then," Donegan remarked.

I started out the door. Billy followed me. "Stay here," I told him. "Don't need you lurking behind me."

"Got any grub?" he asked.

"Not offering you food."

Donegan laughed. "Billy, take a seat. Let Little Spike get to work. Eats come after we're afloat."

There he was using that name again, Little Spike. Even

119

though my true nature was to be shy, something about this situation brought courage out of me that I didn't know I had. Fine. If he thinks I'm sharp as a spike, so be it. I'll stab him with my wits and words, every chance I get.

I hurried to the lower deck and sat at the galley table with my sisters. "We have a situation. Donegan requested a ride to Westport."

"Westport?" Viorene said. "Not before I'm dropped off in Hoquiam."

"That won't be happening. Didn't want to alarm you, but his request was really a threat. Donegan's gotten into a fix, needs out of town, and won't leave this boat, but said he would at Westport. Way I see it, we don't have a choice."

"From what I saw, I wouldn't trust him. Or that scroungy boy," Viorene said.

"I agree, but what do you suggest?"

"I don't know." She sighed. "How do you get us into these messes?"

"I don't have time for your rants." I turned to Wilmina. "While I distract Donegan, you sneak into the shed and hide the money sack." We had a ladder in the engine room that lead up to the shed. "But first take out twenty dollars and put it into a sock."

"Why's that?" Wilmina asked.

"Donegan suspects we have money and won't be satisfied until he finds some."

"You're going to let him steal it?"

120

"Better than losing the whole wad." Daddy had stashed our fishing-trip earnings all around our boat.

When I opened the pilothouse door, my gut wrenched. I never liked playacting. Wasn't good at it and having to do it now, upset me. I spotted Billy through the window. Relieved to see him out on the deck, instead of inside, I took a deep breath and walked to the back of the pilothouse.

Bedded on the back bunk, the captain curled up on his side. Donegan sat on the nearby bench with his bare feet propped up on the captain and his dirty boots next to the captain's head. I smelled the stench, but held my tongue.

I feared Donegan might hear Wilmina inside the shed, so I had to get him moved. "All fueled for Westport, but first I need to tend to the captain. Could you give me room?"

Without a word, Donegan got up and went to the front window.

I reached for the smelly boots and threw them toward the wheel. "Please put those outside." Much to my surprise, he didn't fuss and did as I asked.

I knelt down to the captain, near the pass-through opening into the shed, and dabbed his neck with my hankie. Wilmina and I had an agreed-upon phrase: *nice sailing day*. Once she heard me say it, she was to transfer twenty bills to a sock, leave it near the entry, and hide the remaining.

"Nice sailing day," I said extra loud for Wilmina's sake. "How much do you know about boats?" I asked Donegan.

"Sailed plenty on clipper ships." He removed the binoculars from the hook, leaned on the wheel, and looked toward the wharf.

"What was your task?"

"Riggin' the sails. And whatever else demanded."

"Do you know anything about boilers? Steamboats are different from sailing ships; they require fueling and watching gauges and water levels."

"Stop jabberin'." He lowered the binoculars and re-hung them. "Don't need a lesson. Long as a boat has sails, I'll do fine. What's that noise?"

I recognized the sound right off. The louver door banging in the wind. It was the quickest escape from the shed. Wilmina must've gone out that way instead of going back down the ladder, but forgot to latch the door. "All I hear is the boat. It creaks and moans with the tide."

He ignored me, opened the pilothouse door, and hollered for Billy. "Heard somethin'. Check it out."

I shot up to the wheel. "Nothing but the wind. You sure are jumpy."

He glared at me, then turned and looked out the window again. As he swiveled his head back and forth, he reminded me of a perched owl searching for prey. Truth was I possessed the same nervousness, but tried not to show it.

The door opened. Billy pushed Wilmina inside. "Found her on the deck."

"I needed air," Wilmina said. "*Nice sailing day,*" she added, giving me a wink.

Our agreed upon phrase. I knew from that, she'd completed her mission.

"Stay off the deck," Donegan told her, "until I tell you."

"Who are *you* to tell us what to do? On our boat?" Wilmina said.

I grabbed Wilmina's arm. "Go below."

She nodded.

"I'm comin' with you, for grub," Billy told my sister as he followed her out the pilothouse door. I was thankful she didn't object and allowed him to tag along.

I turned to Donegan standing beside me. "I'll get the engine started now."

" 'Bout time," he said, sitting down on the front bench.

I opened the throttle and shifted the forward-reverse lever back and forth. *Hiss, thump, hiss, thump.* Hearing the cylinder and piston rod, I throttled wider, shifted forward, and spun the wheel. The *Irene* inched away from the dock and into the river.

River traffic had died. I was grateful for that. The bay wasn't much different. It spanned miles on both sides and not one vessel in sight.

"Good handlin' boat," Donegan said. He pulled a cigar from his pocket, put it in his mouth, and lit it. It sizzled as he sucked and stunk worse than week-old sauerkraut.

I coughed. "Please, take that outside."

"No." He sauntered toward the back where the captain was sleeping and sat down on the bench.

"That smell can't be good for him," I said, craning my neck to talk.

"Neither can this." He sucked on the cigar, leaned down, and blew the smoke into the captain's face. Then he laughed, real mean-like. "Always Mother's favorite. Not so precious now, are you, little brother?"

Not wanting to taunt him more, I turned back around and held my words, but I said plenty under my breath. It appeared, if Donegan didn't have an audience, he was better behaved. After putting out the cigar, he sat sideways on the back bench, leaned against the padded armrest, and closed his eyes.

AT EIGHT KNOTS, roughly nine miles per hour, we had reached Westport in two hours. I pulled the whistle rope and glanced back at Donegan. The sharp shrill startled him awake. Nothing could've pleased me more.

When we passed the tin-roofed canneries, the conveyors clanked so loud, I barely heard my own voice as I yelled back to Donegan. "I'll be pulling into the far dock."

He got off the bench, joined me at the helm, and pointed up at the boardwalk. "Who are those men?"

124

I knew Westport well. Daddy always anchored at the port, waiting for slack tide to cross the bar. Plus during the fall, we hauled skiffs to the canneries, filled with salmon caught in our river traps.

"The Lifesaving Service," I said. "They're stationed here. Surprised you didn't know that."

"Forgot. Haven't been to Westport in years." He grabbed the binoculars. "What're they doing?"

"If not on maneuvers, they watch incoming boats."

Donegan paced back and forth behind me. "We can't dock here. Turn around."

"What? No."

"The law could've telegraphed with our descriptions."

"I don't know what type of trouble you're in, but we had an agreement. I'm docking this boat and you're getting off."

"Watch your mouth or I'll throw you off. Feed you to the sharks."

"You can't man the boiler without me. Besides, it'd look odd if we turned around."

He scratched his chin. "Then, head out to sea."

"Cross the bar now? At ebb tide?"

Ebb tide had a run-out flow and was hazardous to cross.

"Any smart sailor only crosses at slack," I said. "Grays Harbor's one of the most dangerous bars along this coast."

With a slack tide, there'd be no *in or out* or *rise or fall*, but it only lasted a short time before the tide reversed.

"This boat can handle any tide," he said.

"I've never crossed the bar on my own. And I won't do it now." I throttled back.

Just as I cranked the wheel toward the dock, he pushed me off to one side.

"I'll steer us out myself," he said smugly.

I reached for the whistle rope, but he batted my arm away and knocked me down. I landed on my behind.

He sneered. "You act tough, but you're nothin' but a squirt."

"You're not a man of your word," I said, brushing off my overalls as I stood up.

"No insult to me."

He steered us into the channel and increased our knots. "This boat's easy. Appears I don't need *you* after all."

I went to the window. When I saw breakers ahead, I shivered. "It's too dangerous. Go back."

"No."

"Those are wind waves pushed by a westerly. They curl up. Plunge down. I can hear the roar now." I glared at him. "Get us out of this channel."

"Shut your trap."

I stared in disbelief as he steered us into a no-turning-back situation. "They're coming fast. In sets of five," I said, shaking my head. "The middle ones look fifteen-feet high. Ever pass through a wall of water like that? I have. Had to once. In a storm. But Daddy was at the helm."

Donegan yanked the binoculars off the hook and looked through. His mouth popped open. He let go of the wheel and stepped back, letting it spin on its own as if possessed.

His glance showed concern. "Maybe you're right." Shaking his finger toward the wheel. "Go ahead, take it and get us to shore."

"It's too late," I screamed.

He ignored me, stumbled to the front bench, and slumped down on it. His hands trembled.

I reached for the wheel and gripped it tight. My insides shivered so fierce, I thought for certain I might faint. When the pilothouse bell clanged, I wasn't sure if it was my sisters pulling on the engine-room rope or just clanking from the rocking boat.

In front of the wheel pedestal was an opening in the floor, which allowed communication with the engine room below. Grasping the wheel with one hand, I swung to the side of the pedestal, looked down, and saw Wilmina below, waving her hands.

"What's going on?" she hollered. "It's bouncy down here."

"Batten down," I yelled back. "We're crossing into the ocean."

ROUTE FROM GRAYS HARBOR TO PORT TOWNSEND

CHAPTER 12
PACIFIC OCEAN

A WAVE CRASHED OVER OUR BOW. It foamed like a rabid dog, drooled over the deck, and swayed us side to side. The pilothouse's cast-iron bell clanked and clanked. I thought hard and quick about Daddy, what was it he said? "Point, power, plow, and pull back."

I steered the *Irene* in the direction of the last breaker. I remembered Daddy doing the same. He said it gave room to breathe and time to reach the next wave before it breaks.

I repeated his steps aloud. One by one:

"**POINT.**" I pointed the bow directly into the on-coming wave.

"**POWER.**" As our bow and the wave were about to meet, I throttled up.

"**PLOW.**" The *Irene's* bow lifted as she plowed through the wave's face.

"**PULL BACK.**" Soon as we broke through to the other side, I throttled down.

I don't know how many roller-coaster waves we rode, but I repeated the steps and let my hands take over for my head. When the sea finally flattened, I knew we had crossed. Now in the Pacific Ocean, I looked back at the bar, but all I saw was rolling water and cascading spray.

As the *Irene* bounced up and down in the swells, I

released the wheel and shook out my arms. My hands tingled and my arms hung limp. My legs wobbled too. I looked over at Donegan. Bent over on the bench, he had his head cupped in his hands. I almost felt sorry for him, but I didn't say a word.

I went to the captain. He had rolled off the mattress. His hands clenched to the bunk's legs.

"Let's get you back in bed." I pried loose his grip, helped him up to the bunk, and covered him with a blanket.

"Hey girl," he said, and then his voice grew faint. I had to bend down to hear it. "What's goin' on?"

"We crossed the bar. Get some rest. I'll bring up food and water soon."

He nodded and closed his eyes.

The pilothouse door flew open and Wilmina rushed to me. Viorene followed.

"What a ride," Wilmina said.

"Is everyone all right?" I asked, walking up to the wheel.

"We're fine. Can't say the same for Billy," she said. "He lost his sea legs and used a bucket the whole way."

Viorene gave me a no-nonsense stare. "What happened to Westport?"

I jerked my thumb toward Donegan.

She marched over and stood in front of him. "Well?"

Donegan looked up at her, but he didn't speak. Appeared the ride had stolen his voice as well as his nerve.

130

I chimed in. "We could've lost our lives. That was careless of you."

"Knew you could handle it," he said in a non-convincing tone. He stood, weaved past me, and headed for the door.

"No thanks to you," I added.

"Keep your tongue. No mood for it." He opened the door and staggered outside.

"What now?" Viorene said to me.

I sat down on the bench. "I'm still reeling from that crossing. Doubt if any ideas will be popping into my head."

Wilmina sat next to me. "That must've been scary."

I nodded and showed her my shaking hands. "Daddy was with me. Mrs. Hill too," I said, touching her necklace and recalling her words that it'd keep me safe.

"Pacific Beach is up the coast," Viorene said. "They can get off there."

"Fine by me. Go convince him."

Viorene turned and walked out. Before the door closed, Wilmina got up, propped it open with her foot, and stood in the doorway. I joined her to listen. Donegan sitting on the gunwale smoked a cigar. With her hands on her hips, Viorene stood in front of him again.

"Not goin' to Pacific Beach," Donegan told her. "Nothin' there but homesteads."

"It's a good place to lay low," she said. "You can live off the land, fishing and clamming."

"No," he said gruffly. "Need a town. Good size one like Port Townsend."

Truth was Port Townsend was *exactly* where we needed to go. According to Grandma's telegram, Daddy had shipwrecked along the Strait of Juan de Fuca, but I didn't want Donegan to know any of that. I wanted them off the boat.

I piped in. "No. That's clear around Cape Flattery and at least eight hours up the strait. Could take us four days to reach it, pick somewhere closer."

He craned his neck around Viorene and looked at me. "Head south. To Astoria. Could be there by nightfall."

"Cross the Columbia bar on my own? Never," I blurted. "It's known as the *Graveyard of the Pacific* for good reason."

"Long as I get to a decent-size town, don't care if it's north or south."

"What about Hoquiam?" Viorene said. "We could re-cross this bar and be there in hours."

"No way," Donegan said. He tossed his cigar into the water. "Want out of these parts. Not crossing that nightmare again."

I shook my head at Viorene in disbelief of her offer. I agreed with Donegan, I didn't want any part of crossing that bar again, either. We were lucky that we still had our lives.

"Appears Little Spike agrees with me."

"Go below and fix the captain food," I told my sisters.

"I'll hash something out with him."

I removed Daddy's *Pacific Coast Pilot* book from the bookshelf, carried it outside, and opened it to maps. "Port Angeles is closer. What about there?"

"Too small."

"Victoria's a nice city."

"Canada? No, prefer the states."

"Seems to me, you should be more accommodating. You could catch a ferry at any port and let us be on our way."

"Where're you headin'?"

"This isn't about us."

"Maybe going town-to-town with you would do us fine."

I gritted my teeth. "I'll chart a course now for Port Townsend."

"Good," he said. "Could use a nap. Where can I sleep?"

I pondered on where to put him. On the starboard side at the back of the pilothouse was Mama's bunk, but I didn't want him there. Or below, for that matter, but it appeared I didn't have much choice.

"Go to the galley and sleep on my bed, but wait for my sisters to come up."

"Not waitin'." He stood and stepped to the hatch.

"Good riddance," I said under my breath.

Inside the pilothouse, I sat on the front bench, studied the map, and outlined our course. When the door handle rattled, I got up and opened the door. Wilmina walked in first with four tin cups dangling from her fingers.

"Thanks," she said. "Hard to open with full hands."

Viorene followed behind with a kettle on a tray. "Fish broth for the captain," Viorene said, carrying it back to him and setting it on the bench.

"We're having broth too," Wilmina added, handing me a cup. "Donegan kicked Billy off your bed. Billy's in my bunk now. He sure is seasick."

"Hope they stay below the whole trip," I said.

Viorene knelt next to the captain and held a cup to his lips. He slowly sipped. "Did you settle on a place with Donegan?" Viorene asked.

"Port Townsend. I suggested other places too, but he threatened to stay aboard, so I gave up."

Viorene shook her head. "I had a simple day planned. The library then home. Never this."

"All I wanted was medicine for the captain, but we can't change the day. We need to stick together and make the best of it."

"The captain's looking peaked," Viorene said. "Hardly touched his broth." She carried the kettle to the front and set it on the floor. "And had no interest in the medicine, either."

"Thank you both for caring for him."

"Of course," Viorene said. "He's like family."

I smiled at my sister, remembering that she had a caring, nurturing side to her too.

AFTER I ATE, I gathered my courage. I'd never sailed the open sea on my own and my knotted-up stomach reminded me as I stood at the wheel. I was certain by the time we reached Port Townsend I'd have an ulcer big as an orange.

"Time to sail," I told my sisters. I grasped onto the spokes and steered the *Irene* seaward, trying to ignore the squawking seagulls wheeling around our boat.

We didn't give the birds handouts, and after a bit they finally flew off, except for one yellow-billed straggler. It swooped down in front of the windows—squawking and pooping white splats. Mrs. Hill said birds brought omens, both good and bad. But a seagull? It was Donegan's doing that we were sailing north. Could that scavenger gull be a symbol for him? I sure was happy when that straggler bird gave up and flapped toward shore.

Cranking the wheel, I straightened the bow north and bucked a northwesterly. The wind rocked the *Irene*, flapped the edges of our tied-down sails, and formed white caps on the sea. When waves sprayed over our bow, the *Irene* bounced up and down, same as a baby carriage with a broken spring.

"Not another rocky ride," Viorene said. Pressing her hand against the bulkhead, Viorene stood and inched toward the bookshelf.

We never had a shortage of books: *Farmers' Almanac*, poetry, an illustrated flower book, and Mama's favorite, *Little Women*, to name a few.

135

Viorene removed *Little Women,* sidled back to the bench, and plopped down next to Wilmina again. "I'll read this aloud in memory of Mama."

"That would be nice," Wilmina said.

As Viorene read, I smiled at my sisters. Regardless of the circumstances, it felt right being together. I hung Daddy's pocket watch on a nail near the compass. Seemed every fifteen minutes I was checking the time and every half-hour down to the engine room for the boiler. With Donegan and Billy aboard, time couldn't pass fast enough.

At four o'clock, we had been in open waters for over three hours. I spotted Bird Rock in the horizon, throttled down, and steered inland toward it.

Bird Rock, a rock formation almost two-hundred-feet high and half-a-mile round, looked like an island erupting from the sea and marked the entrance into Grenville Bay.

Viorene stopped reading and looked at me. "What're you doing?"

"Heading toward Grenville Bay. Tide's coming in; perfect time for setting crab pots. We can boil the crabs on the deck and have a feast."

"Are you including them?" Viorene asked.

"Maybe if we act civilized, they'll keep their word."

"They didn't last time."

"Worth a try."

"You can't be serious," she said, slapping the book closed. She stood and steadied back to Mama's bunk. "Don't include me."

"I'm too worn out to continue sailing and we have to eat," I told her, but she ignored me and resumed reading the book in silence.

"Crab sounds good to me," Wilmina said, removing the binoculars and looking through them at the Rock. "Guillemots, auks, and seagulls on top."

"Quite an assortment," I said. "That's why it's called Bird Rock. We'll drop hook behind it."

Bird Rock blocked the ocean current and made the half-circle bay smooth as glass.

"Glad this bay has a deep bight," I added.

"What does that mean?" Wilmina said.

"Deep water. Easy for us to turn around. Daddy said that's why the old clipper ships moored here."

I spun the wheel and inched us toward the Rock's northern end. Within one-hundred feet, I throttled off, pushed the lever into reverse, and reopened throttle, to let in steam. With the propeller now in opposite rotation, the *Irene* stopped. I quickly shut the throttle valve again.

I turned to Wilmina. "Ready to set the hook?" We had two anchors off the bow, but it was the Fisherman—an iron shank with two fluked arms that we used for heavy holds. Daddy taught us how to set and weigh anchor using the winch. We were all good at it. Even Viorene, if forced.

While Wilmina waited by the winch, I hurried to the block and tackle, a pulley system that was bolted to our mast. Pulling the lower block with me, I hooked it onto the Fisherman anchor, then waved to Wilmina.

"Use the lowest gear," I said.

As the cable wound, it lifted the anchor and cockbilled it over the water. I signaled again and she reversed the gear. Lowering, the anchor's flukes scraped the hull and splashed into the water. A moment later, the *Irene* jerked.

"We've hit bottom. It's taken hold," I called to Wilmina. "Turn off the winch."

Billy stepped out of the hatch, yawning.

"You feeling better?" I asked as he approached.

He nodded.

"Donegan still asleep?"

"Passed out, more like it," he said. "Had a bottle on him. Guzzled down half. Should be out for hours."

"Uh, huh," is all I said. "You like Dungeness crab?"

"Yep."

"Good, you can help us set the pots."

138

CHAPTER 13
GRENVILLE BAY

I KNELT DOWN next to the lazaret—a five-foot-deep hold, four-feet long and four-feet wide, and built into the aft deck. I leaned into it and pulled out a square-framed netted crab pot, three fishing poles, two hand nets, a pail filled with gloves, and a tackle box. I handed them up one by one to Billy and Wilmina standing above me.

"Where's Viorene?" Billy asked.

"She's staying in the pilothouse caring for the captain." I didn't add that she didn't want to be around him or Donegan. Truth was I partially agreed with her. Billy was tolerable, but not Donegan. I was glad that he was passed out in the galley. Hoped he stayed that way the whole trip.

"Oh," Billy said, referring to my answer about Viorene. He picked up the two-foot-high crab pot and examined it. "So how does this work?"

"Once the crab crawls through the funnel-like opening," I said, showing him a hole in the side of the net, "the crab drops to the bottom, devours the bait, but can't get out."

"How are we going to catch them without pogies?" Wilmina said.

Pogies were a tiny perch-like fish that travelled in schools. Before every trip, Daddy caught them for bait and kept them in a barrel filled with seawater.

"Any fish will do. Pick out a lure, so we can get started."

The weighted wooden lures, fish-shaped and painted bright yellow with splats of red, had at least two shiny dangling hooks attached. Wilmina sat on the deck, straddled the tackle box between her legs, and looked through the assortment. "I don't see my favorite. It had three hooks."

"Doesn't matter. Choose one and I'll tie it on, and let Billy pick one for his pole."

"Not a fisherman," he said. "Rather watch."

I tossed Wilmina's line into the water, then cast mine. As my sinker dropped to the bottom, I raised my pole a bit and twitched it back and forth. "Daddy called this type of fishing, jigging," I told Billy. "Best way to attract a bottom fish."

"Got a bite," Wilmina said. "Help me."

"Already?" I handed my pole to Billy and hurried to her.

As the fish dove down, pulling her fishing line with it, Wilmina's reel spun like a top. "That fish has some speed." I told her. "And look how it's straining the rod, it must weigh at least ten pounds." I wrapped my hands below hers on the pole. "Let's reel it up, then give it slack until it tuckers out."

Fifteen minutes or so passed before the fish gave up the fight. As Wilmina guided it to the boat, I leaned over the gunwale with the long-handled net and scooped it in.

140

"A brown rockfish," I said, unhooking the lure from its mouth. "This is perfect bait."

"They sure are ugly fish," Wilmina remarked.

She was right on that. Rockfish had large-lipped mouths, bulging front eyes, and a spiky spine that ran from its front quarter and almost to its tail.

Still inside the net, the fish flopped back and forth but each flip-flop grew less and less energetic. Once it stopped, I pulled the fish out of the net and laid it on the deck. Reaching for wire in the tackle box, I wrapped it over the fish's body, behind its spiny dorsal fin, and at the base of its tail before securing it to the bottom of the cage.

Billy was still holding my fishing pole. When the pole bowed and he knew he had a strike, he beamed like a kid with a new toy. "Caught one," he said excitedly.

"Appears to be a big one. Don't give it too much run, it'll try to dive and wedge into the rocks."

Billy reeled the fish up, almost to the surface before it took off again, diving deeper. This went on—him reeling up, the fish diving down—at least ten more times. Finally, he got the fish aboard. It was another rockfish, but bigger than Wilmina's.

Billy grinned wide. "It's over two feet long."

"And at least thirteen pounds," I said.

After we caught two more fish and secured them inside the pot, we had a well-baited trap.

As Billy and Wilmina balanced the pot on the gunwale, I guided a pulley over, hooked it onto the top frame, and unlocked the pulley gear. "On the count of three. *One, two, three...PUSH.*"

The cable hummed as the pot plummeted. *Splash.* Now sinking, bubbles formed around the pot until it disappeared. Soon as it hit sea bottom, I locked the gear.

About an hour later, I sent Wilmina to the winch and waved Billy over. He was standing at the bow looking out. Donegan was still passed out below. To our surprise, Viorene strolled out of the pilothouse and up to us.

"How's the captain?" I asked her.

"Sleeping, but I got more broth down him." She turned to Billy. "He can't make it to the privy. I'd appreciate if later you'd help with private matters. I've placed a pail at the back."

He scrunched up his face, but when she smiled at him, he nodded.

"Thank you," she replied. I added my thank you too.

I signaled to Wilmina to start the winch. As the cable wound around the spool, up came the pot swinging in the air. Tiny waterfalls streamed through the netting and exposed piled-up crabs.

"Cut," I shouted to Wilmina, pulling on my gloves.

With a gaff, a long pole with a hook, I directed the pot to the boat and onto the gunwale. Billy and I then slid it off, down to the deck. It banged when it landed and riled the crabs—snapping pinchers, wildly flapping like castanets.

Wilmina raced over. "What a catch. Bet there's close to thirty."

I reached down into the toolbox, pulled out a pipe wrench, and used its curved end to open the lid, and then quickly removed the wrench and shoved it into my overalls pocket. Lowering my gloved hand into the pot, I grabbed hold of a crab. As its claws and legs frantically fussed, I carried it over to the washtub we had filled earlier with boiling water from a deck spigot piped to the boiler and dropped the crab inside the tub to cook.

"Let me try," Wilmina said.

"Have to be careful," I warned. "Those claws slice same as a knife."

"I will. Promise."

With gloved hands, she grasped a crab and gingerly held each side of its shell. Suddenly, one pincher grabbed hold of her glove. "Oh, no," she gasped, shaking her hand back and forth. The crab released, but instead of falling, it clawed onto her thumb, dangled in the air, and then let go, landing on the deck, and scurrying off—all eight legs moving faster than spitting steam.

All of us—Billy, Wilmina, me, even Viorene, joined in the chase.

"Crawled under that crate," Billy said, getting down on all fours, looking under it.

"Don't get too close," I said. "Dungeness move in any direction. Might latch onto your nose."

Billy picked up a piece of wood off the woodpile and poked it at the crab. "It's clawed on," he cried out, pulling the board out with the crab attached as he slowly stood.

We were having such fun laughing and clapping we didn't notice Donegan behind us until he staggered toward Billy, cussing under his breath. "Got a headache," he hissed. He glared at Billy. "What's the matter with you? You know I don't like harsh awakenin.'"

I smelled his liquored breath as he brushed past me. He pulled back his arm and aimed it at Billy's head. Before he made contact, I grabbed the wrench out of my pocket, held it up, and Donegan smacked it instead. Curse words flew out of his mouth. He grabbed his hand, rubbing it. I knew it had to hurt.

Billy, my sisters, and I stepped backwards. I gripped tighter onto the wrench. "No violence on this boat," I hollered. "Leave Billy alone."

"Bah," Donegan growled, opening and closing his hand into a fist. He narrowed his eyes and jabbed his finger at Billy. "I'll deal with you later." He turned and stumbled toward the bow.

Without a word and still holding the board with the crab clutched on, Billy walked to the tub, and shook the crab loose, and then he threw the board onto the deck and walked away.

"Billy, wait," I called out, but he ignored me and disappeared.

"Billy looked mad," Wilmina said.

I nodded. "Wait here while I find him."

I caught Billy at the galley table throwing his pocket-knife into the tabletop. Soon as it stuck, he pulled it out

144

and threw it again. It shocked me to see such disregard for other people's property. "Quit stabbing your knife into our table."

He wiggled the knife loose, snapped it closed, and shoved it into his pocket, then crossed his arms and stared ahead. "Don't need no girl fightin' my battles."

"If you're referring to Donegan, I didn't do it just for you. Did it out of respect for my folks. My daddy built this boat and had strict rules. When you're done sulking, come up for crab."

I hurried back up top. After I spotted Donegan slumped over, sitting on the bow deck, I signaled my sisters over to the crab pot.

"Stand back," I told them as I tossed crabs into the salted boiling water.

Soon as the crabs sank, their shells transformed from purple to salmon pink to pale orange. The crab I had dropped into the boiling water earlier and the one Billy did too, were as bright orange as pumpkins, which meant they were fully cooked. I fished them out and threw them into a washtub of cold, clean water to cool. In less than twenty minutes, the remaining ten cooking crabs were orange too.

"Do you think the captain could eat some crab?" Wilmina asked, piling all the cooled-off crabs onto a platter.

Viorene frowned. "No, I barely got broth and water down him. Another time."

"Start dishing up," I told my sisters. Just as I turned back to the crab pot for more crab to cook, I saw Billy out of the corner of my eye. He was standing near the hatch. "Better get some, before we eat them all."

He sheepishly sauntered over and sat next to Wilmina, who immediately handed him a tin plate with pliers and two cooked crabs.

"Thanks," he said. With his pliers, he cracked a crab, pulled out chunks of white meat, and popped them into his mouth.

After the batch started cooking, I sat down next to Viorene completing the half-circle with Billy and Wilmina. "My favorite is the claw meat," I said, reaching for a crab and breaking off the larger pincher.

"Mine too," Wilmina said as she chewed. "What about you, Billy?" she asked.

Before Billy could answer, Donegan appeared behind him. "Didn't think to offer me any?" he said, slurring his words as he grabbed Billy's plate.

Get your own plate I wanted to say until I remembered Billy's embarrassment of me coming to his aid. I bit my tongue.

Instead of taking crab off of our full platter, Donegan reached into the cooling washtub and fumbled two more crabs onto his plate, but those were still hot, which brought more swear words out of his mouth before he staggered away.

"Donegan appears to be drunk," I said to Billy.

Billy smirked. "Yep. Short-fused when he's drinkin', but less connivin' than when he's sober. Neither one's good."

I didn't reply but nodded, taking it as a warning.

After we cleaned up the dishes, I headed to Donegan. "Sleeping arrangements," I said to him. I picked up his dirty plate. "There's extra bedding in the pilothouse for you and Billy under my mother's bunk."

"Fine," he said, swigging down the last of his whiskey and tossing the bottle overboard. He weaved past me to the pilothouse. I watched until he opened the door and slammed it closed, and then I headed to the stern to join Billy and my sisters.

I sat down on the deck next to Billy. Wilmina was on the other side of him, Viorene next to her. I looked up at the copper sunset reddening into cranberry. "*Red sky at night, sailors' delight—,*" I said.

"What does that mean?" Billy asked.

"*Red sky at night, sailors' delight. Red sky at morning, sailors take warning.* At night, means good weather for tomorrow. A morning red sky points to foul conditions—rain, wind, and maybe a blistering storm."

"Time for bed," Viorene said, standing and reaching for Wilmina's hand. She looked toward the pilothouse. "Don't want to go in there with Donegan. You think the captain's good for the night?"

"I'll check on him," Billy offered.

"Thank you," she said.

147

As my sisters walked away, I turned to Billy. "See you in the morning."

"Hope that sky holds true," he said.

I nodded and prayed for the same. Daddy's *Pacific Coast Pilot* book described the dangers of Washington's northern coast—fog, rip tides, strong currents, ragged reefs, and huge rock masses and jutting cliffs. I touched Mrs. Hill's necklace. "Please let tonight's sky be a good omen."

CHAPTER 14
THE RUGGED NORTHERN PACIFIC COAST

THE NEXT MORNING, I awoke to squawking seagulls. Hope there's no bad omen to them, remembering Mrs. Hill's fit being awakened by crows. Already dressed in my overalls, I put on my rubber boots and walked into the engine room. I peeked through the peep-hole in the firebox door and saw a weak flame. We had thrown in four-footer logs for the night. I pulled on gloves, opened the squeaky door, and threw in more wood. Seconds later, a yellow-red fire blazed.

"Awful soupy out there," a voice said from the ceiling.

I looked up and saw Billy's face. He was staring down through the large hole in the pilothouse floor, poking his head around the cylinder to see me.

Daddy had to cut the hole in the pilothouse floor for the large cylinder of the triple-expansion engine to fit. But it turned out to be a positive: the opening allowed communication from the pilothouse to the engine room below and the engine top kept the coffeepot warmed too.

"Hopefully, it'll burn off soon," I told him, referring to the fog. "How's the captain?"

"Still sleepin'. Not much movement last night."

"Okay. I'll be up shortly."

I went back to the galley to wake my sisters.

149

Viorene and Wilmina's upper bunks hung on each side of the bulkhead toward the point of the bow. My floor-level bed sat between the two and was used as a step to get up to theirs.

I stood at the foot of my bed and shook my sisters by their feet. "Time to get up. Soon as the fog breaks, I'll need help with the anchor."

"Not from me," Viorene said, sitting up and stretching. "I don't remember how."

"Uh, huh," Wilmina said in a sarcastic tone. "You just don't like getting your hands dirty."

I giggled under my breath. Wilmina was right. Viorene had boat skills, but only used them if forced. But truth be told, I was the same when it came to galley chores, especially cooking, so to me it evened out. Poor Wilmina was helper to us both.

"I'll do it, Aggie," Wilmina said, "but Viorene can make breakfast on her own."

"Whatever you two work out," I said. "I've got to tend to the boat."

Soon as I climbed onto the upper deck, fog smacked me in the face and hung like sheets over our mast and Bird Rock. When I opened the pilothouse door, the white haze trailed behind me. Nothing like boiler heat," I said, rubbing my arms as I felt the warmth.

"Any coffee?" Donegan asked, standing at the helm. Billy was sitting on the front bench.

"You'll have to wait," is all I offered.

I walked to the back, leaned down, and felt the captain's head. He barely stirred and didn't open his eyes.

"Don't look too good, does he?" Donegan said, standing behind me.

The whole ordeal disgusted me and I felt like crying, but I didn't dare show weakness to him. "He just needs rest." I stood, headed out the door, and down to the galley.

AFTER BREAKFAST, the fog had thinned, and the sun now fighting through the clouds, exposed the ocean's entrance. "Let's weigh anchor," I told Wilmina, "and get Billy to help; can always use an extra set of eyes with fog."

While I manned the anchor winch, Wilmina and Billy leaned over the gunwale and watched. "It's scraping the hull," Wilmina relayed.

"That's part of pulling it out of the water," I said.

"Good thing Daddy nailed on metal for protection."

She never showed this much interest in the boat before and it pleased me to see it. Must be because I assigned her as my first mate, remembering my excitement when Daddy first called me his.

Once we got the anchor in its hold, Billy and I headed to the pilothouse. Wilmina went below to help Viorene with cleanup. Donegan was nowhere in sight. I figured he must've gone to the galley for more food.

I cracked open the throttle to warm the engine and listened as the cylinders hissed. Opening the throttle more, the high-pressure cylinder pushed the piston rods up and down, bringing a pass of steam to the middle cylinder, then onto the third, restarting the cycle. With each stroke, the *Irene* moved forward. Soon as we cleared Bird Rock and were out to sea, I cranked the wheel starboard, north.

I looked at Billy sitting on the front bench. "In less than an hour, we should see the lighthouse."

"Lighthouse?"

"Destruction Island Light," I said. "It's the only off-shore island along the Washington coast."

The door swung open. "Cold out there," Donegan said, walking in sipping coffee from a tin cup. Its aroma flooded the room as he stepped to the back bench.

"Coffee smells good," I said to Billy.

"I'll get you some." He disappeared out the door.

Donegan called out. "How long to the cape?"

I knew he meant Cape Flattery. "At this speed, at least thirteen hours. Maybe more."

"That long? Can't see how you take livin' on a boat. Train's better. More to do."

"Maybe you should've thought of that before you bullied yourself aboard."

"Smart mouth," he mumbled. "Wake up, old man," I heard him say.

I spun around. "Leave him be."

"Strikin' a nerve with you, Little Spike? What do you think of this?" He tapped the captain's butt with his boot.

I turned back to the wheel and scolded myself for taking his bait.

152

Wilmina banged at the door and mouthed through the window, *open the door.* I stepped over and pushed it open. "Thought it'd be good to have the coffeepot up here," she said as she walked to the front of the wheel, placing the pot on the engine top. Watching Wilmina made me think of Mama. She used to do the same for Daddy. Sometimes, she'd flavor the coffee with vanilla and the sweetness permeated the room. Thinking about her now tugged at my heart.

"Where's Billy?" I asked my sister as she poured me a cup.

"Helping Viorene with cleanup. She offered to read him a book later. He jumped at the chance."

"I don't think he can read," I whispered. "I'm getting that he's had a hard life."

"He's taken to her. And she's showing kindness, treating him like a stray dog," Wilmina remarked.

"Viorene has a good side. She appreciates his help with the captain."

Wilmina rolled her eyes. "If you say so." I chuckled at her response. "Any chance we can anchor near Ruby Beach, row to shore, and search for agates?"

I smiled, remembering Mama telling me of all the rocks she collected there and that the red aggies were her favorite. She told me that's how I got my name.

"Not on this trip," I said in a low voice, feeling regretful that we couldn't. It was a beautiful beach—large offshore sea stacks, tidal pools, and fragmented-ruby

153

gemstones shimmering in the sand, which sparkled like jewels in the setting sun.

Donegan walked up from the back and shoved his tin cup toward Wilmina. "Give me more."

"Add *please* to that," she said as she poured it and handed it back.

"Another smart mouth. You two could learn from your sister. She's better natured. Prettier too." He sneered at me. "Good thing you know boats, doubt if you'll ever snag a man with those looks." He opened the pilothouse door, walked out, and slammed it behind him.

"That was mean," Wilmina said. "And not true. Wish he'd fall overboard."

"Never mind him, he's mean-spirited," I said. "Take the wheel; I need to check the captain again." I knelt down next to him and felt his head. "Still feverish. Could you get his medicine? And some broth?"

Soon as I stepped to the wheel again, Wilmina rushed out the door. A moment later, she returned with a tray.

"Viorene had it ready and was bringing it up. She's got Billy washing dishes now."

"No harm in that."

"I'll tend to the captain, if you want me to?" Wilmina said.

"That would be nice. Thank you."

When the Destruction Island lighthouse came in view, I thought of Mama and Daddy. Once a year, while we stayed with Grandma, they'd visit the island. Called it their special get-away. Captain Hill, the lighthouse keeper, had been Daddy's friend long as I could remember. He claimed to be a distant relative of Mrs. Hill, on her husband's side. Two to three times a year, Daddy sailed to the island on his own to fish and crab nearby. On his last visit, he brought me along.

Wilmina looked through the binoculars. "I see the lighthouse."

High on a rocky cliff, the white tower stretched toward the sky. Its five windows, edged in black and arrowed at the crown, scaled up the side. The glass lookout at the top had a spiked brick-colored roof.

"Wish we could visit," I said. "It's been two years since you and Viorene did."

"Sure was fun climbing the tower and swimming in the lagoon."

"Do you remember Keeper Hill's goats? Nanny and Oscar?"

"Yes, they got into Assistant-keeper Griffin's vegetable garden and ate the lettuce patch," said Wilmina. "Mrs. Griffin sure got mad. Can't we stop and say hello?"

"Maybe on the way back." I did feel guilty for not stopping. I knew it was a lonely post and that all visitors were valued, but I couldn't chance it with Donegan along. Who knows how he'd act or what he'd say or do.

Donegan stuck his head through the door. "Looks like the shed has plenty of room for a person to sleep," he said, referring to the boiler shed.

Been snooping, have you? I wanted to say, but bit my tongue. "It does. It's just that it gets hot from the boiler, but tolerable if you leave the door ajar."

"Good. That's where I'll be ridin'."

Soon as he closed the door, I smiled at Wilmina. "What luck is that; wish I'd thought to put him there at the start of this trip."

"What about the money sock?" she asked.

I had stashed every-day funds into an old sock and left it in the boiler shed for easy access. The remaining money was hidden in the engine room.

"I knew he'd be poking around," I said, "so I buried the sock in the coffee grounds."

WE STEAMED ALL DAY, and by dusk, had reached Cape Flattery, the most northwestern point of the United States. Known as a landmark, its tip overlooked the Pacific and the Strait of Juan de Fuca, Daddy had told me.

"So glad we reached the cape before dark," I said to Wilmina. "And that the weather held."

"You could've sailed by the North Star."

"Not without Daddy."

Crossing into the strait, Wilmina looked through the binoculars again. "There's an island with a lighthouse."

"That's the Tatoosh light. It's not a stand-alone tower like Destruction's. See how it protrudes from the keeper's house, same as our smoke stack from our shed. The island is named after a Makah Chief."

"M*uh*-kaw?" she said.

"That's right. They've been here for centuries. Daddy said they were honorable people and the best fishermen and whalers that ever existed."

I steered the *Irene* into Neah Bay. After we anchored in its half-circle cove, Wilmina and I stood on the deck and looked toward land.

"Totem poles," she squealed. "I'll get the binoculars."

As she raced back with the binoculars in hand, she almost knocked into Donegan who had just crawled out of the shed.

"Watch where you're goin'," he barked as he wobbled toward the pilothouse, disappearing inside.

"I better check on the captain," I told my sister.

I poked my head through the door and looked toward the back. Thankfully, Donegan was nowhere in sight and the captain was still fast asleep. I tiptoed inside past the wheel, peered toward the privy, and found Donegan on Mama's bunk, snoring. Soon as I walked out the pilothouse door, I met Viorene and Billy coming up from below.

"Where are we?" Viorene said.

Before I could answer, Wilmina called over. "Totem poles," she said. "I counted eight. Come look."

With my turn, I viewed beach-weathered houses—an extra-long one stood in the middle—and all had totems nearby. On the graveled beach below, fishnets hung on poles and hulled-out canoes were scattered here and there.

"Aren't the totems fun to see?" Wilmina said. "What do they mean?"

"Totems tell stories and legends about the chiefs, clans, and history," I said. "On our trip to Vancouver, I saw totems with Mama. You and Viorene were babies and stayed aboard with Daddy. Mama called them colorful sculptured art and remarked about their age being older than her, me, and Grandma combined."

"Were they as nice as these?"

"Yes, but back then all I saw was the birds had oversized beaks and the bears had giant teeth. The carved warrior men snarled, as if challenging for a fight. I had nightmares for months, but I was barely six."

"She shouldn't have taken you," Viorene remarked.

"I got over it. What's your favorite?" I asked Wilmina, referring to the totems in the village.

"The thunderbird."

The large eagle-type bird had a bright orange beak, slit eyes, and wings painted red, yellow, and green that spanned out on both sides of the totem.

"I saw it. Did you see the one with the killer whale?" I asked.

"Oh, that's nice," she said, looking through the glasses. "There's one with a red salmon, a huge black bear, and a man on the bottom holding it all up. I could stare at these for hours."

"No more for me tonight," I said. "I'm tuckered out. See you all in the morning."

"I'm coming with you," Viorene said.

"Think I'll turn in too," Billy added.

"Aggie, Aggie," Wilmina cried out. "Come... quick."

"No, you can show me in the morning."

"You must see," she insisted, racing over and putting the binoculars in my hands. "There's a broken hull in the *th*and," she lisped. "It looks like the *Belle*."

CHAPTER 15
STRAIT OF JUAN de FUCA
NEAH BAY

EARLY MORNING, Billy shook me awake.

I bolted up. "Billy? What are you doing here?"

"You gotta come see."

Already in my overalls, I threw off my blanket and pulled on my boots.

Wilmina sat up. "What's happening?"

"Don't know, stay here. And don't wake Viorene." Billy and I raced to the stairs. With daylight breaking, we had light to see. Normally, I would have been up, but fourteen hours of sailing had worn me out. We stepped out of the hatch onto the deck.

"There," Billy said, wagging his finger at two men standing at the gunwale.

They had their backs to us, so all I could see was they were shirtless, had dark copper skin, and thick black hair tied up into a club-knot. The taller man had a spruce sprig wrapped around his bun and an Eagle feather sticking out.

"Hello," I stammered, walking up to them.

When they turned, I saw their red-painted faces and froze. Wearing canvas logger pants, they had similar features: muscular, high cheek-bones, and square jaws. The taller one nodded, and with one arm outstretched, moved his hand sideways. "Makah waters."

Billy gazed in amazement while I talked.

"Yes, we'll be on our way soon."

"Where's the captain?" the taller one asked.

"He's ill, but not contagious."

He turned to the other man and spoke to him in their native tongue. I waited for him to finish, then I cleared my throat. "What do you know about the green boat washed up on your shore?"

With a confused expression, he shook his head.

I motioned him to the gunwale. Billy and the other man followed. "There," I said, pointing across to their village. A movement from the water strayed my eyes down to three long canoes filled with face-painted men. One canoe sat directly below and two more off to the side. I gasped and looked at Billy. He gawked at me with a wide-eyed stare.

The tall man brushed past me and looked in the direction I had pointed. "Gone on boat," he said, steering his finger east.

"The man left?"

"Yes."

I pulled on my hair and touched my jaw. "Did he have yellow hair and my chin?"

He studied my face and nodded.

"How long ago?"

He held up two fingers.

"Two months?" The timeframe was right; Daddy's accident was in May and we were now approaching July.

He nodded again. "Sick," he said, tapping his head.

"What do you mean?"

He turned to the other man and spoke again in words I didn't understand. Then, the other man started dancing all crazy-like. He stuck out his tongue, shook his head, and walked as if half-dazed. The taller man nudged me and pointed at the dancing man.

"Why's he acting like that?" I asked the taller man.

"Mixed-up head," he said to me.

"Him?"

"No." He poked my arm. "The sailor on the boat."

Suddenly, I felt ill. How hurt was Daddy? I wanted to ask more, but before I could, Wilmina appeared at my side.

"What's happening?" she asked excitedly.

"Don't say a word," I instructed.

"Okay," she said as she kept her eyes fixed on the men.

The taller man smiled at her, then turned to me again, and tugged on my sleeve. I was wearing one of Daddy's red and white plaid shirts. "Trade," he said.

"You want this shirt?"

"Yes," he answered.

"Daddy has another one hanging in the galley; I'll get it," Wilmina offered, racing away.

I looked at the taller man again and asked, "How sick was the man on the boat?"

He shrugged, motioned to his friend and the two men

headed off to our bow, scanning our deck as they walked.

"Better hope they don't see somethin' else they want," Billy remarked.

"This must've been how it was a hundred years ago, offering to trade," I said, recalling the history lessons. "Except for their clothes, they're keeping to the old ways. I'm glad to see it. It's sad when traditions get lost." Thoughts of Mama and Daddy flashed into my head. We had traditions too.

Wilmina sped toward me with two shirts. "I took Daddy's blue one too. Where'd they go?"

"At the bow." I lifted the shirts in the air and shook them. "Hello," I hollered.

Soon as they reached us, the taller man pulled out cut-up pieces of smoked fish from his pocket and exchanged it for Daddy's shirts.

"Thank you for letting us stay," I said. "Can we go ashore and look at that hull?"

He nodded, then gave the blue shirt to his friend, slung the red and white one over his shoulder, and headed to the gunwale. The other man followed. We scurried behind him.

The taller man faced the water, and with the swiftness of a cat, leaped over the gunwale and landed upright into the canoe. It tipped side to side as he sat. When the second man jumped, the canoe swayed again.

"Goodbye," Wilmina said, waving.

The taller man looked up and smiled, then tapped the

side of the canoe. With all eight men paddling at the same time, they skimmed away like a water-bug. The other two dug-out canoes, eight rowers in each, raced behind.

Billy shook his head. "When I saw their painted faces, I wasn't sure what to think."

"I had the same concern until I remembered Mrs. Hill coating me with red ochre."

He looked at me puzzled.

"It's a yellowish-orange clay found along the riverbanks that turns red after it's baked. Mrs. Hill smeared mine on with bear grease, said it protected my skin from the sun. I'm guessing that's why the men had it on their faces."

Wilmina giggled. "I remember that. Mama scrubbed and scrubbed, but couldn't get it off."

"I know. It took almost two weeks before I looked normal again."

Billy interrupted us. "Where do you think they're going?"

"They had harpoons. Must be going to sea. For a humpback or a gray."

"They hunt whales in canoes?" Wilmina asked, giving me a cockeyed stare.

It was hard to imagine. We'd seen our share of whales, knew their massive size, grace and playfulness. We'd also seen them after being killed when the whaling boats towed them to the cannery. The whalers made a game of it. With colorful flags flapping on their masts, they'd holler and blast their horns as they paraded the dead whales through the channel. It was the saddest thing I'd ever witnessed. I considered whales beautiful creatures.

"Yes, they hunt whales," I told my sister. "It's the Makah tradition, but they respect it and don't destroy a pod. They only kill as many as they need, use every part—unspoiled meat, blubber even the teeth and bones—and honor them in a ceremony."

"They honor them on their totems too," Wilmina added.

"This is their land and their waters. If I'd been thinking, I should have rowed to shore and requested permission to anchor."

"They seemed happy with the shirts."

"Best not mention any of this to Viorene. She'd shake in her boots the rest of the trip."

"Don't say nothin' to Donegan either," Billy said. "He's a coward and would make rude remarks. Ain't much character to him."

I had seen proof of that firsthand, but Billy saying it out loud? I wondered now what type of hold Donegan had on him. "Need to get to shore."

"Donegan won't tolerate that," Billy said. "He'll want to get movin'."

I thought a moment. "Tell him our anchor's stuck and we had to wait on the tide."

"Still don't explain you goin' to shore."

"Went to see the totems," I said. "Help us get the dinghy lowered before he gets up."

166

Billy and I pushed the rope-ladder under the taffrail. Unrolling, it banged against the stern. I pulled the pulley over to the dinghy, hooked it on, and signaled Wilmina to turn on the aft winch. We knew the noise would wake Donegan, so we hurried. Soon as the dinghy landed in the water and Wilmina cut the gear, I sped down the ladder, unhooked the pulley, and left it dangling in the air.

Wilmina scaling down behind me, jumped into the boat. "We can eat the smoked fish for breakfast," she said, sitting down at the stern thwart.

When I heard Viorene's voice, I looked up and saw her wrapped in a blanket, leaning over the railing, staring down at us. "Where are you going?" she said. Donegan and Billy were now at her side.

"To shore. Won't be long."

"You're leaving me aboard with these scoundrels?"

I glanced at Billy. From his expression, it appeared Viorene's hurtful words had stung. He lowered his head and walked away.

"I'm sorry," I told my sister. "Did you want to come?" Truthfully, I hadn't thought beyond getting the dinghy into the water and now felt bad leaving her behind.

Before she could answer, Donegan spouted, "No, she's fixin' me food. You two get back here," he said, muttering more words under his breath.

I mouthed *I'm sorry* to my sister again, then slid the oars into the water, looked over my shoulder, and pulled.

Wilmina's oars lockstepped to mine.

"Can't believe I get to see a real village with totem poles," Wilmina said excitedly.

"Totems are impressive up close."

Soon as the dinghy grounded, we jumped out, pulled it to the beach, and ran to the hull, bending down to examine it. "It's the right shade of green," I commented, "but it's been shattered, for sure." We dug around it to expose more. "This is part of the starboard hull and it has a flat-bottom, same as the *Belle.*" The hull was the watertight portion of the boat. I could tell by the curvature of the wood that it was Daddy's boat.

"Look." Wilmina said, touching the hull. "A shipworm hole shaped like a heart. The *Belle* had one just like it."

A salt-water shipworm, known as a teredo, was a wood-eating menace of wooden boats and structures.

We didn't notice the young boy until he said *hello.* No taller than four-feet, he had acorn skin, dark-brown hair, and a pearly-white smile. I stood and lowered my eyes to him. "This is our father's steamer. A man from your village gave us permission to come ashore and examine this boat. He left with a group in canoes."

"Whale hunters," he corrected. "Come," he said, motioning us to follow.

Leading us past beach-weathered houses, all sizes and shapes, I had to pull Wilmina along. Every time she saw a totem, she dug in her feet until we stopped. "These are beautiful up close. Look at that bear's nose and the carved feathers on the Thunderbird."

168

The youngster continued walking on without us.

"You can look at these later," I had told her, scurrying until we caught up with the boy.

He stopped in front of a rectangular, flat-roofed structure. It had split-planked cedar walls, no windows, and a five-foot hole in the center used as a door.

"What is this large building?" I asked.

"My great-grandfather lives here." The boy's English was good, so I knew he attended school.

"Is this a longhouse?" Mrs. Hill had told me that many years ago members of the same clan: mothers, fathers, grandparents, sisters, brothers, aunts, uncles, and cousins lived in longhouses, some sixty-feet long. They shared food, parceled duties, and taught skills to the young.

"Longhouses are frowned upon, but my grandfather is an Elder so got to keep his," the boy said. "The white men don't like them. They want families in separate houses."

I didn't press, but it made me feel bad. It didn't seem right that people could tell others how to live, especially since it had been a custom for hundreds of years.

The boy stepped to the five-foot-hole door, parted a cattail-weave mat hanging in front, and crawled through the opening and into the longhouse. Wilmina and I followed. We gasped when we got inside.

"This place is bigger than a grange," Wilmina said, batting her head from side to side.

I nodded, taken aback by it as well.

"Wait here," the boy said, walking away.

169

While I was still gawking, Wilmina had strolled away and up to a carved salmon, painted red and black, hanging on the wall. She traced her hand around it. "Almost life-like."

"The Makah are artistic people," I remarked. "Now get back over here."

"In a minute," she said. "How interesting the way they live," she added as she studied the raised benches lining the walls, separated every few feet by hanging mats. Before I could stop her, she wandered over to one of the stalls.

I rushed to her. "Not polite to snoop." I pulled her back to where we had been told to wait. A moment later, the boy appeared with an old man.

Wrapped in a red and gray woolen blanket, the man had coarse white hair, a leathered face, and several absent teeth. He was holding a captain's hat.

"That's Daddy's hat," Wilmina squealed. "It has his grease stain." She grabbed for it, but the old man held it back.

"Be polite," I scolded, latching onto her arm.

"This is my great-grandfather," the boy introduced.

"Please tell him that she didn't mean any disrespect. Our father's missing. To see his hat excited her."

After the boy translated to the Elder, the old man handed the hat to Wilmina and patted her head.

"Thank you," Wilmina told him as she wrapped her arms around his waist. He smiled, stroked her hair, and spoke in his native tongue.

170

"My grandfather wants to know her tribe."

"Not sure what you mean?"

"Her black hair and olive skin."

"One-quarter Portuguese. We both are, except I don't look it." After the young boy explained, the old man nodded. I cleared my throat. "The men from your village said our father left about two months ago. Can you give us any information?"

His grandfather replied with words and gestures, one of rowing and another of a boat sailing away. "He says that your father rested three days, was rowed out to a boat, and sailed off."

"Is there anyone else we could talk to?"

"No, they're on the whale hunt. Be back in a week."

SOON AS WE CLIMBED aboard the *Irene*, Donegan cornered us. "Took off on a lark, didn't you?" he barked.

"Had to wait on the tide anyway," I muttered, brushing past him with Wilmina. We hurried down to the galley to Viorene. "We found the *Belle*," I said, bursting with excitement as I told her. "Right shade of green."

"And we have Daddy's captain's hat." Wilmina pulled it out of her pocket and handed it to Viorene. "Our first clues to finding him."

"That doesn't prove a thing. All boat captains wear that hat. And you know green and white are the most common colors for fishing boats."

There it was, Viorene's black and white view, putting

171

dampness on the brightest speck of good news. I ignored her comments. "Knowing Daddy survived inspires me even more to find him."

"The only thing inspiring me is getting those two off this boat and going home."

"Don't you want to find Daddy?" Wilmina asked in a surprised-hurt tone.

"I'd love to find him, but we have no idea where he went. Or if he's even alive."

"He's alive," I blurted. I started to tell her about the red-painted men who had boarded our boat, but I feared that might spark more phobias, she already had too many as it was. I looked at Wilmina. "Let's not say more, she needs time."

Wilmina glared at Viorene. "Two votes outdoes one. That's all I'm saying."

Viorene shook her head. "You two are always against me."

While my sisters stayed below, I went atop and commissioned Billy's help. "Need to hoist the dinghy and weigh anchor." He did as I asked, but not with the same enthusiasm as before.

"Sorry about Viorene's words earlier. She didn't mean anything bad. She was upset."

"Ain't no concern to me, either way." I could see by his face, he was lying. He followed me into the pilothouse, sat on the front bench, and stared out the window.

I stood at the wheel and craned my neck to check on

172

the whereabouts of Donegan. He was sprawled on the back bench with his eyes closed in a quiet snore. Nothing could have pleased me more.

BY LATE AFTERNOON, we had reached Port Angeles. Not the preferred town of Donegan, but knowing Daddy had sailed this way, we had to stop. I slowed our knots and headed into the harbor.

"What are you doin'?" Donegan asked, getting off the back bench coming toward the helm.

"Thought we'd anchor here tonight and row to shore to stretch our legs."

"Told you I wanted Port Townsend." Donegan scowled. "Can't be but four more hours."

"Townsend's a busy port. Best to wait until morning."

He studied my face. "Port Angeles tonight, huh?" He pondered for a moment, then spoke. "Might be a good idea, after all." By his tone, I knew he had mulled up something no-good, but I had to chance it to find Daddy.

After we anchored, I tended to the captain, but he barely sipped the water that I held to his lips. The instant his head hit the pillow he passed out.

Billy walked up behind me. "Ain't lookin' good."

"Yes," I said. "Maybe it would be best if my sisters stayed behind to watch him."

"Ain't happenin'," Donegan said. "We're all goin'. Think I don't see past your tricks, Little Spike? You row us to shore, strand us, and take off in this boat."

173

"I'd never do that." Truth was if an opportunity allowed, I'd do that very thing. "But we can't leave him alone."

"Don't matter if someone's here. He's just lyin' there like a dead fish."

Much as I wanted to disagree, I couldn't. Without a doctor, all the captain could do was rest. When I went below and told my sisters we all had to go, Wilmina jumped at the chance to search. Not Viorene, she fussed.

With everyone inside the dinghy, it sure was tight. Donegan sat at the stern, me at the bow, and Billy, Wilmina, and Viorene scrunched together on the middle thwart.

"Not a bad little rower, Little Spike," Donegan said.

Soon as our portside hull rubbed against the dock, he jumped out of the dinghy, tied onto a piling, and waited for us to get out. Wilmina stepped onto the dock first. He grabbed her arm.

"She'll be comin' with me. That way, I know you won't be skippin' town."

Wilmina squirmed. "Let go of me."

"I demand you release her," I told him, clutching onto his sleeve.

When he jerked his arm away from my grip, he backhanded my face. It didn't appear that he smacked me on purpose, but he wasn't sorry for it either.

"Teach you to keep your distance," he said, pulling Wilmina with him.

Viorene and I followed, keeping in step best we could up the long dirt road to a wild-west type town: wooden buildings on each side of the street, planked sidewalks, and horses and buggies tied up to posts. Billy dashed in front of us and disappeared into a store. I figured he did it to stay away from Viorene.

"Not much of a town," Viorene whispered.

"It's got everything needed. General store, blacksmith, livery, and feed. Even a nice hotel."

"Not big enough for me," she said.

"You sure are snooty for someone raised in the woods."

She sighed and shook her head.

Donegan led us into a saloon and up to the bar. One handed, he unbuckled his belt, pulled it off his pants, looped it around Wilmina's waist, and re-buckled it. "Sit down," he told her.

Wilmina looked at me.

I nodded and she sat on the floor.

Donegan lifted up a stool, put one leg inside Wilmina's belt slack, then he sat atop the seat, trapping her. The bartender leaned over the bar and laughed. "Need a belt for those two?"

"No, one will do, but I could use a bottle," he continued, plunking down a dollar.

Viorene scowled at me. "This is disgraceful."

"I agree, but he's got the upper hand. Stay with Wilmina while I make inquiries about Daddy."

"You *can't* leave us here," she said.

"He won't let anything happen. He needs us." I bent down to Wilmina. "I'm sorry, I'll be back soon as I can."

"I'm fine," she said, stretching out her legs. "Sure is noisy though."

A bottle broke against a wall, and Viorene squatted down next to us. "It's not safe in here. Drunken men hollering, swearing, and throwing bottles, there's sure to be a fight."

I pushed an empty stool off to the side and made room for her to sit. "Stay low, next to Wilmina."

At the saloon door, I stopped and looked back at my sisters. Viorene, nervous as a spooked horse, twitched her head side to side. Not Wilmina. She scanned the room taking it all in. I hesitated and considered going back, but then I thought of Daddy and hurried out the door.

Once I got to the dock, I jumped aboard the first fishing boat I saw, went to the hatch, and knelt down. "Hello. Anyone here?" An older man poked his head up. "Excuse me sir, I'm looking for my father."

"No one here, but me. Get off my boat."

"Please. My father went missing two months ago in a shipwreck near the Makah Village. He was picked up by fishermen. Do you know anything about that?"

He paused and scratched his chin. "No, but the *McMillan* fishes in those parts." He climbed out of the hatch. "There it is," he said, pointing. "Fourth one down, but I doubt if anyone's there. Probably at the saloon."

"Thank you." I hurried to the *McMillan*, but the old fisherman was right, everyone was gone.

Back at the saloon, the crowd had grown. I elbowed through to my sisters and leaned down. "You two, all right?"

"Viorene's in a pother, but I'm fine," Wilmina said. "What'd you find out?"

"Daddy might've sailed on a boat named the *McMillan*. The crew's here. I need to talk to them." I looked at Viorene. "Come, help me ask."

"I'm not talking to drunken fishermen."

Donegan saw me and looked down from the stool, eyeing me suspiciously. "Where'd you disappear?" The half-empty bottle and slurred voice gave away his condition. "What're you up to, Little Spike?"

"Nothing."

I waited until he turned around and poured another drink, then I went over to six men playing poker. I never liked talking to strangers in a group and my shyness kicked in. I inhaled a deep breath and tapped a man on his shoulder. "Excuse me," I said, barely above a whisper.

He shrugged me off, so I quit tapping and stood behind him like a lump.

"Can't you see we're in the middle of a game?" he snapped, craning his neck to look at me. "What'd you want?"

I leaned toward the smoky table. "Any of you from the *McMillan*?"

"Might be," another burly man responded. "Why?"

"My father was shipwrecked two months ago and rescued near the Makah Village."

He thought a moment. "Big Swede? Muscular, blond hair? I didn't correct him that Daddy was German and nodded. "Left on the ferry. Don't know where. Only worked for us a couple weeks. He didn't know his own name, but he knew the fishing trade."

"Is there anyone who might know more?"

"Doubt it. He wasn't much of a talker. Seemed confused most the time."

"Thank you." I turned to go back to my sisters and saw Billy on the outskirts stalking four men. I moved to the side and watched him. Faster than a dog snatching a bone, he slipped his hand into a man's pocket, lifted out a wallet, and shoved it into his coat. He side-stepped and did the same thing to another man. I don't know why I was surprised, I had suspected him and Donegan as crooks, but to see it first hand, shocked me and I felt betrayed. I headed over to him, but he saw me and bolted out the door. I hurried to Donegan and shook his arm. "Time to leave."

"Not ready," he slurred, jerking my hand away.

I leaned in. "Billy's been caught."

Donegan spun around on the stool and scanned the room. Without another word, he jumped up and darted toward the door, bumping into people on his way out.

I tilted the stool and released Wilmina. As she stood,

the belt fell to the floor. She kicked it to the side and extended her hand to Viorene, pulling her up to her feet.

"What's happening?" Wilmina asked.

"Never mind," I said. "Hold hands," I told my sisters. "One of you grip tight to my suspenders." I parted through the crowd. "Excuse us, excuse us," all the way to the door.

We barely got to the road, when we heard a voice call out, "I've been robbed."

I grabbed my sister's hands. "Run...fast as you can."

CHAPTER 16
STRAIT OF JUAN de FUCA

WE RACED DOWN THE PLANKED DOCK, and with darkness falling, I almost tripped over my feet.

"Where's the dinghy?" Viorene asked, panicked.

Before we got to the end of the pier, I heard oars slurping though the water, coming toward us. "Didn't think we left you? Did you, Little Spike?"

Soon as Donegan angled the bow against the dock, I held Viorene's hand and steadied her down into the dinghy, then Wilmina. I went last and climbed over the thwart to the stern. Billy sat where I needed to be. "Unless you plan to row," I said, "move."

Avoiding my glare, he darted his eyes, up, down, and side to side, then got up, stepped over the thwart, and sat down next to Wilmina but faced the opposite direction of my sister. With his back to me, he hunched forward and hung his head. When I clenched my lips, Wilmina gave me a funny stare. "What's wrong?" she asked. I shook my head and quickly slid the oars into the water.

Under different situations, I might have explored Billy's state of mind. Did he feel guilty? Ashamed? Or was it just his way of life? Now, as I looked at him sitting before me, I didn't ponder further. I only considered him a thief.

"Pull," I told Donegan, trying to lockstep our strokes.

Much to my dislike, I had to admit Donegan's rowing was clean, swift, and some of the best I'd ever seen. Good as my daddy's, hard as that was to choke down.

After we boarded the *Irene,* everyone scattered. My sisters to the galley, Billy who knows where, and Donegan to the bow. I rushed into the pilothouse to see the captain. He was fast asleep, same as he was when we left. I felt his clammy forehead and dabbed it with a damp cloth that I had wetted from the nearby pail filled with water. After a bit, I lit the lantern and went outside. As I stood on the deck shivering from the cold air, I looked toward the town and thought about Daddy. Where are you?

Donegan broke my concentration when he called out. "Little Spike." A flame illuminated his face as he lit a cigar. "Get me some hot brew."

I didn't answer him, but when I saw that he'd dropped a burning match on the deck and stood unconcerned, I hurried over, stomped it out, and tossed it overboard. "You can wait on your coffee," I said. "We're leaving *now* for Port Townsend. I want you *off* this boat tonight." My boldness shocked me. Normally, I'd cower and scold myself for not sticking up for my beliefs, but something mustered inside of me now.

He stared ahead as if I wasn't there. "Upset are we? No one to blame but yourself. Wasn't me who suggested goin' to town."

"Not for you to steal and get us involved."

"Settle down, Little Spike. Everythin' worked out."

"Stop calling me that. Doesn't make a bit of sense."

He didn't reply. Instead, he sucked on his cigar and blew out smoke.

I spun around to walk off, held up the lantern, and saw Billy by the mast. "You're nothing but a thief and no better than Donegan," I said. "For the rest of this voyage, stay away from me and my sisters."

Biting his lip, Billy nodded and sauntered past me.

I couldn't read Billy's face, but as I watched until he disappeared, I felt disappointed by his actions and realized I didn't know him well enough to expect either good or bad. What did it matter? In four hours or so, they'd be off this boat, which couldn't be soon enough for me.

"Little hard on him, don't you think?" Donegan said.

I tightened my hands into a fist and stomped away, heading toward the hatch. Soon as I entered the galley, my sisters, sitting at the table, stopped talking when they saw me. "What's going on?" Viorene asked.

I set the lantern down and sat across from them. "Need help weighing the anchor."

Viorene gave me a stupefied look. "Tonight?"

"Have to. Don't want the *Irene* tagged as a thieving boat."

"Thieving?" she said, surprised. "Why would *we* be suspected of that?"

"Didn't you hear the men yell from the saloon? About being robbed? Why do you think we ran?"

"To get away from Donegan and back to our boat."

I looked at Wilmina. "You know the truth?"

"No."

"Billy's a pickpocket. He's the one who robbed the fishermen."

"What?" Viorene said.

"Donegan must've made him do it." Wilmina defended.

"Doesn't matter. He should've refused."

Wilmina looked at me strange as if I'd betrayed her. "It's not his fault," she said.

"Don't agree," I said. "Mama and Daddy said to *never, never* steal. No matter what."

Viorene interjected. "Finally, you're talking sense. We should row to shore and get the authorities."

"No, we'd be tied to their crime," I said. "Best we get out of these waters and them off this boat." I turned to Wilmina. "Help me with the anchor. And don't give me any backtalk about Billy."

Wilmina huffed and followed me to the upper deck. After we weighed anchor, she headed back to the galley without a goodbye or see-you-later wave. I walked into the pilothouse, and much to my dismay, there sat Donegan on the front bench, to the right of the wheel. I scanned the room for Billy, but it appeared that he was nowhere in sight. I knelt down to Captain Murphy and felt his head again. Not even a squirm. "We'll get you help soon," I whispered under my breath.

Standing at the window looking up at the night sky,

Daddy's voice popped into my head. "You can do this," I heard him say. His words sounded so clear as if he was standing next to me. "Okay," I muttered, and then I sheepishly glanced over at Donegan, but saw that he was too liquored up to notice me talking to the air. Daddy had taught me to navigate by the North Star, but never to a slivered moon and a few twinkling stars, like tonight. You can do this, repeated in my head, but this time it was my voice doing the convincing, not Daddy's.

After I removed the *Pacific Coast Pilot* book from the bookshelf and set it on the pedestal next to the lantern light, I flipped to the chart I had marked earlier. Along with latitude and longitude dimensions, the next few pages were littered with lighthouses along the strait and a full description of each. The first light coming up would be the New Dungeness—a fixed white light sitting atop a tower one-hundred-feet above sea level—illuminating the entire horizon as it shined almost eighteen-nautical-miles out.

I gripped the wheel, throttled open, and headed us out into the strait. After a bit, I spotted the shining beacon and pointed the *Irene* toward it. In the distance, a deep-throated *Eeee...ahhh* echoed through the waves, keeping true to the foghorn intervals described in the book. As we plowed ahead, the light's refraction grew brighter and the *Eeee...ahhh's* six blasts, then resting twelve seconds or so in between, magnified louder and louder. Even though I knew the horn wasn't for us, hearing it comforted me.

As we approached the light, preparing to pass, the

brightness blinded me a bit and the horn forced me to cover my ears. During the foghorn's brief silence, I yanked our whistle rope, and as it shrilled like a teakettle, I mouthed a *thank you* to the light for guiding us this far.

Suddenly, the pilothouse door flew open and a cold air penetrated the room.

"Was that the dinner call?" Viorene said, carrying in a tray of hot biscuits and gravy. My stomach growled from the smell. Wilmina behind her held the coffeepot one-handed and tin cups hanging on her fingers in the other.

"Sorry for acting mad at you," Wilmina said, nuzzling up against me.

"Sorry from me too," Viorene added as she set the tray on the side bench. "You know we love you."

I smiled. "I love you too."

"Blah, blah, blah," Donegan remarked as he eyed Viorene's tray. "Dish me up a plate," he told her, and then he sneered at Wilmina. "And you, get me coffee."

A scowl crossed Wilmina's face. "Why should I?"

Donegan got up from the bench, snatched a cup out of her hand, and held it out. "Pour," he said. When he turned toward me, I smelled his stale-liquored breath. I nodded to my sister to do as he asked.

Pouring, Wilmina tilted the coffeepot and it sloppily streamed out. Some splattered on Donegan's boot; either he didn't notice or didn't care. Soon as Viorene handed him a plate, he stepped back to the front bench and started shoveling food into his mouth and slurping coffee.

Wilmina handed me a filled cup, then set the coffeepot atop the engine. "Can I find Billy and give him some food?" she asked.

Even though I was still angry with Billy, I didn't want to upset her again. "Okay," I said, "but it's too dangerous walking the deck at night. Best you can do is shout-out and see if he comes."

She opened the door. "Billy, Billy," she called out. "Come get food," she repeated over and over until Viorene walked over and closed the door.

"You're bringing in cold air," Viorene said. "Dish up a plate for Aggie and take the wheel so she can eat while I tend to the captain." As I stood above Viorene eating fast as I could, she looked up and whispered. "He's barely breathing."

I quickly swallowed. "I know. Soon as we dock, we'll get him to a doctor, but all we can do now is keep him cool."

Viorene's face filled with worry as she propped up his bedding. "And try to get water down him."

"Much as he's sweating, doubt if it'd do much good," I said.

She nodded, stood, and took my empty plate. "Come on, Wilmina," Viorene said. She clutched onto Wilmina's arm as they headed out the door.

Back at the wheel, I tried ignoring Donegan until he pulled a cigar from his pocket, stuck it in his mouth, and patted his pockets for a match.

"Your matches got tossed," I said. I had thrown them overboard with his discarded lit match.

He scowled and shoved the cigar back into his pocket. "Be glad to be off this boat and away from you."

"I'm in agreement with that."

He smirked and nodded. "Imagine you are."

WITH THE NEW DUNGENESS LIGHT at our back, another white light shined in the distance, but this one also flashed red. The pilot book called it the Point Wilson Light—the entry into Admiralty Bay and Port Townsend.

Soon as we entered the bay, I veered away from three clipper ships anchored inside the inlet. Beyond them, I saw a floating dock, a wharf, and side-by-side warehouses. All of it so well-lit by kerosene lanterns and streetlights, it seemed like the middle of the day.

"We'll hook out here," I said. "No room at the dock, otherwise those ships would be tied on to it."

"They never are," Donegan remarked. "They lineup and wait their turn. There's already a clipper at the wharf being loaded."

"How is it you know so much about this harbor?" Then I remembered Billy saying he lived here at one time. I wondered if that meant Donegan, as well.

"Don't be makin' talk with me now. You had your chance and snubbed me the whole trip." He pointed to a vacant spot off the starboard side. "Pull in there. I'll handle the lines." He went out the door and met Billy at the bow.

188

While Donegan talked, Billy bobbed his head up and down. Sure wish I could hear that conversation, I thought. But maybe not.

I throttled off, pushed the lever into reverse, and reopened the throttle, to let in steam. With the propeller now in opposite rotation, the *Irene* slowed. Soon as I closed the throttle again, she drifted toward the dock.

Donegan picked up the line, twirled it above his head, and lassoed it to a piling, cinching it tight. Quick as I'd ever seen him move, he darted to the stern, grabbed that line, and tied it on too. With his final bowline knot, the *Irene* jerked and stopped.

When the pilothouse bell clanged, I knew it was my sisters pulling on the engine-room rope below. I went to the front of the wheel pedestal, looked down at the opening in the floor, and smiled when I saw Wilmina's grinning face looking up. "Can we come up?" she asked.

"Not yet, wait until they're off the boat."

Heading toward the pilothouse door, I looked at Daddy's pocket watch. Ten-thirty. No wonder I'm tired. As I stepped outside and breathed in the brisk air, tinny-sounding piano music and a deafening din echoed from the wharf above. "Sure is noisy out here," I remarked to Donegan.

"Over fifteen saloons in this town," he said. "Closest one is at the top of this dock. I'll be headin' there now." He turned to Billy. "Collect that five dollars from her."

Before I could respond, Donegan leaped off the boat.

"That payment was for Westport, not a journey around the cape," I grumbled to Billy.

"Advise you pay it."

I could see by his face he wasn't threatening, but giving advice. "Fine, wait here." I went inside the pilothouse. The opening to the shed was next to the captain's head. I reached into the hole, felt for the sock I had hidden in a tin can, and pulled it out. Untying it, I heard the door creak, so I blocked the sock with my leg and peeked over my shoulder, expecting it to be Billy. But it wasn't, it was Donegan instead.

"That's where you stashed it." He grabbed the sock out of my hands. "Old sailor trick. Knew you wouldn't go for the money with me around." He reached in and pulled out dollar bills, shoving them into his pocket.

I jumped to my feet. "Give me that back."

"No doin'," he said, walking away with the sock. "Took old Captain Paddy's papers too." Captain Paddy was Captain Murphy's nickname. "He's lookin' mighty sickly. Don't think he'll last long."

"You have no right to those. I insist you return them."

He pulled the captain license from his pocket. "Good likeness, don't you think?" he said, holding the picture next to his face.

"So what?"

"One thing about this port, it's a county seat and it abides by laws. Better be able to produce a registered captain or they'll claim this boat."

"Not if we pull out now."

"Willin' to go without one of your sisters?"

"Leave them alone. Or I'll personally report you as a kidnapper and a thief."

"Settle down, Little Spike." He went to the door and called out for Billy.

Billy slowly walked in, holding a piston rod.

"Is that from our boat?"

"Sure is," Donegan said, taking it from Billy. He turned to me. "Boy ain't much of a sailor but he sure has a knack for machines." Donegan examined the rod. "Looks to be part of the engine."

I glared at Billy. "How dare you damage our boat."

"Ain't damaged," Donegan said. "Just disabled for a spell. Right Billy?" He patted Billy on the back. "I'll keep hold of this rod. Maybe use it as a cane. You'll get it back when *I* say it's time to go."

CHAPTER 17
PORT TOWNSEND

THE NEXT MORNING, I headed uptown and found a doctor's office on the second block. "He's really sick," I said, studying the doctor who now at second glance didn't appear as professional as Doctor Simpson back home. This doctor had greasy blond hair, shifty eyes, and a red nose, like Donegan's after a day of drinking. Plus scuffed-up shoes and a rumpled suit that appeared a size too small for his bulk.

He grabbed his bag. "We'll take my buggy," he said, motioning me to follow him out his back door. Soon as we reached our boat, he made me wait outside as he examined the captain. Moments later, he came out shaking his head. "Serious infection," he said. "Need to get him transported to the St. John Hospital for the sick and poor. It's run by the Sisters of Providence."

"Okay," I said, still hesitant of this doctor, but also relieved that the captain would be getting proper care.

"Got any money?" he asked. "They don't charge the poor, but he'll get better care if you can pay. And you owe me two dollars for my time. And two dollars for a wagon transport."

I pulled four dollars out of my pocket and handed it to the doctor. I had retrieved ten dollars earlier out of the money sack hidden in the engine room.

"The wagon should be here within the hour," the doctor said. "Have someone waiting on the wharf to escort the drivers to your boat. I'll meet you at the hospital."

While my sisters stayed aboard the *Irene*, I rode in the back of the wagon with the captain. The box wagon had four large spoke-wheels, little padding on the floor, and was as bouncy as any I'd ever felt. Two younger men sat at the front, atop a squeaky springboard and guided two horses along.

I placed the captain's head in my lap and stroked his brow, but he never opened his eyes. As the wagon climbed a winding road, magnificent views of the bay below spanned for miles. When we finally reached the hospital, two Sisters, cloaked in black robes, greeted us. I followed the stretcher as the drivers carried the captain into the hospital.

The doctor approached and examined the captain again, and then he turned to me. "Four dollars for one week will pay for a daily wash, a fresh gown, three meals, and a clean bed in a shared room."

I reached into my pocket, handed him the money, and watched as he paid a Sister.

"The Sisters aren't used to infections like this," the doctor told me. "Pay me another two dollars," I had already paid him two, "and I'll check on him throughout the week."

While I counted out the money, the doctor gave me firm instructions. "Understand this. I may have to make fast decisions, without consent." He removed a paper and a pencil from his pocket, wrote out those words, and had me hold the captain's hand to make an *x*, but it was really me writing, not the captain. A Sister signed off as a witness.

After I kissed the captain's forehead, the Sister pulled me off to the side. "Wait seven days to visit," she said. "He needs rest."

TRAPPED AT THE DOCK with a disabled boat and the captain in the hospital, we didn't have much choice but to wait. After four days, I visited the doctor's office, *rest and time* was all he offered. Plus, he extended the captain's hospital stay. "Another week," he said, which required more money to him and the Sisters.

I reached into my pocket for the additional money, but stopped short. "I can pay the Sisters myself. I plan to visit the hospital tomorrow."

"Nope. Your grandfather needs his rest." The doctor assumed that the captain was my grandfather and I saw no need to correct him. "I'm going up tomorrow to check on him," the doctor continued. "Stop back in and I'll give you an update."

Much as I wanted to trust the doctor, something in my gut set off alarms, but I also realized that I didn't have much choice with that either. I pulled out the money and set it on his desk. Heading back to the boat, I spotted Donegan ahead walking into a saloon. I stepped to a store window, pretending to gaze while watching Donegan out of the corner of my eye. Thankfully, it appeared that he didn't notice me, but I'd have to pass this saloon to get back to the dock.

Every step closer, my stomach tightened. Right before I reached the saloon door, I took a deep breath, and then ran all the way to the boat. Not that seeing Donegan could be avoided; he had become a daily routine. Since arriving to this dock, he returned nightly so drunk he could barely make it aboard the *Irene*. He never brought Billy. And I never asked where Billy might be. He only inquired once about the captain, then spouted, "Waste of time puttin' him in a hospital; he's already close to dead." But every morning Donegan demanded coffee, food, and money. I held firm and reminded him about the money he had stolen from the sock and told him that was all we had. "You got more, certain of that," he would bark.

Today, Donegan had tried to barter. "Ten dollars for the piston," he said.

"Not paying you another cent," I snapped back. "Even if I had it." I walked away.

Truth was I didn't need the old rod. I had found a blacksmith, paid him two dollars to make a new one, and install it by the end of the week.

After Donegan had swallowed his final drops of coffee, he threw his tin cup onto the deck, climbed over the gunwale, and slid down to the dock. "See you tonight, Little Spike," he said, whistling as he walked away.

Much as the entire situation grated on my nerves, I was

grateful for the opportunity to search for Daddy. Every evening after the boats pulled into port, my sisters and I canvassed the dock. While Viorene stayed aboard and surveyed with binoculars, Wilmina and I went from boat to boat. One time, we thought we had a lead, but it turned out to be a sailor playing a cruel game. It sure got us mad, but that was the way with boatmen. Some made jokes and others walked away without listening. Then there were those who tried to be helpful. "Have you checked here or done that?" they'd say as they wished us good luck.

The next morning after Donegan had left I went to the pilothouse and pulled out the logbook. The last entry was by Daddy, March 1, 1898. I brushed my fingers across his handwriting, turned the page, and picked up a pencil and wrote.

DATE: *July 4, 1898. Independence Day*
VESSEL: *The Irene*

Next was the captain slot. I tapped the pencil on my chin and pondered what to write. I piloted the *Irene*. Does that make me a temporary captain? Or is it Captain Murphy by default? I remembered Donegan calling him, Captain Paddy. Must be for Patrick, his first name. Or maybe a childhood nickname his father gave? I decided to adopt it as my captain name, so it could serve for us both.

CAPTAIN: *Captain Paddy #2*

Looking at it written, it seemed right. I went to the next heading in the book and wrote after the description.

ROUTE: *Port Townsend, Washington*
NOTES: *Captain Murphy (Captain Paddy #1) recovering in the hospital.*

Wilmina knocking on the pilothouse window brought me out of my thought. I looked up.

"Come outside," she mouthed. I closed the log and joined her on the deck.

"Listen." Horns trumpeted, drums *rat-tat-tatted*, and a lone tuba burped in and out, deep and low. "A parade. Can we go?"

"Don't think it's wise to leave this boat. Donegan and Billy could sneak aboard."

"We haven't seen Billy since we docked. Donegan only comes at night. Pleeese, pleeese can we go?"

Something in my gut told me no, but looking at her excited face, I caved in. "All right, but we need Viorene's vote."

Much to my surprise, Wilmina convinced Viorene, but only after she promised to dress up. Besides the pants, shirts, and overalls we wore daily, there were dresses with proper accessories packed in a chest—petticoats, leggings, ribbons, and boots, to name a few.

"Can't I just put on a clean shirt?" I said.

"No, this is a holiday," Viorene said.

198

I changed out of my overalls into my blue and yellow calico dress, but I refused ribbons in my braided hair.

Viorene furrowed her brow. "You don't look patriotic."

"I don't need to. You and Wilmina got that covered."

Viorene had tied red ribbons in Wilmina's hair and dressed her in a red, white, and blue striped sailor dress. She finished her off in a white petticoat, white leggings, and black boots. Viorene wore red hair ribbons too, but they didn't stand out like they did in Wilmina's black hair. But Viorene's sea-blue dress sure brought out her eyes.

"You both look nice," I commented. But as always Viorene stood out, even when she didn't try. At five-foot-five, she was the same height as me. Dressed up, she looked more like fifteen than her true eleven. No matter her real age, when she tossed her curly blonde hair and showed her dimples, boys melted like bear grease.

UP THE FIRST BLOCK to downtown, patriotic banners hung from the storefronts, but other than noisy chatter from the saloons, the town was locked-up tight. I feared at every saloon Donegan would spot us, so before we crossed in front of one, I peeked into the doorway. I'd decided if I saw him or he saw me, I'd send my sisters to the festivities and I'd go back to the boat.

After seven saloons and no sightings, we continued walking and took turns carrying the picnic basket and the two blankets we had brought.

"The music appears to be coming from up there," Viorene said, pointing to the bluff above downtown.

Following the winding road leading up the hill, I realized it was the same road to the hospital.

"Sure is a steep grade," Viorene said, "but what a view."

Water spanned in every direction—the harbor below, the strait beyond that. I had already seen the view riding with the captain to the hospital and knowing we were so close, I wanted even more to see him, but then I remembered the Sister's sternness, telling me to stay away.

"That sign says courthouse," Wilmina remarked, looking at the red-bricked building with three stories, turrets, and a tall clock tower on one side. "Sure is big."

"What about all the fancy houses?" Viorene cooed. Living in a stately house was Viorene's dream.

Two and three-story homes of every architectural design dotted the hillside. Some had turrets and attic dormers—windows jutting out of a roof—and gingerbread gable trim. But the most common features were the laced window-shades, the wrap-around porches, and the water-view balconies.

Wilmina grabbed my hand. "I see the band. Come on," she said, pulling me with her.

Luckily, the sun had burnt off the fog and promised a nice day. Red-white-and-blue flags, banners, and bunting hung everywhere we looked: booths, tables, band gazebo, and park benches, to name a few. Even a reddish weenie dog—short-legged, long and skinny with floppy ears—trotted past with a tiny flag draped over its back as its patriotic-garbed owner held onto the dog's leash.

We spread out our blankets on a patch of grass near the bell tower, put down our picnic baskets, and sat.

"I'm glad we came," Viorene said.

I smiled at her and nodded. "Feels like the old days with Mama and Daddy."

Wilmina stood. "I'm going to explore. Wanna come?"

"Aggie, you go," Viorene said. "I'll stay here."

Wilmina tugged me from booth to booth. One had homemade candies and cakes. Another one, cookies and pies. We opted just to look, but planned to come back.

Three ladies dressed in lacy gowns and fancy feathered hats stood outside the most elaborately decorated patriotic booth I'd ever seen.

"Hello," I said to a middle-aged woman wearing a bright red ostrich-feathered hat with blue-jay feathers mixed in and a stuffed white dove perched on the top. "What a pretty hat," I told her, admiring it.

"How dare you," she scolded.

"I didn't mean any offense," I said quickly.

Another woman walked up and spouted, "Remember the Maine." She handed me a pamphlet that showed a sketch of a half-sunk ship, and then she stabbed her finger toward Wilmina while focusing her eyes on me. "Why would you bring *her* to this event? Don't you know we're at war?"

I read the pamphlet.

SUPPORT THE SPANISH-AMERICAN WAR BUY BONDS, MAKE DONATIONS, DO ALL YOU CAN TO WIN THIS FIGHT

I had forgotten all about the war. Right then, I thought of Grandma. This *is* why she wanted Wilmina hidden. Why didn't I remember that?

The woman grabbed the pamphlet from me. "Get out of here. *Now,*" she demanded. "Before we throw you out."

Wilmina looked at me. "What'd we do wrong?"

"You're Spanish," the woman snapped. "I can tell from your skin and hair."

Wilmina turned to her. "No, we're German and Portuguese."

"And proud to be," I said loudly.

"Portuguese have Spanish blood." She looked at me. "Sisters?" I nodded. "Lucky for you, you don't take after your sister."

I grabbed Wilmina's hand and pulled her away. After a few steps, Wilmina stopped me. "I don't understand," she said, sniffling.

I knelt down in front of her. With my kerchief, I wiped the wetness off her cheeks. "Sometimes, people can't see beyond their ignorance. Always be proud of who you are."

I boiled with such fury I was sure I'd punch the next person who gave me reason. As we neared Viorene, I saw three teenage boys standing at the edge of our blanket talking to her. We sat down next to her.

"Who's this?" one blond boy asked.

"My sisters," Viorene replied.

"Even the black-haired one?"

"Yes," she answered.

"We *all* have Portuguese blood," I blurted, standing up. "Is that a problem? I'm in no mood for further ridicule."

"All right, all right," he said, holding up his hands. "Doesn't matter to me."

"Seems to matter to those close-minded women over there. How dare they hurt the feelings of a little girl."

Viorene looking at me, stood. "What happened?"

"The Spanish-American War. Seems anyone with olive skin and black hair is accused as a traitor."

"Someone said that?"

"Implied it."

Viorene bent down, gathered up the food, and loaded it in the picnic basket. "Help me roll up the blankets."

I swelled with pride for her fast action and quickly did as she said.

Without another word, the boys walked away.

All the way to the boat, Viorene and I talked of uninformed people and the right and wrong of judgments. Wilmina sulked and walked ahead, kicking a rock.

"Don't forget about pig-headedness," I piped in. "Some people can't be convinced, even if you shove it in their face."

"You're not helping," Viorene said to me. "Best we soothe Wilmina's feelings, not get her riled up again."

Wilmina stopped and spun around. "They had no right talking to me like that. I should go back and tell them."

Even though I agreed, I knew Viorene was right—some fights you had to let go. "No, not worth the hike back up, but I'm glad you're mad," I told Wilmina. "Makes *you* the better person for walking away."

Closer we got to the *Irene*, I felt comforted. "Good to be home." I shimmied up onto the gunwale and over onto the deck. Viorene handed up the picnic basket and the blankets. "Here's the step stool," I said, lowering it to my sisters. Holding my hands, Viorene stepped up onto the stool, sat on the gunwale, swung her legs around, and slipped down onto the boat. Wilmina did the same. With a gaff, I lifted the stool aboard.

"Is that hammering?" Viorene said.

I stopped and listened. Sure enough, *bang, bang, bang.* Metal on metal. "It's coming from below. Must be the blacksmith, he's early." I rushed to the hatch, flew down the stairs, and into the engine room. I stopped in my tracks. "What are you doing here?" I said coldly.

He dropped his wrench and jumped down in front of me. "Came to fix it," Billy said. "Felt bad for what I done."

"Does Donegan know you're here?"

"No. I snuck away."

Wilmina called down from the opening in the pilothouse floor. "Aggie? Is it the blacksmith?"

I went over to the engine, looked up at the ceiling, and saw her face. "No, it's Billy. He came to fix the rod."

My sister's footsteps dashed across the deck and scurried down the stairs. Wilmina skidded in first. Viorene behind her.

"Surprised you'd show your face," Viorene said.

He shamefully looked down. "Soon as it's fixed, I'll be on my way. Then, you can sail off."

Truth was, leaving sounded awful good but we couldn't depart without the captain. "Won't be able to go for at least another week," I said.

"You don't understand," Billy said. "Donegan's been drinkin' all day. He's out of money and offered up this boat. Once he showed the captain's license, the bar owner fronted him two-hundred dollars."

CHAPTER 18
PORT TOWNSEND

FULL HEAD OF STEAM—that's what was needed.

Billy had fixed the rod, but it required testing and couldn't be done without steam. My sisters waited in the pilothouse. I stayed below in the engine room with Billy.

"Looks good," Billy said. "Be on my way."

"Be obliged if you waited until we tried it out. Let's get the boiler ready," I said, heading to the woodpile.

After he tossed boards onto the furnace wood-grate, I dipped a stick into the sap bucket, threw it onto his pile, and struck a match. The fire crackled and then it burst into flames. I closed the firebox door. Even though the engine had been out of commission, we kept the boiler tank filled with water.

"Won't have full steam for at least an hour, probably longer," I said.

He nodded and followed me back into the galley and sat at the table on the opposite side, but wouldn't look me in the eye.

"Appreciate you coming back," I told him.

He sighed. "Gnawed at my gut the whole time."

"At least you owned up to it. Suppose we've all done things we're not proud of."

"Yep," he said. "Done with thievin'. Plan to go to Montana. For railroad work."

Excitement rose in my voice. "Is Donegan going?"

"Nope, just me, but I gotta try. Ain't nothin' else for me."

"Glad to hear that you're thinking straight, but pounding spikes requires muscles. How old are you again?"

"Thirteen goin' on fourteen."

"You sure don't seem it." When he furrowed his brow, I feared I had insulted him. "What I meant was..."

"Don't matter," he snapped. "I was a sickly kid. That's why I got sold to Donegan, but he had use for me."

"Sold?"

"Donegan's a crimp." I'd heard the word before to describe a no-good who would steal, kidnap, and do almost anything dishonest to get a buck. That sounded like Donegan. "Don't care to talk about it," Billy said. "How much steam is needed for testin'?"

"At least another half hour to give us enough to start the engine and see if your fix holds."

"It'll hold," he said. "I'm good with machines; learned a lot when I worked in the pig-iron factory."

"Seems to me, machinery work is what you should be pursuing. At fourteen, my daddy learned all about boilers from working the tugs. Maybe you could do something like that?"

"No one's goin' to give *me* that kind of chance."

Much as I wanted to argue the point, I couldn't. He was right. One look at him—scrawny and shy—they'd make a joke, crush his pride, and he'd be forced back to an unlawful life.

"Back to leavin', Billy said, "you need to disappear from this harbor. Donegan's got eyes on stealin' this boat."

"But we can't leave. The captain's still in the hospital. The doctor extended his stay five more days. Plus we're searching for our Daddy. Why can't we just anchor out in the bay? He can't get to us there."

"No, he'll find a way to get aboard. You need to get the captain outta here too."

"Why's that?"

"Donegan wagered money that the captain will be dead in a week. Got two freckled-face thugs checkin' at the hospital and reportin' back."

I gasped. "What...? You really think they might hurt the captain?"

"No, they're just wharf rats. Always workin' angles for easy money."

"Wait a minute, freckles?"

"Yep, the Andrews brothers. There's four of 'em and they all look alike: ginger-colored hair, freckled skin, and skinny as fishin' poles. But it's the two younger ones workin' with Donegan."

"That sounds like the drivers who transported the captain to the hospital."

"More than likely."

"Do you think the doctor's in on this?"

"It's hard to say. Nothin' or nobody's safe around

209

Donegan. Last I heard the wager on the captain was up to two hundred."

I grabbed my chest, trying to slow the thumping beats. "Stay here," I told him. "I need to talk to my sisters." I raced to the pilothouse and up to the front bench where my sisters were sitting. "We have a big problem," I told them, panic rising in my voice. "The captain's in danger and so is the *Irene.* We have to move this boat and we need Billy's help. I'm going to ask him to stay."

Viorene gave me a disbelieving stare. "Stay? Are you forgetting he broke our engine?"

"But he fixed it too. I'm telling you that we need his help. He was raised here and can guide us on where to go."

She leaned back and crossed her arms. "I say *no.* It's time for us to go to the authorities."

I looked at Wilmina. "What about you?"

"I'll do whatever *you* think best, Aggie."

"Always siding against me," Viorene said, glaring at Wilmina before turning back to me. "Here's a simple answer, if the engine's fixed, then get him off this boat and head for home."

"And leave the captain behind? Didn't you understand what I said?"

"You're overreacting like you always do. The Sisters will keep watch. We can send money and have the captain put on the train when he's better."

"Where to? Are you forgetting I sank the *Molly Mae?*"

Wilmina interjected. "And what about Daddy? We're close to finding him."

Viorene threw her hands into the air. "What a mess. If Billy stays aboard, keep him away from me."

I spun around, and yanked the *Pacific Coast Pilot* book off the shelf and rushed down to the galley again. I slammed the book down onto the table, flipped to the Port Townsend section, and shoved the book toward Billy. "Where should we go?"

He tapped on the page. "Port Hadlock," he said. "Town's called Irondale. 'Bout nine miles south of here. Sparse, not much left but sawmills, which makes a good hide'n place."

"But I have to get to the hospital first."

"Wouldn't advise it, best you get the boat gone first. And once Donegan sees the boat missin', those ginger-headed thugs will be on the hunt. Donegan will make sure of that."

"Will you stay aboard and help us? Would be better than you sleeping on the streets; I'm guessing that's what you've been doing."

He nodded. "Can't believe you'd offer for me to stay. I'm sure your sisters don't want me here."

"They agreed to it."

"Even Viorene?"

"Can't say she'll be friendly, but if you prove you've changed, she'll come around."

"Don't *you* need proof?"

"My gut's telling me to trust you."

He looked down so I couldn't see his face. "Never had anyone give me a second chance."

AFTER A HALF-HOUR or so while waiting for our steam to bank, we heard rowdy yelling coming up the dock. Billy jumped up, climbed onto my bed, and looked out the porthole. "Donegan. Know that drunken howl anywhere. That's the bar owner with him." He turned to me. "Is there enough steam now?"

"Might be, but won't do any good without untying us first."

"I'll stall him to give you time."

Before I could stop him, he leaped off the bed and bolted past me to the stairs. I followed him, but by the time I got up to the deck, he was already off, racing up the dock.

I darted into the pilothouse and hollered to my sisters, "Donegan's coming. We have to untie the lines. Now!"

Wilmina jumped up, and to my surprise, so did Viorene. As I headed to the bow, my sisters ran toward the stern. While I loosened the bowline knot, I watched Billy bouncing side to side in front of Donegan as if trying to tell him a story.

"Get out of my way," I heard Donegan say, but Billy ignored him and kept up with his act until Donegan caught Billy's arm and then threw Billy to the ground, stepping over him.

"Need help at the stern," Viorene cried out. "The knot's too tight."

"Coming," I said, but first racing over to the metal toolbox and rifling through the hodgepodge of tools: screwdrivers, wrenches, and nuts and bolts until I found a hatchet and pulled it out.

"Out of the way," I told my sisters as I leaned toward the line, and chopped and chopped.

Donegan saw me, ran to the piling, and grasped at my arm, trying to catch it with each chop. "Stop it," he growled. In his drunken state, he was slow and sloppy. When I accidently nicked his arm, he jerked it back.

"Get the gaff," I told my sisters as I continued axing. After the frayed line finally broke through, I dropped the hatchet, grabbed the gaff from Wilmina, and pushed the hooked pole against the dock.

The *Irene* creaked and barely moved, not more than half-a-foot. Then suddenly, as if an angel had appeared, a rogue wave bounced beneath us and carried the *Irene* at least seven-feet away from the dock, leaving too much of a gap for a sloppy-drunk Donegan and an over-weight bar owner to jump aboard.

Donegan stood before me, shaking his fist.

The bar owner walked up. "What's going on?" he said to Donegan.

"Orphaned misfits," Donegan said. "They won't be goin' far with a broken part. We'll get a tug to push 'em back to the dock."

"Only kids aboard?" the bar owner said.

"Three girls. Could sell 'em as housemaids."

"No interest in that," the man said. "Only want the boat."

"It's not for sale," I said. "Belongs to our father."

"You see a father aboard?" Donegan said to the bar owner. "Besides I have legal papers to sell it." Another tactic used by crimps—forgery, I figured.

"Holding you to your word," the bar owner said. He turned and walked away.

Donegan waited until the bar owner got out of earshot. "Little Spike, not too late to strike a deal with me."

Our eyes locked. I could tell he was searching my face. Maybe hoping my expression would reveal hidden money aboard. Statue-like, I didn't blink or move.

When Billy walked up, I broke the stare-down with Donegan and focused on Billy. "You, all right?"

Before he could answer, Donegan seized Billy's arm and shoved him against the piling. Billy fell backwards and landed on the ground, and as he sat up, I saw blood oozing from his nose and mouth. If I'd been within reach, I would've whopped Donegan with the gaff.

"Have explainin' to do," Donegan said, yanking Billy up to his feet and dragging him along as he staggered away toward the wharf.

Wilmina tugged on my arm. "We have to help him."

"Wish we could, but for now he's on his own. Come on," I said, leading them down to the engine room.

214

At the boiler, I opened the try-cocks one by one—bottom, middle—and water mixed with steam flowed out of both. The top one, only steam hissed out. Thank goodness, everything in order and enough steam built up to get us out of here.

"What now?" Wilmina asked.

Removing my gloves, I pondered a moment. "Stay down here and watch the piston rod," I told her. "Viorene, I need you up top with binoculars. Don't want Donegan seeing us pull out of here. He'd have us tailed for sure."

"Where're we sailing?" she asked as she followed me into the pilothouse.

"South of here, about nine miles. To Irondale, near Port Hadlock. Billy's idea."

Viorene huffed. "You sure we can trust him? This could all be a trap."

"Viorene," I said, tempering my frustration best I could. "He tried to help us. You saw for yourself."

She paused, then heaved a sigh. "Yes...it did appear that way." She removed the binoculars from the hook and looked through the glass. "All clear."

I prayed as I opened the throttle to warm the engine. *Hiss...thump...hiss...thump.*

Wilmina hollered up from below. "Everything looks good."

I took a deep breath, opened the throttle wider, and pulled the lever to forward.

The *Irene* moved with ease, but as I fretted about Billy, the captain, Daddy, and piloting a boat that might break, my stomach knotted like a thousand tied-up ropes.

CHAPTER 19
PORT HADLOCK - IRONDALE

AS WE PULLED UP to Irondale's weathered dock, it reminded me of the Aberdeen one we had tied onto back home—same sorry shape with missing planks.

"Looks like a ghost town," Viorene said, referring to Irondale.

She was right about that: deserted buildings, shambled shacks, and a closed-down foundry.

Wilmina looked through the binoculars. "I see some men going into a building."

"Probably a saloon," I said. "Billy said there's a working sawmill here."

"Can we go to town and explore?" Wilmina asked.

"Tomorrow. Let's just hope our boat doesn't get noticed."

"What are we going to say if we are approached?" Viorene asked.

"Keep it simple; that Daddy's asleep and wanted to dock in a quiet spot."

IN THE TWO DAYS since we had arrived, we had explored what little there was to see—one saloon, a general store, which opened only on Thursdays according to a· sign, and a far-off sawmill that we could hear and smell. To pass our time, we washed clothes, scrubbed down the

217

deck, played cards or checkers, and waited on Billy to show up. But I already decided, Billy or not, I'd walk to the hospital tomorrow to see the captain; figured the nine miles by boat would take two hours or so by foot.

As I linseed-oiled the wheel, Wilmina walked into the pilothouse and plopped down onto the bench. "I'm bored. It's so nice out; can we explore the foundry today?"

"It's nothing more than a closed-up factory."

"Better than sitting here," she said. "All Viorene wants to do is read."

"Guess it would be good to stretch our legs. Ask Viorene if she'd like to come."

"I already mentioned it to her. She told me that she had no interest in seeing a dirty old building."

WALKING UP THE DIRT ROAD toward town, we heard the sawmill buzzing in the distance.

"Look," Wilmina said, pointing. "The general store opened early. Do you have any money?"

"I reached into my pocket. "Yes, actually I do." I still had money remaining from the ten dollars I had taken to pay the doctor and the hospital.

"Good," she said, "I'm going to get some candy." She raced ahead of me and into the store.

"We're from the boat," I heard her tell the clerk as I walked in behind her.

"Boat?" the man said.

"Yes," I answered. "Our father just got back from a

218

long fishing trip and wanted a quiet place to catch up on sleep. Surprised to see you open. Your sign said Thursday."

"I never pay that any mind. I come once a week when I feel up to it."

Wilmina tugged on my sleeve. "Look at all the candy," she squealed.

Right then, Mama's words flashed into my head. "Wilmina," she'd say, "ration your sugar." I smiled at my sister. "Not too many," I told her as I looked about.

All the shelves were caked with dust and lined with what a sawmill worker might need or want: canned corn, pork and beans, flour, sugar, and salt. And another whole shelf was dedicated to chewing tobacco—colorful tins of every shape and size, each one with its own picture: a Wild Tiger, Mallard Ducks, and my favorite, a funny-looking man instructing how to chew and spit. Wilmina picked out three peppermint sticks and didn't show a lick of concern about their crusted tops when she popped one into her mouth. "Got one for you and Viorene," she said, sliding them into her pocket. "Is it okay if I go outside with these?" she asked the clerk. "My sister will pay."

"Sure," he said, and then he called over to me. "Give you half-off on a tobacco tin. Bet your dad would enjoy one."

No, I started to say and then I remembered that the captain liked to chew. I picked up the tin with the funny-looking man and brought it to the counter.

Wilmina poked her head through the door. "Aggie. Billy must've passed when we were in here. He's halfway to the boat."

I quickly paid the clerk, shoved the tin into my pocket, and followed my sister to the road. As we sprinted, Wilmina hollered out to Billy. Finally, he turned around. She ran up to him first.

"Hi Billy," she said.

"Hello," he replied as I skidded up. He had a black eye and scraped-up nose.

"I'll let Viorene know you're here," Wilmina said, "and to get food ready." She sped off.

I studied his face. "You, all right? We were worried."

"I'm fine, but Donegan and his thugs have been watchin' close, so I had to be careful with my steps. Walked extra blocks, hid out in a store, took off in one direction, turned around, went the other, then came here."

"Surprised he's keeping you with him?"

"Long as I earn my keep, he won't let me go."

I knew that meant stealing, so I didn't pry.

"Got news," he said, "but I'd like to wait until we get to the boat. Thought it might be better if you were sittin' down."

"This sounds bad," I said, panicked. "I can't wait. You need to tell me now."

"Okay," he sighed, lowering his eyes and then inching his gaze back up. "Gangrene took the captain's leg."

I gasped and stared at Billy's somber face. "Did I hear

you right? He lost his leg?" Tears welled in my eyes as I watched Billy's watering too.

He nodded. "Got cut off two days back."

As I fought down the bile threatening to invade my mouth, I clutched his arm.

"I went to the hospital yesterday," he said, "couldn't see him, but spoke to a Sister. She said he's holdin' his own."

I straightened up and looked at him square on. "I have to see him."

"It's too dangerous. The thugs know what you look like."

"I don't care. I *have* to go."

He hesitated. "Let me think on it," he said, looking up at the sky in deep thought.

Suddenly, an idea popped into my head. "I could dress like Viorene," I blurted, "and fix my hair."

He studied my face. "Well...that might work; they ain't lookin' for a dressed-up girl. But you'd have to go on your own. Can't be seen with me or your sisters."

"My sisters," I said, biting my lip. "How do I tell them?"

"Sometimes just spittin' it out is the best."

While I waited in the pilothouse with Billy, trying to figure out the right words, Wilmina walked in carrying a tray. "Salmon, pickles, and bread," she said, setting the tray down on the side bench.

I reached for her hands, pulled her with me to the

221

front bench, and faced her. "I have bad news about the captain."

Her mouth flew open and wetness flooded her eyes. "He's dead, isn't he?"

"No," I said, patting her hand. My voice trembled as I said, "but...he lost his leg."

"Oh, no," she said, shaking her head as tears cascaded down her face.

I hugged her and glanced up at Billy, feeling helpless on what more to say. Thankfully, he spoke up.

"But he's gettin' fitted for a peg one," Billy said. "Be walkin' before you know it."

"Really," Wilmina said, wiping her cheeks with the back of her hand.

I swallowed the hard lump in my throat, but still felt like I could puke, but I held it back. Had to for my sister's sake. "That's right," I said in a confident tone. "I'm going to see him today."

"I want to go too," she said.

I shook my head. "We can't leave the *Irene* unprotected and it's too dangerous if we all go." I stood. "Visit with Billy while I get ready." I hurried to the galley and found Viorene on her bunk reading a book. "Need your help," I told her, choking back tears.

"What now?" she said.

Before I could answer, I broke into sobs.

She slid down off her bunk and sat next to me on my bed, rocking me back and forth, as I relayed the news.

After she wiped her wet face with a hanky, I told her about my plan. She stood, walked over to the closet, and took out her frilliest pink dress. "This should fit you; I let out the hem."

I quickly undressed out of my overalls, and slipped Viorene's long pink dress over my head. Circling me, Viorene straightened and aligned the pink ribbons on the bloomers, showing below the skirt. "Sit," she told me, grabbing a comb. "You can't wear braids." I folded my hands into my lap as she brushed my now wavy hair and pinned it back with a large pink bow.

"You look nice," she said softly, handing me a mirror. "I'm sure the captain will think so too."

"Uh, huh," I said, looking at my reflection, not sure what more to say. "Thank you."

"Of course," she said.

"It'd be polite if you said *hello* to Billy. He's been a big help and is escorting me to town."

She didn't respond, so I figured the answer was *no*. But she followed me, and soon as she walked through the pilothouse door, she smiled. "Good to see you, Billy."

I could tell by his face that he was shocked. I was too. But that was Viorene. Sometimes, she'd do the opposite of what a person might expect. He gave her a quick nod and glanced downward.

I turned to my sisters. "Keep a close eye on this boat. Untie the line if anyone suspicious approaches. You can always row to shore to get me later."

223

"Okay," Viorene said, trying to sound confident, but I could see anxiousness in her face. Not Wilmina.

"Don't worry, Aggie," Wilmina said. "We can do it."

"I know. And I'll be back soon as I can."

CHAPTER 20
PORT TOWNSEND

AT THE OUTSKIRTS of Port Townsend, I looked at Daddy's pocket watch again, then at Billy. "Less than two hours to get here. Made it faster than I thought."

"Yep," he said, "but now we're in the not-to-be-seen-together part." He pointed to a side street. "Up that road to the bluff and another twenty minutes you'll be there. I'll check on you later in the week."

Before I had a chance to thank him again, he had disappeared around a corner. I peered over my shoulder— no one in sight—and raced along the street. Huffing and puffing, I finally reached the top of the hill and looked down at Port Townsend, way off to the left.

Along the dirt road in the distance, I spotted the hospital; it appeared like a castle through the trees: two squared towers on each side of the brick structure; four floors, each with ten windows evenly spaced; and a tall gold cross atop a steeple roof. With each step closer, my worry for the captain and fear of being caught spun in my brain.

As I approached, I took a deep breath and started up the wide steps to the cave-like porch leading to a thick mahogany door. I pushed it open, slivered through, and with a bit of a struggle, got it closed. Now standing inside the foyer all I saw was hallways: left, right, and straight, and beyond the large oak desk in the center of the room, a staircase climbed to the upper floors.

A Sister wearing a black tunic, white headdress with a black veil, and oversized silver cross that dangled from her neck, approached with a no-nonsense look, which shattered my nerves even more. I shoved my jittery hands into my coat pockets.

"Hello," I said. "Came to see Captain Murphy. I mean Patrick Murphy."

"Are you a relative?" she inquired.

Billy had instructed me, if asked, to say that I was a granddaughter. I sure didn't want to lie to a Sister, but I rationalized that I loved the captain like a grandfather, had known him my whole life, and with the captain's life in peril, it was really a fib of necessity, and I was sure God would understand.

When I hesitated, the Sister answered for me. "Granddaughter?"

I nodded, and without a word, I followed her to the large desk.

She shuffled through several charts, selected one, and while reading it, motioned me to follow. I trailed behind her in silence as her footsteps echoed on the wooden floors. She finally stopped at a door, opened it, and pointed me to the room. "Don't stay long. He needs his rest."

"Thank you, Sister."

She nodded, and as soon as she closed the door, I

226

smelled antiseptic right off and gagged. It reminded me of Mama—the day she had died. I held my hand over my mouth and looked at the six wrought-iron beds lining the wall, each filled with lifeless men. Charts hung off the brass footboards.

Once my stomach settled, I tiptoed from bed to bed and stopped at the chart that read—*Murphy—amputated leg.* My gut wrenched and my heart pounded clear up to my throat. I slowly came up the side of his mattress and reached for his hand. "It's me, Aggie," I whispered, leaning down and kissing his forehead.

From his contorted face, I knew he was in pain and it anguished me to see it. Suddenly, his eyes squinted open. I gasped and leaned closer. "I love you, captain. I've been so worried."

He quivered a weak smile and faintly squeezed my hand, shaking it back and forth.

"I'm so very, very sorry," I started to say as his eyelids drifted shut.

I stood motionless and looked down at his near comatose face. Sadness, remorse, and fear throttled me into uncontrollable sobs. My shoulders vibrated and giant tears plopped from my cheeks onto his gown. I didn't hear the door or Billy's voice until he walked up to me and gently touched my arm.

"Aggie, I'm sorry. Know this is private, but ..."

I jerked my head up, saw it was Billy, and wiped my face with the sleeve of my coat. "What're you doing here?"

"Ran into the red-heads," he said. "Told me they were deliverin' supplies to the hospital and could use my help. Acted like friends, even offered to buy me lunch, so I played along. I had to warn you. You gotta go now."

"No, I need to wait until he wakes up again."

"Can't chance it," Billy said. "As it is, they're watchin' me and will be gettin' aggressive for answers, so I gotta figure a way out of here too."

I sighed and stared down at the captain again, tears watering in my eyes so bad that everything blurred.

"You're runnin' out of time; come on." He latched onto my arm, bringing me with him to the door. He peeked out, turned his head side to side scanning the hall, then pulled me out of the room and double-stepped me toward a side door. "Quarter-mile up there's cleared-out woods for you to hide," he said. "Wait until the wagon passes. Keep away from the hospital. I'll come see you soon as I can."

No sooner had he pushed me outside than I heard a voice say, "What are you doing, Billy?"

"Nothin', gettin' air," he said, quickly closing the door.

I sprinted to the supply wagon, ducked behind its large wooden-wheel, and watched through the spokes as the door swung open. When I saw a ginger-headed man looking out, I froze like a possum. Soon as the door closed, I darted toward the road and didn't stop running until I reached the cleared-out woods.

IN THE FOUR DAYS since visiting the hospital, I busied myself with chores, but every time I thought about the captain, my stomach twisted with worry. Then more sad memories of Mama flooded my head and I got sick over those, but what nested in my brain, was all the *what if's*. What if...I hadn't talked the captain into sailing the *Molly Mae*, then he wouldn't have lost his home or his leg. What if...I had gone to Daddy sooner when Mama got so sick, maybe she wouldn't have died. And what if...I'd been caught by Donegan's thugs? Thank goodness, Billy came to warn me. That could have cost me the loss of the *Irene*. And if I got sent back to Grandma, that would've meant the loss of being with my sisters, the captain, and finding Daddy too.

That afternoon while studying charts, I heard a knock on our hull, looked through the window, and jumped up when I saw it was Billy. I dashed out the pilothouse door over to the gunwale. "I'm so happy to see you. Have you seen the captain?"

"Yep," he said as he climbed aboard. "Sittin' up and eatin' puddin'."

"Really?"

He nodded. "But Donegan's actin' like a caged dog. Another bar owner paid up the wager, and is pressurin' Donegan to find this boat even more. Donegan's got forged papers sayin' it's his to sell."

"I have papers too. Real ones. Locked away in a strongbox."

229

"Hope it don't come to that. 'Cuz you bein' a kid, you'd probably lose."

"Don't want to think about it," I said. "It was pretty scary at the hospital. How'd you get away from the red heads?"

"After we completed the delivery, I climbed into the wagon and sat near the rear. Soon as it took off, I jumped out and high-tailed it into the back woods."

"Surprised they didn't come after you."

"They tried, but it's thick with underbrush and I was too fast."

I leaned against the wheel and heaved a heavy sigh. "What a mess."

"Appears to be," Billy commented. "Not sure how, but Donegan knows you visited. The captain says for you to stay away. Wants you sailin' the *Irene* back to Port Townsend. You're to dock next to the *Lucy Elaine*. Ask for Captain Pete."

"Who?"

"He's related to Reynolds, the man in the next bed. Reynolds overheard the captain and me talkin' and offered to write a note. I delivered it yesterday. You're expected."

"How do you know you can trust him? He could be working for Donegan."

"The captain trusts him," Billy said, "and he seems like a nice man, so were the people at the dock."

"I don't know; this whole thing sounds fishy. The captain might not be thinking straight. I say we stay put."

"The captain figured you'd put up a fuss." Billy handed me a crumpled note.

After I read it, I shook my head. "All it says is...GO."

"There's your answer. Besides, now that Donegan knows that you're still around, he'll have his thugs checkin' every cranny of this harbor. Only a matter of time 'til they find you."

"I don't know what to do."

Billy gave me a befuddled stare. "Ain't you been listenin'?"

"Yes, but I'm uneasy about it all. How long before the captain can travel?"

"At least another two weeks. Has to learn to walk with a peg."

I lowered my eyes and sighed. I hadn't thought beyond the captain being sick and now having to learn to re-walk. How hard will that be? When I looked at Billy, he quickly spoke.

"I'm to get more carin' money. The captain said twelve dollars, most will go to the Sisters, but wants two dollars extra, just in case."

"Does that include the doctor?"

"Didn't say," Billy remarked. "Ain't seen much of him. Maybe he figures the captain's on the mend."

"All right," I said, heading to the pilothouse with Billy at my heels. I knelt down to the shed opening at the back and pulled out a gunnysack. Earlier in the week, I had refilled the sack with thirty dollars for quick cash. I

231

counted out twenty. "Fourteen for the captain and six for you," I told Billy as I stood.

He shoved the wad into his pocket. "Thanks, can use it for eats. Most days, I hide in the woods and visit the captain when it appears safe. The Sisters think I'm seein' Reynolds."

"Sounds like you trust Reynolds."

"Yep, especially after I met Captain Pete."

"Guess I will too. You might as well stay aboard and ride to the port with us."

CHAPTER 21
PORT TOWNSEND

ENTERING PORT TOWNSEND'S HARBOR, I spotted the empty slot next to the *Lucy Elaine*. Her gunpowder-gray hull, troll lines, and cramped pilothouse mirrored most of the weathered fishing boats lining the pier. I shut off the throttle valve and steered us toward the dock. A large man with gray-streaked hair stood at the piling, hollering. I opened the side window to hear.

"Angle more," he said, motioning me into a cockeyed slant.

"That's Captain Pete," Billy said.

I nodded. "Awful odd angle he's guiding us to. Could you go out and check with him?"

Billy sprinted out the door. "Yes, that's right," I heard the captain tell Billy. Billy turned around and gave me a thumbs-up.

After our stem touched the dock, I hurried out to the deck.

"With your boat angled, that clipper's tattered sails," he said, pointing to a tall ship, "will block anyone from viewing your boat from the top of the wharf. It split its keel and not moving anytime soon."

"Oh," I replied, looking at the leaning ship again, then up at the wharf. "Good thinking."

"Been known to have a quick wit," he chuckled. "I'm guessing you're Aggie."

"Yes, hello. And you're Captain Pete."

"Yep. I recall you girls from before, asking about your dad. Ever find him?"

"No."

"Don't know your full story, but was asked to watch after you. You can count on us. Seadogs stick together." I smiled, remembering Captain Murphy saying that very thing when the tugboat crew pulled the *Molly Mae* out of the mud.

"Speaking of family." He pointed to a large man coming up the dock. "My son, Leo." Leo was a younger version of his dad, except his hair still had color, light brown.

Soon as they tied the *Irene* to the dolphin, a group of pilings tied together, Captain Pete jumped aboard. Leo headed to the *Lucy Elaine*.

"My sister's cooking venison stew," I told the captain. "Should be ready in about an hour, if you'd like to join us."

Mama had jarred deer, elk, even bear. All shot by Daddy and enough to last at least two years. She had jarred fruit jelly and soups too.

"My stomach's already growling," he told me with a boisterous laugh, and then he yelled over to Leo. "Come over in an hour; the girls are fixing us supper."

BY THE END OF THE FIRST WEEK, we had settled into a routine, which all centered around Viorene's cooking. Captain Pete and Leo provided most of the food—fish, potatoes, fresh berries, flour and sugar, and whatever else Viorene requested. When they fished, they commissioned friends along the wharf to guard us. Only thing—we had to feed them too. And because it wasn't safe for us to leave the wharf, Wilmina and I got roped into meal preparation; my least favorite chore. I had never showed an interest in cooking. Mama would try, but after a bit, even she gave up and sent me off to help Daddy on the boats. But that wasn't going to happen; the fishermen had to eat, Viorene needed help, and there were plenty of potatoes to peel.

This morning while my sisters worked below in the galley, I tended to the boiler, greased the worm gears, and oiled the wheel with linseed, but stopped when I saw Billy walking up the dock. He was now living aboard in our pilothouse, but left every morning, returning later with news, except last night he didn't come home at all.

I raced out of the pilothouse "Where have you been?"

"The thugs had me in a chase," he said, chortling, "but I fixed them good. When I saw the Port Angeles ferry pull into the dock, I joined in with the passengers getting off. Even paused a couple times making sure the thugs saw me."

"Weren't you concerned they were going to nab you?"

"Nope, but they took my bait like a rat to cheese; got 'em thinkin' you're in Port Angeles. Watched as they boarded the ferry and waited until it pulled out. They should be gone most of the day, so I figured it'd be safe for us to visit the hospital."

"I sure would love to see the captain," I said. "But do we dare?"

"You ain't gonna get many chances. And if we're careful, should be fine."

I WORRIED THE WHOLE WAY to the hospital, especially as we headed through town, passing the bars. Soon as we entered the hospital, the Sister behind the desk jumped up and motioned us forward. "Quickly, both of you," she said, leading us to a closet filled with cloaks. "Wait here until I come for you." Before we could ask what was happening, she closed the door, leaving us in darkness.

Holding onto the cloaks, I lowered to the floor and sat. "This isn't good. What do you think is happening?"

"Hard to say," Billy replied, plopping down beside me, "but wouldn't be surprised if Donegan's involved."

"I knew we shouldn't have come."

"Too late now, besides it don't do no good worryin'."

I rolled my eyes and groaned. It seemed forever before the door creaked open. I squinted from the light. Billy stood and pulled me up to my feet. "What's going on?" I asked the Sister.

236

She put her finger to her lips. "Shhh..."

Following her down the long hallway, we tiptoed past the stained-glass windows of the chapel with muffled prayers echoing from inside. Soon as we got beyond, the Sister increased her pace and her footsteps grew louder on the wooden floors, which flared my nervousness even more. She finally stopped at a door and motioned us into a sparsely furnished room with one bed and a chair. "Wait here," she said before hurrying away.

A moment later, *clip...clip...clip* ricocheted down the hall. The door flew open and there stood Captain Murphy upright on a peg leg.

"Captain," I shrieked, rushing to him and wrapping my arms around his neck.

He smiled and stroked my cheek. "Glad to see you, Aggie-girl."

"I'm so happy to see you." As I looked down at his leg, my lip quivered.

He lifted my chin with his finger and gently spoke. "No one's fault, understand."

Before I could reply, Billy interjected. "You're doin' good with that fake leg. Better than the last time I saw you."

"Aye," the captain said, grinning. "Doc says I should be ready in two weeks, but I'm itchin' for sooner."

"Did you know we were put into a closet?" I said.

He nodded. "Donegan was here; just left. He acts like a carin' brother, but the Sisters know he can't be trusted."

"Are you sure he's gone?" I asked, panicked. "What if he sees us, or worse, follows us back to the boat?"

"Watched him from the window," the captain said. "He caught a ride with the old doctor. The two of 'em probably back at the saloon now, guzzlin' down whiskey and conjurin' up more plans."

"The doctor who's been caring for you?"

"The same. Hard to trust anyone in these parts."

After Billy told the captain how he led Donegan's thugs onto the ferry, the captain howled. "It seems to me, this might be good timin' for me to scoot out of here."

"Now?" I said. "How?"

"Already worked out details with Sister Anne. The bread man is a close friend of hers; she said to let her know when I'm ready. He should be arrivin' shortly."

I studied the captain's pale face and frail body. "Are you well enough to leave?"

"Can rest on the boat, good as I can here. And with so much no-good stirrin', probably safer too."

I glanced at Billy. He glanced back at me and shrugged.

"Got any money on you?" Captain Murphy asked. "Might need to pay the man."

I pulled out my five-dollar gold piece, the one I had earned helping Daddy in the cannery. "Can't think of a better use for it."

"Soon as the wagon arrives, you young'ns hop in the back; I'll go talk to Sister Anne now."

238

WE GOT THE CAPTAIN into the back of the wagon, making him as comfortable as anyone could in a hard buckboard, but the ride to the dock went just fine. As I waited under the blanket with the captain, Billy jumped out and raced to the *Irene*.

Before long, Billy and one of our fishermen friends, Bud, appeared at the wagon. Leo lagged behind carrying a board and panted as he approached. It was clear his over-sized body strained from running too fast.

"Let's get him onto the board and out of here," Leo said. The two men helped the captain out of the wagon and onto the makeshift stretcher, then lifted it into the air. As they hurried down the dock, the captain's legs dangled off each side. Billy jogged behind them.

I turned to pay the bread man.

"No need, Sister Anne explained. And if anyone asks, I'll say I dropped him off at the Seattle ferry."

"Thank you." I shoved my sentimental coin back into my pocket and shook his hand. "You're a good person."

"Just following God's ways," he added.

Right then, Mama popped into my head, she used to say that very thing. Thinking about her, tugged at my heart. When I reached the boat, the captain was already aboard sitting on the gunwale. Leo and Billy stood off to one side with Viorene. Bud was gone, but Wilmina had plopped down next to the captain, peppering him with questions.

"What does it feel like to walk on a wooden leg?" I heard her ask. "Does it hurt? Do you sleep with it?"

I pulled on her arm. "Give the captain some air."

"Aye," he said, trying to stand. Suddenly, he stumbled backwards toward the gunwale.

Leo rushed over. "Let me help." He steadied the captain to his feet, clutched his arm, and escorted him toward the pilothouse. Viorene darted ahead, holding the door open as the captain hobbled through. Leo entered next, then Viorene and the rest of us followed.

With all six of us now inside, we were crammed like pickles in a jar: Leo behind the wheel, Viorene at the back bunk fluffing up the pillows, Billy next to me, and Wilmina plunked down on the front bench next to the captain. Good thing Captain Pete was at the market, otherwise, he would've been in here too.

Wilmina wrapped her arms around the captain's neck and kissed his cheek. "We sure missed you."

He smiled at her, then glanced at me teary-eyed. "Missed you all."

Billy shuffled places with Viorene, so she could come up to the front to the captain. "Your bed's ready, if you need to lie down."

"Thank you." He patted her hand. "Might shortly."

"Can I get you something to eat?" she offered. "Coffee and blueberry pie?"

"That would be a treat." He looked at Leo. "Bet you'd join me in a cup and a bite."

"Always have room for one of Viorene's pies."

"Thanks for watchin' after my crew," the captain said.

"They've been a joy. Bet Dad and I've gained ten pounds from all the good cooking."

"I'll get the food now," Viorene said, inching toward the door.

"Need help?" I asked as I opened it and stepped out to let her by.

"No, I'll carry it up on a tray."

Soon as I came in again, Captain Murphy spoke. "Need all you young'ns to go. I'd like to speak to Leo in private."

I looked at him quizzically. "But not me, right?"

"Nope, you too," he replied.

We single-filed out the door.

Standing next to the pilothouse, drizzle wetted my face and I frowned. I looked at Billy and Wilmina and puckered my lips.

"Little rain makin' you mad?" Billy said.

"No, private talks do. Can't trust the outcome of them."

"Any place to listen in?" he asked.

Wilmina gave me a devilish grin. "The boiler shed."

We rushed toward the shed's louvered door. "Shh...," I said, opening it.

"Maybe I should be the listener," Billy offered. "In case, the captain calls for you."

I nodded, held the door as he climbed inside, and quietly closed it behind him. After a bit, Billy poked his head out and motioned us inside.

I turned to Wilmina. "Been thinking, we can't all have disappeared. Do you mind helping Viorene with the food, but don't tell her that we're spying. Say Billy and I took a walk."

She pouted. "Why do I have to go? It was my idea to sneak into the shed."

"Wilmina, please. I'll fill you in later." Truth was I needed to hear the news first. Might not be good, and if it wasn't, I'd have to figure out a way to sugarcoat it.

She huffed. "Okay."

I crawled inside and faced Billy. "They seemed like old sea mates," he said. "Each told a story. Then, the captain explained he needed his help. Went on to tell him about Donegan and the red-heads. Leo assured him that they had been watchin'."

"Can't see why that couldn't be said in front of us?" I mumbled.

"The captain made Leo *promise* to get you girls back to your grandmother, if anythin' happened to him. Just in case, is how he put it."

"Suppose it made him feel better to say it, but I can assure you that would never happen. Never, never, never in hundred-thousand-years."

"May not be a concern," Billy said. "As we were bringin' the captain back to the boat, a man off the barge stopped me. I told him last week to keep his ears to the ground and I'd pay him a dollar for any worthwhile news. Anyway, he told me that a boat builder fittin' your dad's looks had been workin' at the boatyard. Good thing I still had some of the money you gave me so I could pay him. Figured we could check it out tomorrow."

"No. We need to go NOW!"

He shook his head. "They quit early, besides we've had enough commotion today; need to be rested when squirrelin' around town."

"Can't we just go see? Maybe some are still working."

"No," Billy said. "The thugs are back now. And what about the captain? You can't just leave."

"I'd tell him what's happening and make sure my sisters and Leo keep a close watch. He'd be excited to hear this news."

"Tomorrow mornin'," Billy insisted. "I'm too tired to take it on."

I frowned and reluctantly nodded.

"What 'bout Wilmina? Ain't she gonna ask what Leo and the captain were talkin' about?"

"I'll tell her they just told stories. No reason to upset her about the grandma part, and I don't want to say anything about Daddy either, until we know more."

He nodded.

That night before bed, I handed Billy a bucket filled with items from the captain's trunk. I set the tobacco tin from the Irondale store on the top with a note attached: *Welcome home, we love you—Aggie, Viorene, Wilmina & Billy.* "When he's not looking, put this next to his bed."

"What is all this?" Billy asked.

243

"Personal things I rescued off the *Molly Mae.* He doesn't know they got saved. That tobacco tin is a gift. I added your name." He nodded with an appreciative grin. Right then, I realized he'd probably never been included in anything resembling a family celebration.

When I got into bed, I stared up at the ceiling praying under my breath that tomorrow we'd find Daddy and wishing I could leave right now to see. "Calm down," I told myself as I sat up.

"You awake?" I asked my sisters.

"Yes," Viorene said.

Wilmina answered yes right after.

"Billy and I are going to the open market tomorrow, early before breakfast. He's hoping to find new boots."

"Are you sure it's safe for you to go?" Viorene said.

"Yes, we'll be careful."

"All right," she said. "I'll make a list. You can take a basket."

I hadn't figured on my made-up story developing into a shopping trip. I just needed a fib to look for Daddy without sparking their hopes.

"Eggs, jarred fruit, or whole chicken would be nice," Viorene said. "Anything else that looks good."

"Fine," I said, but now annoyed and trying my best not to show it.

"That sounds like fun," Wilmina said. "What time are we leaving?"

"No. I need you to stay and help with the captain."

"Viorene will be here. I wanna go."

"Another time. Too many of us might alert Donegan or his men. I'll make it up to you, promise."

THE NEXT MORNING Billy and I left at first light. Along the wharf, he looked side to side and over his shoulder more than once. I did the same.

He pointed to a tin-roofed warehouse. "Over there."

Five times larger than any building I had ever seen, it was drafty as all get-all. Workers hammered, sawed, and bladed. Some painted hulls. As we walked through sawdust, it smelled like a forest of evergreens. We went from skeletal hull to skeletal hull of a fishing boat, a ferry to a full-size schooner, looking at all the muscular blond-haired men. Most had beards.

I approached a worker and described Daddy, but purposely omitted his name, in case he wasn't using it.

"Sounds Swedish," the worker said. "Could be Hans or Ansel, arrived from the old country several months back."

"He wouldn't have an accent," I told him.

He thought a moment. "There's John. Not much of a talker. He's been working on the *Claudina*. She's out at the pier, being stocked to sail off to the Klondike."

"Thank you." We hurried outside.

"There she is," Billy said, pointing to a large clipper ship with the name *Claudina* etched and painted white on her stern.

As we walked the ship's portside hull, I scanned her deck, looking for blond-haired men and admired the ship's clean lines: chocolate brown trimmed in red, three masts, rope-woven riggings, and starched-white sails. A thick black stack mid-ship told me she was a steamer too. "What a beauty," I remarked. When we reached her bow, I stopped and yanked on Billy's arm.

"What's wrong?" he asked.

I leaned over the dock railing for a closer look at her prow. Carved on it was a black-haired woman, draped in a flowing green gown. She had rosy cheeks and lips, brown eyes, and curls streaming down her sides. "She looks like Mama. This has to be Daddy's work."

"Does he have that skill?"

"He built the *Irene* and did all types of carvings: table-sized hulls of his boats, dolls, and animal figurines." I excitedly looked around. "We need to get aboard this ship."

I raced over to the roped-off gangplank, unhooked the rope, and started up the plank with Billy behind me. From nowhere, a guard appeared, grabbed our arms, and pulled us back. "Only authorized workers allowed."

"Please, I have to check the ship. My father might be aboard."

"Wait until he comes off."

Billy stepped forward. "We're looking for the man who carved the woman on the prow."

"That's John," the guard said. "Gone for the day."

"You sure?" I said.

He gave me an irritated look. "Not blind. Come back tomorrow. Better make it before dawn, she's scheduled for an early sail."

"Tomorrow? What time?"

"Early," he snapped. He walked away.

I ran over and stopped in front of him. "Any chance you know where he lives?"

"Not his nursemaid. Quit bothering me." He turned and headed to the boathouse.

Billy rushed over and put his hand on my arm. "Wouldn't bother that guard again."

"His growl doesn't bother me." I reached into our basket, removed a piece of deer jerky we had packed for a snack, and hurried to the guard again. "Could I offer you this, for an answer?"

He snatched the jerky out of my hand. "Ask."

"Do you know the story behind the carved woman?"

"Heard he got it from a dream."

"Anything else about it or him?"

"No. Now git."

When the guard walked away again, I dashed back to Billy. "Did you hear?"

He nodded. "That's somethin' for sure."

Standing at the ship's prow again, I twisted forward and studied every inch of the carving, focusing on the lips. "Remarkable." I turned to Billy. "Mama had a lopsided smile. See how he's got her lip lifted on one side?"

"Yep. She sure was pretty."

"Yes," I murmured. "She was."

"Take your time. I'll wait on the bench."

When my neck kinked, I straightened and walked over to Billy. "Better get to the market."

"Thought that was a made-up story?"

"It was until my sisters gave me a list. They're looking forward to fresh eggs."

AT THE MARKET, we found most of Viorene's request—jarred blackberries and peaches, fresh eggs and chickens. Except the chickens were alive.

"We can't take a live chicken aboard a boat, "I said.

"Why not? If you got hens, you'd have fresh eggs."

"No room and too much work."

"Only teasin'," he said. "They chop off the head after you pick it out and pay."

"You do it." I handed him fifty cents. "Just the sound of that makes me squirm."

"You?" he said. "Miss hack-up-a-fish with one blink."

I shrugged. "Fish don't have a personality."

In less than five minutes, Billy sauntered toward me carrying a brown paper wrap stained with blood and chicken feet sticking out.

"Oh, oh," I said. "Viorene will fuss about the mess and the feet."

"I'll pluck and clean it," Billy offered. "Gulls will even eat the feathers if there's meat attached."

248

On the way to the dock, all I thought about was Daddy and the carving of Mama. Has to be him, repeated in my head. Just as we stepped onto the wharf, Billy grabbed my arm and pulled me behind a crate. "Get down. See that wagon. It's the red-heads. Know their horses."

"You think they found the *Irene*?"

"Hope not."

CHAPTER 22
PORT TOWNSEND

SOON AS THE THUGS left the wharf, my stomach twitched with nervous flutters as we darted up the dock toward our boat.

"Of all days to be carrying berry jars," I complained, slowing my pace so they wouldn't clink or break. "Anyone following us?"

"Not so far," Billy said.

When we reached the *Irene*, my sisters rushed out of the pilothouse and to the gunwale. "What did you get?" Wilmina asked, taking the basket from me. Billy and I climbed aboard.

Viorene stopped short when she saw the dead chicken that was missing its head. "It still has feathers," she said. "I'm not cleaning that."

I glanced at Billy with a told-you-so look, but truthfully, it wasn't a foreign task to any of us. Whenever Daddy returned from duck hunting, he'd cut off the heads, but we all shared with the plucking and cleaning.

"I'll do it," Billy offered, lifting the chicken out by its feet and taking it over to the stern.

My heart was still thumping like a runaway horse—partly from seeing the thugs at our dock and partly from knowing that Daddy was close—that I blurted, "We found Daddy."

Wilmina gasped. "You did?" and before I could finish, she raced to the pilothouse. "Captain, captain. Aggie found Daddy."

Viorene's eyes widened. "Where has he been? Why didn't he come with you?"

"Well...uh...uh..." I took a deep breath. "Maybe tomorrow."

"Tomorrow?"

"He had left for the day."

She furrowed her brow. "Did you see him or not?"

"Well, not exactly... but I saw a carving that he did...of Mama on the prow of a three-mast steamer."

"A carving?"

"Yes. I talked to the guard. He described Daddy head-to-toe: blond, stocky, perfect smile."

She scowled. "That doesn't mean anything. Half the men in Port Townsend are Scandinavian."

Much as I wanted to argue the point, I couldn't. Yes, Daddy was German, but with his blond hair and stocky build, he could've passed for Finnish, Norwegian, or Swedish.

"I'm telling you that it was Daddy's work."

"You don't know that for sure; anyone could've carved it." Her voice quivered, but I wasn't sure if it was anger, disappointment, or sadness; maybe all three. And for that, I felt bad, but I didn't let it derail my thinking.

I was thankful when Wilmina hollered from the pilothouse door.

252

"Come inside," she said. "The captain wants to hear."

Viorene huffed, followed me into the pilothouse, and sat at the side bench, crossing her arms. When I told about the carving, Wilmina had me describe every detail. Not Viorene. She rolled her eyes as if I had exaggerated the whole thing. I was grateful for Captain Murphy's open mind.

"Seems to me, this needs further investigation by all three of you lasses," he said.

"We'll go early," I added.

"Take Billy with you to scout out trouble."

Viorene looked at the captain. "I'm staying here. You shouldn't be left alone."

"Nope, you'll be goin'. Captain Pete and Leo can keep me company. You need to see the carvin' for yourself. And hopefully find ya dad. You wouldn't want to miss bein' there for that."

The next morning, Wilmina walked ahead with Billy. Viorene and I followed. She fussed the whole way. "Sure this isn't a waste of time?" she kept saying, but I could hear by her tone a hint of hopefulness too.

At the ship-building pier, crowds had formed around the *Claudina*. We couldn't get close. Excited voices laughing and talking so loud we could hardly hear above our own.

"Who are all these people?" Wilmina asked.

"Prospectors," Billy said. "Goin' to the Klondike. To dig for gold."

We stayed together and elbowed through, but were stuck in the middle until the guard unhooked the gangplank rope. Scruffy-looking men carrying duffle bags and picks boarded the ship, single-file. As the crowd thinned, we moved toward the ship. Wilmina got there first, leaned over the railing, and looked at the prow. She kept reaching out trying to touch it, but it was too far away. Viorene, next to Wilmina, bent forward and studied the carving up and down.

Wilmina turned to me, tears pooling in her eyes. "She's beautiful. It is Mama."

"There is a striking resemblance," Viorene said, "but we have to keep our hopes tempered."

"I'm certain for good news," I said.

Billy stood next to me, looking through the binoculars combing the crowd. "Might be able to talk to the guard."

I looked at my sisters. "Stay here."

"If we are forced to move," Viorene motioned to a nearby bench, "we'll be sitting over there."

"Okay," I said.

The guard was a different one from yesterday. I hoped he'd be friendlier. "Excuse me, sir."

He leaned down and cupped his ear. "Speak up."

"Have you seen John? The man who carved the prow?"

He looked up at the ship then pointed. "Right there, starboard deck." Before I could ask him more, another herd of prospectors advanced. "Move to the side," he said.

I followed Billy closer to the hull, lifted the binoculars, and trembled as I focused the lens. "It's Daddy," I whispered. My heart raced. "Billy, it's him."

"Glad to hear," Billy said.

"I've got to get up there." I handed Billy the binoculars and rushed back to the guard. I waited a moment, stepped between a gap in the line, and when I approached the guard, he gave me a strange look.

"Only ticket holders and crew."

"I need to get on the ship. I'll pay to get aboard."

"You got a hundred dollars for a ticket?" The disbelief on my face must've told him no. "Didn't think so," he said. "Stand back, let these men through."

"Pleeese. I *must* speak to John. He's my father," but in the middle of my pleading, the crowd roared again, "To the Klondike."

"Can't hear above the noise," the guard said. "Goin' up in a bit. I'll have him come down."

As he pushed me out of the line, I shouted, "Tell him his daughters are here."

He nodded and returned to taking tickets. Just then, Billy walked over.

"Not sure if he heard you," Billy said. "Best to wait 'till the crowd thins again."

I followed Billy back to our previous viewing spot and focused the binoculars on Daddy again. Watching him, my stomach panged with a yearning to be with him. More than I'd ever felt in my whole life.

255

I hadn't realized Billy left to get my sisters until Wilmina yanked on my arm. "Billy said you found Daddy. Can I see?" I handed her the binoculars and pointed.

Wilmina squealed when she saw him. "It's Daddy. Viorene, I see Daddy."

"Let me see," Viorene said excitedly. Viorene's hands shook as she looked through the lens. A moment later, she gasped. "It *is* him. I can't believe it," she said, choking back tears.

Billy tapped my shoulder. "Guard's goin' up."

With every step the guard took, my heart pounded harder. When I saw him talking to Daddy, I was certain I might faint. "Daddy's coming to the rail," I said.

When Daddy saw us jumping up and down, waving our hands, and screaming, he smiled and waved back and then walked away.

"He must be coming down." Wilmina said.

"Yes, I think so," I said, following him through the lens. "Appears to be going toward the gangplank. Now he's talking to someone. Let's give him another minute." But as it turned out, that minute changed the course of our lives. I'd been so engrossed watching Daddy I hadn't noticed the gangplank being cranked up to the ship.

Wilmina tugged at my sleeve. "Aggie, it's going up."

I lowered the binoculars and looked at her. "What?"

The gangplank!" she shrieked, pointing.

"No!" I screamed, racing over to where the gangplank had been roped off. I funneled my hands around my mouth and yelled. "Lower the gangplank, lower the gangplank." Billy and my sisters ran over and shouted along, over and over until our voices grew hoarse. Looking through the binoculars, I paced back and forth and scanned the ship's deck.

"Do you see him?" Wilmina said. "Do you see him?"

"Quiet."

Once I found him again, I stopped and magnified the lens. Focusing on his face, every smile line and wrinkle came into clear view. Thoughts flew through my head. *You saw us. You waved. Even if you are confused, plain common sense should tell you that we're from your past.* As I continued watching him talk and laugh with two other men, it struck me that I was seeing a joyful carefree man. The way he was before Mama died. And as much as I wanted to be pleased that he was happy, panic wrenched in my gut from the realization that he might be sailing off. I shook my head and muttered under my breath, "This can't be happening. Please, no."

I kept glued to his face until he turned his back and walked away. I froze and stared through the lens at unknown men as waves of disillusionment and dread swept through me. I felt queasy, so I inhaled and exhaled slow and deep before lowering the binoculars.

"What's wrong?" Wilmina said. "You look sick."

"I'm fine," I said, looking down so she wouldn't see my watery eyes. When I glanced up at Viorene, she nodded and slipped her hand into Wilmina's.

257

"Time for us to go," she said, trying to sound strong while blinking back her own tears.

For that instant, I wished we had never found Daddy.

I stared up at the regal ship again and listened to the voices coming from her decks; all in high spirits, whooping and hollering, "To the Klondike." I wondered if one of those might be Daddy. I squared my shoulders and turned to my sisters again.

"Viorene's right; time for us to head back."

Billy looked at me surprised. "The ship hasn't left. We can keep yellin' and wavin' our hands."

I sighed and shook my head. "No, I've been searching for a ghost."

"What'd you mean?" Wilmina said. "Daddy's not dead."

"Don't mean Daddy. I'm talking about our way of life. Ever since Mama died, nothing's been the same."

"We were doing all right," she said in a defending tone.

I smiled at her. "Yes, *we* were, but not Daddy. He was like an empty clam shell."

When the tugboat blasted its whistle, pulling the *Claudina* away from the pier, my sisters and I watched in silence. Finally, Wilmina spoke. "He must've thought we were strangers."

"Probably so," I said, "but he remembered Mama. Even if she came in a dream, means pieces are coming back. So maybe someday..."

258

"Someday he'll remember us?" she said, finishing my sentence before she broke into sobs.

"Yes," Viorene answered, gripping Wilmina's hand tighter. And all the way back to the *Irene*, Wilmina cried and cried. So much, her eyelids swelled up like a puffer fish. After we climbed aboard, Viorene pulled Wilmina toward the hatch. "I'll draw you a bath."

Billy and I headed to the pilothouse. Leo, Captain Pete, and Captain Murphy were playing poker on an old apple crate. Captain Murphy sat sideways on the front bench with his peg leg propped up, and Leo and Captain Pete were on upside-down metal pails. When Billy and I walked in, they glanced up. No one said a word. My glum face must've told them not to ask.

Captain Pete put down his cards, stood, and motioned for Leo to do the same. "We'll be on our way," he said, patting my shoulder as he passed. "Tell Viorene we'll skip supper tonight, breakfast too." He turned to Billy. "Come along, I'll give you a tour of our boat."

Leo gave me a heart-felt smile and gently pushed Billy out the door ahead of him.

"Come sit," Captain Murphy said to me, lowering his leg to the floor.

No sooner had I sat, tears gushed out. "Daddy looked right at us. We waved, jumped, and screamed, but he just walked away."

Captain Murphy pulled me to his chest, and as I wept, he stroked my hair. "At least you know he's alive."

259

After a bit, I sat up and wiped my face with the back of my hand. "Thought if he saw us, he'd remember and everything would be the same."

"Ya dad's been awful sad since your mother passed. Maybe his brain is givin' him time to heal."

I locked my eyes onto the captain's and slowly nodded. "Those memories flooding back could be as raw as the day Mama died, couldn't they? Sure don't wish him that pain again."

"Aye, and you thinkin' like that shows you're walkin' in grown-up shoes."

"What should we do?"

"Between you and your sisters to decide."

That night, my sisters and I were so spent, Wilmina bedded down early and Viorene read in her bunk.

"Can I turn out the light?" I asked her.

"Yes. Good night," Viorene said, closing her book and setting it at the foot of her bed.

The next morning, Viorene, first up, treated it like another normal day. Even cooked up extra pancakes, eggs, bacon, and coffee to share with Leo and Captain Pete, who had planned to eat uptown.

Maybe her preparing for disappointment has its merit, I decided, still feeling as if I'd been punched in the gut.

While I sat at the table sipping hot tea, Wilmina sat down next to me. She glanced at Viorene busy at the cookstove, leaned in, and whispered in my ear, "We need to find Daddy and tell him who we are."

Just moments before, Viorene had announced to both of us that she wanted to head home. "We'll see," I said.

Wilmina smiled. "I know you agree."

But the truth was, I wasn't sure what to do. All night I weighed every scenario and still hadn't come up with one pin-prick idea worth sharing.

When my sisters headed off with Leo and Captain Pete's breakfast, I carried Captain Murphy's to him and sat while he ate.

"How you feelin'?" he asked.

I shrugged.

"Have you girls made up your minds?"

"Wilmina wants to find Daddy. Viorene votes for home. I'm wobbly on what to do."

" 'Tis a hard one."

"Surprised you're not forcing us back to Grandma's."

"Thought about it. Can't get over that she wants to separate you girls. Life will carry you away soon enough."

"Mama used to say sisters are sisters for life, but the most precious are the young years shared."

"True enough. Lost my family sooner than I should've. Don't want it happenin' to you."

I knew he was referring to the people in the picture album, but I also knew not to ask. He'd offer if he wanted me to know.

"Meant to thank ya for savin' my things. But it was foolish to go near the *Molly Mae*. Sinkin' boats can take ya under quick. I should be scoldin' ya."

261

"I know."

"But it means a lot to have me treasures, so I'll forgive ya. But next time, Aggie-girl, ya gotta listen to what I say. Especially, somethin' as serious as that. Would've broke my heart if somethin' happened to ya."

"I'm sorry. I'll listen from now on. I promise."

"One thing I'm goin' to insist ya do is telegraph your grandmother to let her know you're all safe. I'm bettin' ya haven't done that."

"No." I wanted to add that letting her know our whereabouts would be dangerous, but I knew he wouldn't agree. "I'll do it later; maybe before we leave port."

"Nope. Want it done today. And I want a receipt."

"A receipt?"

I WAITED CLOSE TO AN HOUR for Billy. He had wandered off. Finally, I gave up and headed uptown on my own. I was extra careful, looking over my shoulder every few steps, and before I knew it, I had landed in front of the telegraph office. I pushed the door open, walked up to the work counter, and pondered on what to say. I feared that the instant Grandma read it she wouldn't trust the message and would notify the authorities to look for our boat. After writing out the note and ripping it up three times, the clerk called over.

"Need help with that?"

I sighed. "Don't really want to send it because it will show from Port Townsend, but I promised I would do it."

"For an extra two dollars or so, I can have it transmitted from Seattle and forge a return reply."

"You can?"

"What does it need to say?"

"We found Daddy and we're all fine. See you soon. Love, Aggie, Viorene, and Wilmina."

"Simple enough," he said, scribbling it down as I spelled out my sister's names. "I'll give it to the ferry dispatcher and have him forward it to our Seattle office. That way you've met your promise and haven't revealed your location."

After I paid and gave him Grandma's address, he handed me a phony reply, stating *received*, but I had to pay another fifty cents for that. I stuffed the reply telegram into my pocket and hurried out the door. When I reached the *Irene,* I saw Billy sitting on our flat-roofed shed.

The shed, no higher than my waist, attached to the back of the pilothouse and housed the upper portion of the boiler drum, the tank that stored our steam. A tall smoke stack that connected to the drum sat atop the roof and stretched toward the sky.

Climbing aboard, I headed to Billy. "Want company?"

"Sure," he said, scooting over for me to sit. "Where you been?" he asked.

"Telegraph office," is all I offered. "What about you?"

"Took a walk; needed it for thinkin'." He turned to me. "So, have you girls decided on what you're doin'?"

"No."

He nodded. "Ain't sure where I'll be goin', either. Been tumblin' that Montana idea in my head again."

"Working the rails? I thought I talked you out of that." Before he could answer, a raggedy voice called out from the dock, "Well, well..."

I froze, then looked at Billy who had the same shocked expression on his face that I knew mine was sporting.

"If it ain't Little Spike and Billy-boy."

My heart thumped. I slowly turned and looked at Donegan, sneering as if he'd won a prize. I glanced at the thin man standing next him. This man's beady eyes, greasy-brown hair, and sly grin deepened my worry.

"Pretty smart to dock this boat under my nose," Donegan remarked. "Saw you go into the telegraph office. Careless of you not to notice it's across from Sweeney's Bar."

Billy leaned toward my ear. "That's Sweeney," he said, referring to the man with Donegan. He was a different bar owner from the one before.

"Waited until you headed back, then followed you," Donegan added.

Billy latched onto my arm and pulled me with him across the roof. Just as we reached the other side of the shed, Billy jumped down first onto the deck.

"Don't wait for me," I told him. "Get the captain." Soon as I got down, Donegan and the bar owner had come aboard and cornered me at the stern.

"Best be packing up," Donegan said. "This boat's sold with official papers drawn up."

Before I could respond, Captain Murphy hobbled right up to Donegan. "Is that right?" he said.

Billy rushed to my side.

Sweeney looked back and forth at the two brothers and shook his head. Side by side, the captain and Donegan did look like twins.

"You no-good," Captain Murphy said. "Did it ever bother you that your crooked ways broke Mother's heart?"

"Baaa," Donegan said, pushing the captain back.

The captain stumbled. Luckily, Billy and I caught him.

"Not too steady are ya, gimp?" Donegan smirked.

The captain faced his brother again. "Tell me, how is it you sold a boat that you don't own?"

Sweeney spoke up. "Papers showed him as the registered owner. This boat belongs to me now."

The captain looked at Sweeney. "Sorry mate. Those papers were forged. I'm guessin' he used my captain's license to get 'em."

"Don't care," Sweeney said. "I've got notarized papers stamped by the port authority, listing me as the owner."

"So you're a crook too. Are ya?"

"I'd call myself a person of opportunity."

"Crook's the right word to me," Leo's bold voice said as he climbed aboard.

Leo stomped past us and up to Sweeney, blocking

265

Billy and me from Donegan's and Sweeney's view. "I'd suggest you men leave, unless you want us filing charges for fraud."

"Try it," Sweeney told Leo. "I'm an important man in this town, with high connections. You people need to get off *my* boat. My men will be here shortly."

"Is that a threat?" Leo said.

"Just a fact."

"Psst...kids," a voice said behind us.

Billy and I turned and saw Captain Pete squatted down behind the back of the shed. We hurried to him.

"Sure glad to see you and Leo," I told him, "but this sounds bad. Could he really steal our boat?"

"Not if we can help it, but we gotta act fast."

CHAPTER 23
STRAIT OF JUAN de FUCA

WITHOUT BEING NOTICED, we got the *Irene* untied at the bow and she drifted from the dock.

"What's goin' on? Why we movin?" Donegan yelled, coming toward us. He eyed me standing behind Captain Pete and jabbed his finger as he spoke. "Your trickery might've worked last time, but not now."

Captain Pete stepped to the pilothouse wall and grabbed a gaff—a long pole with a sharpened hook on one end—then thrust it toward Donegan like a spear. "That's far enough," he told Donegan, then craned his neck. "You kids get."

Billy and I scuttled past Donegan to the hatch and down the companion stairs into the galley. Wilmina was at the table and Viorene on her bunk looking through the porthole. "Are we afloat?" she asked.

"Yes," I said, "we have to leave now. Both of you come into the engine room so I can explain while we work." As I checked the try-cocks and talked, my sisters and Billy tossed wood into the firebox.

"How long before we have steam?" Billy asked.

"It's already banked. Boiler's been on the whole time."

Suddenly, we heard footsteps rushing across the deck.

"Sounds like a scuffle," Billy remarked.

"We need to get to the pilothouse. Come, on," I told

Billy, leading him to the engine-room ladder. As I climbed up, Billy was directly behind me. I stopped on the top rung and called down to my sisters. "Stay below. If you hear anyone coming, hide."

Once inside the shed, Billy and I crawled over to the opening and into the back of the pilothouse. We ducked below the windows and cat-stepped to the helm.

At the wheel and still stooped over, I opened the throttle, barely letting the cylinders warm. I grasped onto two spokes, drew myself up to full height, and spotted through the window, Leo, Captain Murphy, and Captain Pete in a stare-down with Donegan and Sweeney on the starboard deck. I quickly cranked the throttle wider. The *Irene's* engine purred like Mama's pedal sewing machine as we slowly backed away from the dock.

"Better hurry," Billy told me, now looking out the portside window. "Sweeney's thugs are racin' up."

Right then, Captain Murphy hobbled into the pilothouse. "Good work, Aggie-girl. You too, Billy."

"Did you see Sweeney's men?" I said.

"Aye, but they're no worry unless they commission a boat." He sat down on the front bench and rubbed his thigh at the base of his wooden leg. "I needed to get off this peg. Leo says to head west on the strait."

"Okay," I said, spinning the wheel starboard to angle our bow and shift us into forward.

"Look what Leo snagged," the captain said, waggling an envelope in the air. "Me papers."

"Without a struggle?" Billy asked.

"Leo's size commands respect, but we could use an ear to what's goin' on out there."

"I'll do it," Billy said, heading to the door and out.

"It feels good to be underway," I told the captain, "just wish those two thieves weren't aboard."

"We'll figure a plan."

We hadn't gone but three knots, when a commotion erupted. "Something's going on out there," I said.

"Can hear it," Captain Murphy said, getting up off the bench and over to the window. "Donegan's got a hold of Billy. That no-good is draggin' him over to the gunwale. Not on my boat," the captain barked, limping out the door.

I half-watched as I steered. At my glance back to Billy, I saw him grab onto Donegan's arm, throwing Donegan off balance, then I refocused to steering the boat when I heard....*Splash...Splash...*

I looked over and saw Captain Murphy frantically waving his arms, hollering, "Stop the boat. Stop the boat!"

I throttled down, putting the *Irene* into a drift, and helplessly watched as Leo raced to the pilothouse for one of the gaffs hooked to the outside wall.

Holding the gaff into the air, he rushed back to the gunwale with it, leaned down, and extended the pole toward the water. With all of the turmoil, I hadn't noticed the whereabouts of Sweeney until I caught him out of the corner of my eye, slinking toward the pilothouse. Panic quaked through me as I dashed over to the door, and just as Sweeney reached for the knob, *click*. I slid the bolt to lock.

Rattling the handle and pounding on the door, he scowled at me through the door window. "Turn this boat around," he demanded.

I shook my head and backed away.

Staring at me, he nodded with an evil-smile and softened his voice. "I'll give you my papers if you let me in," he said, lifting them out of his pocket and pressing them against the glass.

Even though he couldn't get in, he scared me nonetheless. "No. I don't trust anything out of your mouth."

"Let me at the wheel," he hollered, hammering at the door again.

I just stood back and let him pound. But I was sure relieved when I saw Leo, Captain Murphy, and dripping-wet Billy walking up behind him.

Leo grabbed Sweeney's collar and tugged him back. I quickly unlocked the door and let Captain Murphy and Billy inside, then relocked it. I yanked a quilt off the back bunk and handed it to Billy. "What happened?"

"Donegan threatened to throw me overboard if we didn't turn the boat around. Figured if he was makin' me go, he was comin' too."

"Quick thinking, but you must be freezing. I have extra overalls below. Want me to get them?"

He nodded.

On my way to the galley, I stopped and watched as Captain Pete fished Donegan out of the water with a gaff. Leo was standing guard over Sweeney who was sitting on the starboard deck watching too.

Donegan grabbed onto the gunwale but he slipped backwards, hanging on only by his fingers. Leo, with his large bulk, rushed over and easily maneuvered him aboard. Donegan now on all fours headed toward Sweeney, but mid-crawl he flopped down onto the deck, shivering like a wet dog.

"Serves you right," I muttered as I headed to the hatch.

"What's going on up there?" Viorene inquired when I walked into galley.

While telling my sisters about Billy and Donegan going overboard, I gathered more blankets, the overalls, socks, and draped one of Daddy's shirts over my arm.

"Can we come up and see Billy?" Wilmina asked.

"Maybe later," I said. "Please stay down here until I signal you."

After I got back to the pilothouse and handed Billy the dry clothes, I went outside to talk to Leo and Captain Pete, who were now sitting on the boiler-shed roof. "Sweeney showed me his papers," I told them. "They're in his coat pocket. Should we try to get them?"

"Won't do any good," Leo said. "I'm guessing he's got a notarized copy filed with the county."

"Daddy's copy is in a strongbox, in the engine room."

271

"That's good to know," Captain Pete said, "but it might not be needed." He pointed to a fishing boat entering the harbor. "The *Rusty Slipper*. Bud's boat." He stood and waved his arms. "Tell Captain Murphy to signal for a red-to-red stop."

Red-to-red meant that both boats would be coming up portside, on their left.

I yanked the cord, and as our whistle shrilled, the *Rusty Slipper* blared back with its deep-throated horn. When it brushed up beside us, Captain Pete tossed over our ropes and jumped aboard.

Sweeney stood up and watched. When he thought no one was looking, he sprinted toward the *Rusty Slipper*, but Leo chased behind and caught him by his arm. A moment later, the pilothouse door flew open. "Have a seat," Leo said, pushing Sweeney through the door and onto the side bench.

I glanced out the window at Donegan, but he was still sprawled-out on the starboard deck like a dead fish.

"So here's your choice," Leo told Sweeney. "Either you write out a document, reassigning this boat to Aggie's dad or you can stay aboard for a long ride to who-knows-where. Might drop you off on a vacant cliff."

"Told the girl, I'd give her these papers," Sweeney said. He reached into his pocket, pulled them out, and threw them at my feet.

I quickly picked them up.

"Think we're dim-witted," Leo said. "We know you've

272

got another set filed, but you can write forged, null, and void on the bottom of these. And sign it. Did I mention that the sheriff's a personal friend?"

"Told you, I have connections too," Sweeney barked, standing. "I'll be catching a ride with that fishing boat," he said, referring to the *Rusty Slipper.*

"Don't think so," Leo said, shoving him back onto the bench. "Aggie, start the boat and get ready to head us out." He turned to Billy. "Go tell Captain Pete what's going on."

Billy jumped up and headed for the door.

"Wait," Sweeney said, now glaring at Leo. "Hand me the papers and a pen."

After Sweeney signed, Leo examined each page and folded them. "Now give me your identification with a note authorizing me to have it as proof. I'll get it back to you."

Sweeney growled under his breath as he wrote the note, then he opened his billfold, tugged out a card, and flung it to Leo.

Leo tucked the card and the note into the papers and placed them all into his coat pocket. "I'll try to get these filed today," he told us, "which means that there's no time for a proper send-off. Soon as we're aboard the *Rusty Slipper*, I'll toss back your lines and you get moving. I'll have Bud wait until you're well on your way."

"Good plan," Captain Murphy said.

I rushed over to Leo and hugged him tight. "Thank you. Sure going to miss you and Captain Pete."

"We're going to miss you too." He pecked my cheek.

"Tell your sisters we said goodbye." He extended his hand to Captain Murphy and shook it, and then shook Billy's. He turned back to Sweeney. "Time to go." When they got outside, Leo yelled to Donegan who hadn't budged an inch. "Get up; you're going for a ride."

Donegan stumbled to his feet and then shambled past the pilothouse window, rubbing his arms. When he reached the *Rusty Slipper*, Leo steadied him aboard next to Sweeney who was standing on the *Rusty Slipper's* deck taking it all in.

As I watched through the portside window, I caught Sweeney's glance. He nodded at me with his evil grin. Goosebumps popped all over my body. Right then I knew if he had a chance, he'd get revenge. And even with him being contained, he scared me something fierce.

WE SAILED OUT OF THE HARBOR into the strait and the captain blasted our whistle for a final goodbye.

"Seems as if we're leaving long-time friends," I said.

"Aye," Captain Murphy replied, sitting down at the front bench again. "Good people affect you like that. Doesn't matter how long you've known them, they're honorable, hard-working men. You saw it right off. The way they helped us today, pure quality."

My sisters rushed into the pilothouse. "What's going on?" Wilmina asked, sitting next to Billy on the front bench. Viorene stood next to me.

I quickly told them what had happened.

"I wish we could have said goodbye," Viorene said. "Are we heading home now?"

"No," Wilmina blurted. "We're going to find Daddy. Right, Aggie?"

"One situation at a time," I said.

Annoyance crossed Viorene's face. "I better have some say-so in this." She glanced at Captain Murphy. "Do you need anything before I go below? Pillows fluffed up, coffee?"

"No, but thank ye for askin'."

Soon as Viorene walked out the door, Wilmina started pestering. "You're not going to listen to her, are you?"

Much as I had wanted to find Daddy, part of me wasn't sure anymore if we should. "Still calculating," I told her. "I'll let you know soon as I figure it out."

She frowned. "It's not right if we don't look for him."

I sighed. "Wilmina, it's been a trying day; we'll talk about it later."

She huffed and removed the binoculars from the hook. "Maritime Quarantine Station," she read from a far-off sign. "What is that?"

Billy spoke up. "Checks foreign boats for diseases: cholera, malaria, smallpox, and others."

She lowered the binoculars and looked at him. "How would they know?"

"When a boat's infected, men are sick. Real sick."

"Oh," she said.

"They have to burn sulphur pots to fumigate," Billy

continued, "and put the men into isolation; any sailor showin' symptoms goes into a pest house."

"A pest house?"

"A stand-alone building out in the woods. My dad died in one."

I gasped and looked at the captain. He stared stone-faced back at me.

Normally, Billy was close-mouthed about his past. I figured it could take years to know his full story, if we ever would, and then to share something as sad as this. I bit my lip and glanced at the captain again. Thankfully, he broke the silence.

"Sad thing to hear, Billy," Captain Murphy remarked. "Doesn't take much to infect a ship."

Billy nodded. And that was that.

"There's a lighthouse on a long spit," Wilmina said. "Black on the top, white at the bottom, and it's sitting on the roof of a grayish house."

"That's the New Dungeness Light," Billy said. "Used to play out there when I lived in these parts."

Captain Murphy stood. "Enough of this chatter, I'm goin' for shut-eye. Wake me, Aggie-girl, if anything arises." He hobbled to the back of the pilothouse and slumped down onto the mattress.

While Wilmina and Billy took turns with the binoculars, the looker described an animal or a site and the other two had to guess what it was. After an hour or so, Viorene brought up the coffeepot and poured us all a cup.

Another several hours, jelly sandwiches. Even the captain joined in on that. After everyone ate, Viorene gathered up the dishes and disappeared below again. Every half-hour, either Billy or I checked the boiler. His machinery skills proved to be a big help. But all along the way, Daddy never left my mind and neither did Sweeney. I kept looking over my shoulder for boats or strange sounds, fearing it might be the authorities signaling for us to stop.

After a bit, "Arf, arf, arf," echoed over the water. Wilmina leaped to the window. "Sea lions. Look at them all. Five bulls, seven pups, and the rest are cows."

"Bet their barks could rouse a ship five miles off," I said, and then I looked at the captain, but he was fast asleep. "Surprise he doesn't wake up from all that clatter."

"Can't get past their smell," Billy added. "Bad as rotten fish." He nudged Wilmina. "Let's go below for a game of checkers."

WITH THE SEA LIONS in the distance, the captain still asleep, and everyone else below, I listened to the hissing cylinders and thought of Mama. She called it the breathing of the boat. Said it soothed her soul. It soothed mine too. She'd sit up here for hours and write in her journal. Daddy never engaged her in conversation. It was always Mama who broke the silence. She'd get him laughing so loud we kids could hear him from the galley.

Standing here now, I was seeing the *Irene* through different eyes. I turned and looked at the boiler stack

277

spewing white smoke into the air. It was nothing but a cigar-shaped stack, but it was built and mounted by Daddy and this boat couldn't run without it. What a marvel was that? And the triple-expansion engine—three side-by-side square cylinders hissing steam that stroked the piston rods, down to the wheels, crossheads, and pedal-like cranks on the floor—all necessary to drive this boat. As the cylinders hissed again, I recalled the day Daddy named one after each of us girls. What an effort on Daddy's part to get them running so smooth.

Right then, I realized every part of this boat was built from memories and love. And even if Mama and Daddy weren't with us in flesh, their spirits were in every crevice of this boat.

The captain's rustling brought me back to the present. "Finally awake?" I said.

"Aye," he answered, pulling himself up to the bench. He tied on his leg and hobbled over to me.

"Just passed Port Angeles," I told him.

"Have you picked a course?"

Before I could answer, a boat appeared in the distance at our stern, blowing its whistle and blasting its horn. My stomach knotted. I turned to the captain.

"Do you think Sweeney turned us in?" I said, and then the telegram sent to Grandma popped into my head. What if it was sent from Port Townsend by mistake? She could've notified the authorities. That thought scared me as much as Sweeney did.

The captain scratched his chin and looked through the binoculars. "Does seem odd for it to be chasin' like that," he remarked.

"My gut's telling me *not* to stop," I said.

"Sometimes the gut knows better than the brain."

I cranked the throttled wider and increased our knots, but the boat continued its pursuit, blasting its horn. I kept looking over my shoulder. It wasn't until I spotted the Makah Village that my stomach finally calmed as I knew the ocean was at the next bend.

Suddenly, a shadow crossed our bow. "Look," I said, squinting up to the sky. "An albatross."

"That it is. Not so certain of itself on land, but at sea it shows full command. I'd say the same of you. On your way to being a full-fledged captain. A *grand* one, indeed."

"You saying that means a lot." It truly did as I always lacked confidence, even when sailing with Daddy. But being forced to the wheel like I had been on this voyage built courage in me that I didn't know I had.

I peered over my shoulder again. "The boat's still following."

"Aye. Time for you to pick your fate."

I looked up at the albatross again. "Mrs. Hill said omens would come."

"Goin' to let the bird decide, are we?"

"Daddy called the *Irene* an albatross."

"Sure it's the bird decidin' and not your heart?"

WHEN WE CROSSED from the strait into the Pacific Ocean and waves splashed our hull, I throttled up to eight knots. *Hiss, thump, hiss, thump,* the engine's rhythmic beat in unison to the albatross, scooping and zigzagging through the sky. Seems fitting to be following an albatross, I thought. After all, I'm a gawky girl and the *Irene's* a gawky boat, but at sea we're as *grand* as that bird. That's what the captain said, and who'd know better than a grumpy, old peg-legged sea captain who I couldn't love more?

"So, we're headin' to Alaska, are we?" Captain Murphy said. "Might not be an outcome you like."

"Better than being cursed with what-if's, should-have's or wish-I-had's, don't you think?"

"That's a fact."

I clasped Mrs. Hill's beaded necklace hanging around my neck, kissed it, and whispered, "Thank you for sending me a sign."

I cranked the wheel starboard.

And as the *Irene* plowed through the waves...up and down...at full steam, she soared like an albatross...North...

Alaska bound.

RESOURCES

Pacific Coast - Coast Pilot of California, Oregon, and Washington. (WA Printing Office 1889.)

Tacoma Ledger, November 28, 1920, Captain Paddy Pride of Harbor, by Kenneth Chute, Ledger Staff Correspondent.

The Alaska Sportsman, October 1954, Man the Pumps! by Fred Cline as told to Paul Taylor.

1885-1913 Grays Harbor, by Robert A. Weinstein, The Viking Press & Penguin Books 1978 (Fred Cline—pg 181, The Ships on the Harbor—boilerman on the tug *Traveler* in overalls, wool jacket, and seated on a box).

The Packard Cormorant, Summer 1989, Packard People: Fred Cline—Boatbuilder, Mechanic, Fisherman and Packard Man, by Robert F. Ryan, M.D.

The North Coast News, August 23, 1989, Lone Tree Presentation, by Kimberly Fisher.

Daily World newspaper, *Newton district had another school,* by Ade Fredericksen, Daily World columnist—interview with Agnes Cline Taylor (Fern Hill School).

The Keeper's Log, Wntr 1998, The Lone Tree Light, by Captain Fred Cline as told to Paul Taylor.

Images of America Ocean Shores 2010, by Gene Woodwick, (Arcadia Publishing). Aggie Taylor pg 24.

The Indians of Cape Flattery. At the Entrance to the Strait of Fuca, Washington Territory (1870), James G. Swan (Smithsonian Contrib. to Knowledge pub. Jnl 1868).

Indian Legends of the Pacific Northwest, by Ella E. Clark. *(University of California Press*, Berkeley and Los Angeles, California, 1953.)

1982 letter written by Agnes Cline Taylor (79)— recording her life on the Humptulips, fishing trips, facts about the boats, and the 1914 Alaskan voyage (age eleven) on the *Irene*, stopping at Destruction Island and Neah Bay where she saw totem poles in the Native American villages.

Red Sky at Morning—from ancient mariner rhyme— Earliest known versions: Matthew 16:2b-3 (approx. 1395).

ABOUT THE AUTHOR

Karen Taylor was raised in Grays Harbor County, Washington State. As a child, she spent most weekends reading at the Hoquiam Library until closing. Her father, a historian and steam collector, wrote throughout his life for various Pacific NW magazines. His love of steam and writing was passed down to her.

Karen worked as a project-control manager for an aerospace contractor in San Diego. She now resides with her husband in Washington State.

GLOSSARY

AFT/ASTERN: TOWARD THE STERN; the back.

ANCHOR: METAL OBJECT LOWERED from the boat by line or chain that rest on or digs into the water's bottom to hold the boat.

BAR: USUALLY AN ENTRANCE of a river or harbor that is plagued with mountains of sand formed by the sea.

BATTEN DOWN: PREPARING FOR ROUGH SEAS or weather by closing all portholes, hatches, and other openings on the boat.

BERTH: BED OR BUNK in a boat.

BILGE WATER: A MIXTURE OF SEA WATER, fresh water, oil and sludge.

BLOCK: A PULLEY on a boat for directing line.

BOILER: A CAST-IRON CAULDRON. Its main function is to convert water to steam to power the engine.

BOILER DRUM: TANK that stores the steam.

BOILER PEEP HOLE: A SMALL OPENING used to check the fire without opening the firebox door.

BOW: THE FRONT of a boat.

BULKHEAD: A WALL within the hull of the boat.

CAST OFF: TO LEAVE a dock; let loose.

CHART: NAUTICAL MAP.

CHEHALIS: *(She-hay-lis)* FROM LOCAL NATIVE AMERICAN word meaning *sand*. The largest of five rivers that flow into Grays Harbor Bay at the eastern end.

COCKBILLED: AN ANCHOR SET AT AN ANGLE as it hangs over the bow ready to be dropped.

COURSE: DIRECTION boat is being steered.

DINGHY: A SMALL ROWBOAT carried or towed by a larger boat.

DOLPHIN: PILINGS TIED TOGETHER.

DOCK: A FLOAT, pier or wharf.

ENGINE ROOM: ROOM that houses the boiler, triple-expansion engine, steering gears, etc.

FIREBOX: BOILER FURNACE.

FISHERMAN ANCHOR: ALSO KNOWN AS ADMIRALTY and the most common anchor shape known: an iron shank with two fluked arms.

FORE OR FORWARD: TOWARD the bow.

GAFF: A POLE with a sharp hook.

GALLEY: A BOAT'S KITCHEN and living quarters.

GREEN-TO-GREEN: PASSAGE OF TWO sea-going vessels moving in opposite directions on their starboard (right).

GUNWALE: PRONOUNCED *GUNNEL* is the outer railing or upper edge of a hull.

HATCH: AN OPENING in the deck of a boat.

HELM: THE OPERATING components of a boat: wheel, gauges, throttle, etc.

HOQUIAM: *(Ho-kwim)* LOCAL NATIVE American word meaning *hungry for wood* ; a lumber town in western Washington; one of the five rivers that flow into Grays Harbor Bay.

HULL: WATERTIGHT portion of a boat.

HUMPTULIPS: (*Hum-tu-lups*) FROM LOCAL NATIVE AMERICAN language meaning *hard to pole or chilly region;* a region in Western Washington; one of the five rivers that flow into Grays Harbor Bay.

KNOT: SPEED of one nautical mile per hour.

LAZARET: a storage area on a boat.

LINES: ROPES of the boat.

LIGHTHOUSE: A NAVIGATION tower with a light and a fog horn.

LOG: A NAVIGATIONAL book.

MAKAH: (*Ma-kah*) AN INDIGENOUS PEOPLE who have inhabited the northwest tip of Washington State for centuries.

MAST: A VERTICAL spar which sails are set.

NOR'WESTER: NORTHWEST wind.

OAR: A LONG ROD with a paddle or blade at one end used for rowing.

OFFSHORE: AWAY FROM shore toward deep water.

PILOTHOUSE: GLASS-ENCLOSED room from which the boat is controlled. Usually U-shaped.

PORTSIDE: The LEFT-HAND side of the boat.

PORTHOLE: A SMALL round window in a boat.

RED-TO-RED: PASSAGE OF TWO sea-going vessels moving in opposite directions on their portside (left).

ROWBOAT: A BOAT propelled manually by a rower using oars.

RUDDER: A VERTICAL BLADE at the stern that can be turned by the wheel to change direction when in motion.

SHIP THE OARS: PULLING THE OARS OUT of the water into the oar locks to stop rowing.

SLOUGH: SWAMPY AREA of water connected to a larger body of water.

SOU'WESTER: A FRESH WIND from the southwest.

SPRAY: FLYING water.

STARBOARD: The RIGHT-HAND side of a boat.

STEAM DONKEY: Steam-powered winch.

STEM: THE BOW'S forward tip.

STERN: The back END OF A BOAT.

TAFFRAIL: THE rail at the stern.

THWART: A CROSSPIECE spreading across the gunwales used as a seat in a rowboat.

THROTTLE DOWN/BACK: REDUCE speed.

THROTTLE UP/OPEN: INCREASE speed.

TRIPLE-EXPANSION: A COMPOUND STEAM Engine that operates THREE cylinders at different pressure levels.

WAKE: TURBULENCE behind a vessel.

WEIGH ANCHOR: TO HEAVE or pull up the anchor from the sea floor.

WINCH: A MECHANICAL DEVICE with the aid of pulleys, cables, and a spool used to hoist or release heavy loads.

Made in the USA
Columbia, SC
14 November 2021

48941692R00181